For Cotter, my son.
Who taught me all I know about patience
and unconditional love.

RESERVED

a love story

TRACY EWENS

RESERVED

a love story

ISBN: 978-0-9908571-7-4 (print)
ISBN: 978-0-9908571-6-7 (e-book)

Book design by Maureen Cutajar
www.gopublished.com

Chapter One

Makenna Rye Conroy was naked again. The cool cotton sheets of her familiar bed tangled around her bare legs as she opened her eyes to the morning sunlight peeking through the shutters. She could smell bacon and hear giggles and the low rumbling of his laughter from the kitchen. The room was soft as her eyes traveled past framed pictures perched on the large teak dresser opposite the bed. The walls were white—they were always white—which was strange because the walls of her bedroom were actually light blue, but every time she had this dream, the walls were white.

The alarm clock was going off in her light blue reality, but she willed it away and stayed in the dream as she wrapped herself in a large white robe at the foot of the bed. More white. She padded barefoot to the bathroom and brushed her teeth, never looking into the mirror above the sink. As she walked out of the bathroom, she ran her hand along the back of a gray Persian cat lounging on the arm of a red upholstered chair. "You don't own a cat," her brain always reminded her at this point in the dream, as if it was trying to prepare her heart for what was about to happen.

Kenna touched the cool glass doorknob, and the laughter grew louder as she walked down the hall. She could hear Paige, an older

Paige that he would never know, explaining in animated conversation why Peppermint Patty was her favorite Peanuts character. Makenna put her hand on the wall as she turned into the kitchen. Their daughter was sitting crisscross on the counter with Fritters, the stuffed pig, in her lap. She got Fritters on her second birthday, something else he would never see. Paige smiled at her with a front tooth just now starting to grow in. Their daughter aged with each incarnation of the dream, but he stayed the same. Of course he did; that made sense. Paige was giggling and he stood by the stove holding a wooden spoon; one of the spoons they bought during the trip to northern California Adam had surprised her with when she was feeling huge and pregnant. It was made of redwood, like their salad tongs.

Makenna kissed Paige on her soft cheek and reached overhead for a cup as she had done a hundred times before in this dream. Instead of a cup, she pulled down the bouquet of flowers—wild flowers she'd carried at her wedding in one of those frilly chapels along the strip in Las Vegas. The bouquet was a last-ditch effort by her subconscious, a reminder before she faced him, that this was all a dream. Once she turned, her heart would race and she would reach out for him. He always looked so real, clad in nothing but pajama bottoms, and she'd touch his face as she did every time. Her head wanted her heart to know that it would be all right and she would wake up soon. She put the flowers into a vase of water, tickled Paige, and turned to face . . . Holy shit!

Makenna sat bolt upright in her light blue bedroom and threw the covers off her legs. She was sweating and gasping for a full breath. She'd had the dream before, in the first few months after Adam was gone. It had been an odd combination of heartbreak and comfort. There were mornings she would awaken crying because all she wanted to do was slip back into the dream and stay with him for a moment longer. But as the years went on, the dream became less frequent and the ache less paralyzing. She was at the point now that she could follow the dream, visit with him, touch his face, and then say good-bye. She'd made peace with it, but this was not the same dream. This was some kind of cruel joke.

His sloppy bleached blond hair was not falling into his face as he stood at the stove making his famous hotdogs and eggs. He was supposed to wrap his arm around her waist after she put the flowers in water, kiss her, and say, "Good morning." That was how it always played out. She would kiss him back, hold his face, and then just as Paige asked if they could go to the park, his face would fade into a soft light and Makenna would wake up. That was the dream, the same dream for over five years since Adam had fallen asleep at the wheel trying to make his way home to her and their newborn baby. The same dream since he'd died. Adam was immortalized in that dream, the only place they were all together. It was a snippet of a normal she would never have.

Makenna glanced through the dark blue morning of her bedroom to the clock that read 5:07. If this had been a normal morning, she would grab a Coke from the refrigerator, turn on CNN, and check her e-mails for a few minutes before waking Paige to get ready for school. On typical mornings that was the ritual, but the dream had changed and nothing felt typical.

She turned on the shower and, standing in the bathroom, tried to play that part of the dream through her awake mind. The turn into the kitchen, the flowers, and then the shirtless man in the kitchen was—dear God. She squeezed her eyes shut, hoping to erase the image, but nothing worked. Slipping out of her pajamas, she stepped into the warm spray of the water.

She should probably be taking a cold shower because something was terribly off. Maybe it was her hormones, or maybe she needed to have sex more desperately than she realized. Turning her face to the spray, she closed her eyes, lathered her hair, and desperately searched for some explanation. There had to be a logical reason why when she turned to find her dead husband, *he* was standing shirtless in her kitchen instead. *He* was making her daughter breakfast.

Him.

How did her mind even know what that looked like? How did it know that he wasn't model perfect or that his abs weren't cut in that way Kenna always thought of as too much gym and not

3

enough sunshine? Instead, he was big, rolling shoulders, flat lovely abs, and a chest dusted with hair. How could she know him in such detail, right down to the way his narrow hips barely held up his—

Makenna quickly rinsed the shampoo from her hair and rubbed her eyes open. *This stops right now*, she thought. There was no way in hell she was going to start her day thinking about him or picturing him in her shower. He made her crazy; that was a real-world fact.

Maybe it was something I ate last night, she thought, trying to take her mind in a different direction.

Makenna stepped out of the shower, wrapped herself in a towel, and looked at her nightstand. She'd fallen asleep reading *Girl on a Train*. That could be it. She had propped and re-propped her pillows, struggling to get in a few more pages because she had to know if the guy in the book, the one who seemed like a bastard, really was one. That was the last thing she remembered thinking before she slid down the stack of pillows and into sleep.

Sure, that was it. She was lost in a twisted fictional world and it had messed up her mind, her sleep pattern, or whatever. That's why he was there. It made no sense and didn't even come close to explaining . . . him, but she got dressed and decided she would accept it as her truth for now. Brushing her teeth and quickly pulling her wet hair into a bun, Kenna walked into the kitchen to pop waffles in the toaster for Paige. It was time to get up, time to start their day in the real world. One of Paige's bedtime books read that "dreams are wishes come to life." Kenna sure as hell hoped not, because her life was just fine and she no longer had half-naked wishes.

When Travis McNulty's face hit the mat for the second time that morning, he was seriously questioning why the hell he took up boxing. It was a great workout, no question, but beating the shit out of himself or rather, letting his sparring partner, Brick, beat the shit out of him was getting old. The man's name was Brick for Christ's sake. Why would anyone get in a boxing ring with Brick?

"You all right, bro?"

In his mind, Travis answered, "Oh yeah, bro! Never better. Nice shot!" but it came out more like the mumble he gave his dentist when he had his teeth cleaned.

Brick offered his hand, and Travis took it because it was either that or remain plastered to the mat for at least another five minutes.

Rolling his neck and relieved it still worked, Travis took out his mouth guard and loosened his padded helmet. "Thanks."

David, his walking motivational poster of a trainer, nodded to Brick that he was free to go and put his arm around Travis. "That was good. Your core is getting stronger."

David was a middleweight something-or-other in his day. There were plaques and belts framed near the entrance of The Square, his gym, that stood as proof he was a badass. Travis had never been one for trophies or plaques. They'd been extremely important when he was growing up, a clear indicator of value in the McNulty house, despite the fact that they were usually made of plastic or crappy metal. Trophies were the reason he and his two brothers scraped and clawed at each other through their childhood. Whoever brought home the most, went the fastest, it all translated to average, better, and best in their father's eyes. There were three of them, so that system worked out, and even though Travis had spent some time in the better category during his sophomore and junior years of high school, he eventually fell from grace and settled right where he belonged on the family tree. He was average: an easy target for his brothers and a disappointment to his father.

David was different, though, because beneath all his accomplishments, he was a nice guy. An athlete and a good person, not something Travis had much exposure to in his life. David had come into The Yard a few times for lunch when they first opened. He and Travis struck up some conversations, and then one day he invited Travis down to his gym. That was a few months ago, and now Travis came three days a week for an hour.

"My core? Yeah, tell that to my face." Travis tossed his stuff into his gym bag and began unwrapping his hands.

"That'll come. You're getting stronger from the ground up. None of this sissy football flashy muscles bullshit."

Yet another reason Travis loved him. Never in all his years growing up on Team McNulty had anyone used the words "sissy" and "football" in the same sentence. It was refreshing.

"Think of it like building a brick house, no reference to your ass kicker back there intended, versus a straw house."

"Is this a *Three Little Pigs* reference? That's all you got?"

David laughed and patted him on the back. "Good workout there today. I'll see you Wednesday."

"Not unless I see you first. The dinner special is a pork chop on that polenta you love, just sayin'."

"Serious? Damn, man. You're going to fatten me up." David patted his envious abs as if he were Santa Claus.

Travis grinned. "That's the plan. Maybe if I feed Brick too, he'll go easy on me."

David laughed.

"I think he's probiotic."

"Of course he is. The man's a machine."

"You know, Cheryl's been wanting a date night for a while, so I just might send the kids to her mother and stop by tonight."

"I'll keep an eye out for you." Travis dropped the towel over his shoulder and pushed the door of the locker room open.

"Wait, I've got a better one," David said, and Travis hesitated at the door. "It's like cooking. You use fresh ingredients, good meat, that's how you build a meal, right?"

Travis nodded.

"Same thing with your body. Good ingredients."

"You know we usually pound the hell out of our cutlets. Kind of like that?"

Both men laughed.

"I'll keep at it. Thanks for the workout."

"Anytime, man."

Travis showered and by the time he set his foot down at the light on Sixth Street, the beep of his earpiece indicated he had a voicemail. Two actually. *Shit!*

His phone was in his backpack, but he already knew who'd left the messages. Pulling his bike back into traffic, he had to admit there'd been a glimpse of "call me" in Trixie's eyes when he'd thrown on his jeans and made all the right excuses last night. There had been some good times with Trix, but a few . . . nights were his limit. Anything more was too much work and often led to complications.

Occasionally, he'd hook up with a woman and, despite his honesty, she wanted to persuade him otherwise or be the woman to change his ways. He was always up front and made it clear what he was looking for. He never shared numbers or an actual limit with them, but any woman who ended up in his bed knew she would not be putting him in a sweater vest and bringing him home to meet the parents.

Travis parked his bike in front of Nick's, home of his favorite huevos rancheros, took off his helmet, and grabbed his phone. Shortly after he had finished the last delicious bite, his phone vibrated. He ignored it, but it vibrated again, this time with an incoming call. Travis let out a sigh, tapped the answer button, and like his father had always instructed, he "took it like a man."

Chapter Two

*M*akenna dropped Paige off at St. Christopher's Private School and drove to work in silence. No music, no podcast, not even her usual audiobook. She hadn't done it intentionally; it was a beautiful morning and she'd put the Jeep's top down for Paige, who loved to play super flying pig with Fritters. After drop-off, Kenna found herself in a bit of a trance, thinking and listening to nothing but the rush of traffic.

She arrived at work, grabbed her laptop bag off the backseat, and took solace in the knowledge that there were no meetings today, just payroll, some phone calls, and that social media post she needed to come up with to promote the new menu. Details — a whole day of details stretched out in front of her. She would park herself in one of her favorite corners at The Yard, the restaurant she managed for her brother, and work. That had always straightened her out in the past, and it would surely do the trick this time.

Sage's car was already in the parking lot, a good thing because Kenna should probably tell someone. Maybe Sage had a simple explanation that would get her back to normal. That's what best friends were for, weren't they?

Kenna locked her car, entering through the front of the restaurant. They weren't open for a few more hours, so she locked
the door behind her. After plugging in her laptop at the corner
bar table, which had become her office when it was available, she
followed Sage into the back kitchen so she could chop more oranges and limes before the lunch crowd arrived. A few oranges in,
Kenna leaned over and said quietly, "I had *the* dream last night."

"Ooh, wow. It's been a while, hasn't it?"

"Yeah, last time was a week or two before we opened here."

"So, are you all right? I mean, I'm sure you are, but . . ."

"I'm fine, or I was fine until the dream wasn't *the* dream. It was
different this time."

Sage stopped mid-lime and turned to Kenna, who was now
resting her elbows on the counter.

"What? Well, huh, are you sure it was different? It's been a while."

"Yup, it was definitely different."

"But, it's never different. Always the same every time, so what,
the flowers were roses?"

"No, same flowers. They were the—"

"Bouquet from your runaway wedding in Vegas?"

Makenna nodded.

"Was Paige still on the counter in the kitchen?"

Makenna nodded.

"So what was different?"

"I'm not even sure I can say it. It's crazy. You know I'm in the
kitchen and I turned—"

"Come on, babe, don't be this way." Travis's voice filled the
space even before he appeared in front of them holding his helmet
and barely balancing the iPhone between his ear and the raised cap
of his shoulder. "Are you crying? I know. Right, but I thought we
both agreed." He nodded a greeting to both of them and put his
beat-up leather bag into one of the cubbies off the back kitchen.
Hands now free, Travis took the phone and held it away from his
ear while an enthusiastically pissed-off female voice yelled at him.
He shook his head and turned away from them, facing the wall.

"Trix, I get it. You need more and you deserve more, babe. I'm sorry we didn't work out." He kicked the metal baseboard with the tip of his work boot. "Now, let's not end things this way."

The pissed-off female voice hit a crescendo and then went silent. Travis, still facing the back corner, let out a breath and slipped his phone into his back pocket. He appeared to be shaking it off, as Taylor Swift advised through the overhead speakers. When he turned, Makenna and Sage both stared in fascination. It was sort of like seeing an animal in its natural habitat.

Kenna's eyes drifted. *Were those new jeans?*

"Trix?" Sage asked.

Travis grabbed an apron and said nothing.

"That's like a stripper name." Sage wasn't letting up, and Travis grinned.

"Oh wow, you date strippers? You're *that* guy?"

At this, he laughed and tied the apron at his waist. "No, I don't date strippers. Her name is Trixie, but she's a loan officer at JP Morgan. Her parents were a little . . . eccentric."

"I see."

Travis went to the sink and washed his hands.

Big hands. *When did he get the leather bracelet?* Kenna wondered. Huh, his beard had more red in it when it was grown out. *You're staring, Kenna. Cut it out before—*

"How's it going, Ken?"

She pulled her eyes off him and looked at Sage, who seemed confused. *Damn it.*

"See something you like?" He waggled his brows at her. She and Travis had a way of bantering that was usually harmless, but that was before her mind had conjured him up standing shirtless in her kitchen and making her daughter breakfast.

Her face flushed. *What the hell is wrong with you? Fix this, Kenna.*

She rolled her eyes. "You have something on your jeans." She pointed and then quickly turned before he figured out there was nothing there. Kenna pushed through the back kitchen doors and stepped into the bar. She needed her details, the ones she'd been so excited about before Travis arrived wearing that blue Triumph T-shirt. She suddenly noticed how it stretched across his chest.

Her heart was pounding as she grabbed the cool, glossy wooden edge of the bar for balance.

"What just happened?" Sage asked, walking through the door behind her.

"Nothing. I need a Coke."

"Coming right up. Maybe I should make that a double, because you were most definitely looking at Travis like you wanted to eat him."

"I was not."

"You were. There wasn't anything on those jeans. You were scoping his ass."

"I was thinking about something and he happened to walk into my line of sight."

"That's the story you're going with? You were fixed on him like you were seeing him for the first—"

Makenna could see the moment Sage put two and two together. "Wait, oh God." She pushed the Coke across the bar and then one hand went to her mouth. "That's what was different? Was he . . . it was him, in the dream?"

Makenna closed her eyes and continued sucking Coke into her bloodstream.

Sage leaned on the bar. "Huh, well . . . that's weird."

Kenna nodded.

"I mean, it doesn't mean anything. You've just been working too much and he's always here."

Kenna kept nodding.

"It's nothing, honey. Just chalk it up to lack of sleep—or stress. Travis is . . . well, he's super yummy."

"Not helping."

"But, he's Travis. You're not into—"

"Hey, did Garrett deliver the artichokes yet?" Travis asked, pushing through the door.

Both women looked at him, Kenna still hooked up, via the straw, to her Coke. They said nothing.

"What the hell is with you two today? Is it Trixie?" He dropped onto the stool next to Makenna. His leg touched hers, and she called on every ounce of self-control to keep from pulling away from him like he was a live wire.

"Because I'll have you both know that was not my fault."

Sage rolled her eyes and Kenna scooted over, hoping she wasn't being obvious.

"We do not care, nor do we want the sordid details of your stripper escapades," Sage said in her best elitist voice. It was the one she saved for obnoxious bar patrons, drunk or otherwise.

"She's not a stripper," Travis said just under a laugh before he leaned over the counter for a mug and held it out to Sage for coffee.

Kenna stared at the bar because that seemed the only safe place for her eyes at the moment.

"Well, either way, no one cares, right Kenna?" Sage prompted her.

"Right," Kenna said, desperately trying to find her mental balance. This was nuts. It was a stupid dream. Granted, it was *the* dream, the one she'd been having for the past five years since her husband died. The one that had never changed and had always been the same until last night, but that didn't matter. It was still just a dream. *Pull it together, Kenna.* "Right," she said again as if trying to convince herself. She finally looked at Travis. His eyes danced with things Kenna was in no mood to tackle. "Garrett will be here in"—she looked at the clock over the bar—"fifteen minutes with the artichokes. What are you doing with them so I can put it on the specials board?"

Travis's look said he was still trying to figure her out, but he eventually said, "Just roasting them. Garlic, olive oil, and probably a little lemon."

Kenna nodded and picked up her Coke off the bar. "Sounds good." She unplugged her laptop and decided to move to the private dining room.

Travis reached out and touched her arm as he'd done a million times before, but this time, a flood of warmth coursed through her body and her heart felt like it was making its way outside her chest. *This must be what an anxiety attack feels like*, she thought, closing her eyes and trying to redirect her mind. That's when she saw Adam's face, as clear as the morning they moved into their first apartment. Her eyes sprang open and she pulled away from Travis, no longer caring if she looked crazy because all signs now pointed to completely nuts. Something was happening and Kenna knew only one thing with certainty: she wasn't ready.

"Ken, are you all right?"

She stared at him for a beat past comfortable and bowed her head before she started to cry. "Fine." She clutched her laptop and quickly moved to the dining room.

Logan arrived a few minutes later with stupid in love all over his face. That made the third morning in a row Logan Rye, chronic overachiever, was late, and Travis couldn't have been happier for his friend. Just a few months ago, he was practically living at The Yard. Just as Travis was really starting to worry about him, a distraction in the form of Kara Malendar wound him up and took him under. The guy was so in love—it emanated from him. He hummed and took long lunches at the bar when Kara came to visit. They were getting married next year, but Kara's brother Grady was first. His wedding was in four months. It would be The Yard's first catering job, which was both exciting and nerve-racking. Travis and Logan were working on a tasting menu that included a new sea bass entrée they'd put together. They would work up two or three other choices, and whatever Grady and Kate went with would be incredible. He'd make sure of it. Kara was going to be in her brother's wedding, so Logan needed to attend as a guest. That meant the day of the wedding was all his. He lived for this stuff. The heat, the pace; he thrived on it.

"Morning," Logan said.

"Morning. Squash is done and Garrett should be here any minute with the artichokes."

"Yeah, he pulled in behind me. Suppose I should have helped him." Logan threw some things on his desk and washed his hands.

"Hey, do you have any idea what's up with Ken?" Travis asked.

Garrett barreled through the door holding three stacked cardboard crates. "Quit calling her Ken. That's my name for her and now, since you annoy the crap out of her, it's tainted. Yeah, thanks for the help, asshole." He glared at Logan and walked back out the door.

"I just washed my hands," Logan said, holding up his hands and laughing. "No idea what's wrong. I haven't talked to her this morning," he said back to Travis. "Why do you think something's wrong?" Logan picked up one of the chokes and turned it in his hands like a patron at a farmers market.

"I don't know. She was talking with Sage when I got here and I was on my phone dealing with Trixie—"

"Hold up, Trixie? I'd remember that name if you'd mentioned her before."

"Chase loan officer, cried after sex. You've heard of her, I just never shared her name because I was trying to avoid that smirk right there." Travis pointed at him. "Anyway, it's not important. I was on the phone when I got here and when I turned back to them, Kenna was . . . hell, there's no other way to say it, she was checking me out."

"You wish." Garrett returned with two more boxes.

"No, I swear to God. Sage even noticed and tried to cover for her. Then, I'm out in the bar talking to them. She's super quiet and suddenly looks like she's gonna cry."

Garrett and Logan exchanged glances, and Travis could tell they were probably having a whole conversation without words, something they did often.

"Do you think . . . I guess we should tell him?" Garrett said, grabbing two paper towels to dry his hands.

Logan shook his head. "Well, since she's looking at him, she's probably considering him, right? The crying is probably the hormones."

"Tell me what?" Travis felt his heart rate kick up a notch, which was weird, but they were so serious, he wasn't sure what to expect.

"Well, you see, Trav,"—Garrett put an arm around him, almost a choke hold, but not quite—"the reason Ken's looking at you is. . . there's no easy way to say this." He looked to Logan, who nodded for him to get it out. "She's been wanting to have another baby."

"What?"

"Yup. You know, a friend for Paige. She's planning on raising it herself, but she's been talking to us about donors, and I'm . . . well, we're guessing that's why she's checking you out."

"For your sperm," Logan said, raising his eyebrows.

"Shut the hell up." Travis searched for a sign they were dicking with him, but both men were expressionless. "Jesus, this doesn't seem like her. When did she decide she wanted a baby daddy?"

"A couple of minutes ago."

"Huh?"

"Yeah, a couple of minutes ago. That's right about the time we decided to screw with your stupid ass."

Both men collapsed against each other in laughter. Travis shook his head and tried not to join them. Baby daddy, that was a good one.

"Oh man, the look on your face," Logan said, leaning forward and brushing the top of his head in a teasing brotherly gesture.

"Fine. Well played. You got me. Assholes. Now, go away. I've got work to do."

Garrett was still laughing.

"Hey, be sure to tell Kenna this story, will ya?" Travis said, shaking his head and choosing a knife.

"Believe me, we will." Garrett fist bumped his brother and left out the back door.

Travis nodded, resigned to the upcoming embarrassment.

"He won't tell her," Logan said, turning to prep the chokes.

"But you will, right?"

"Damn straight." He broke out laughing all over again.

Travis decided there was no point in continuing to feed the fire.

He began prep work. For the life of him, he couldn't figure out why, for a few seconds there, if Kenna had wanted him, he would have . . . shit. They were screwing with him and he was dumb enough to fall for it. That was all it was.

Chapter Three

The Yard's private dining room was Makenna's favorite space. It sat catty-corner to the kitchen, and the long table was a repurposed turquoise-painted barn door. When they were first transforming The Yard from a hardware store and lumberyard into a restaurant, she'd asked one of the contractors what they could do with the door. The original paint had been peeling and chipping, but the color was great and Logan agreed it needed a place in the restaurant. The guy who installed the kitchen storage cabinets took it back to his shop, sanded off some of the falling paint flakes, and sealed the whole thing. He also brought in a huge tree trunk he'd been saving for a future project; it now acted as the table's base.

Kenna had handpicked all ten of the mismatched chairs surrounding the table and frequently moved them around. The best one, in her opinion, was a high-back purple velvet-and-white wooden armchair, currently positioned at the head of the table. She liked moving furniture, any furniture, when she had important things to consider or when she was stressed and couldn't sleep. Garrett once said she should just put everything on wheels.

When she occupied the corner bar table, Kenna felt plugged into the buzz of the restaurant. It was where she monitored the heart of her brother's place, but the dining room was where she went to get work done and to focus. It often seemed like she was tucked away, hiding, although she was most definitely not hiding. She was simply removing distractions so she could concentrate on her work.

It was Friday, mid-lunch rush, and it turned out she did have a meeting with Logan to discuss getting a new air conditioner before next summer and some new spice vendor he wanted to start using. The meeting had cut into her day, and now she had more things on her to-do list than she could possibly complete in the four hours before picking Paige up from school, but she was going to give it her best shot.

After Kenna finished the kitchen and server schedule for the coming week and emailed it to Logan for approval, she pulled her headphones out and rested her head back on the chair. The gorgeous multicolored glass fixture created by her brother's fiancée, Kara, glistened above. There was never a lot of natural light in the dining room even in the daytime, so the fixture was usually on. Kenna still marveled at the glass pieces, each of them different but soldered together to somehow form one unique display. It was an incredible piece of art that cast beautiful jewels of light down on the table.

Kara used to be a food critic for the *LA Times*, but now she had a little studio in downtown Pasadena where she worked on her glass lamps full-time. Makenna had started loving her because she made her brother happy, but now she found she loved her in her own right. Their family gained another person, a woman, which thrilled Paige. The last time Kara had come over for dinner, they'd played Pictionary, and Kara's face beamed when Paige asked to be her partner. The two of them proceeded to beat the pants off the rest of the family. That may have been when Makenna knew her brother had picked a good one. Paige was a great judge of character: if she liked someone, it was always a good sign.

Kenna brought up QuickBooks on her computer, clicked on the Taxes section, and sent in the tax payment for her last payroll.

Pushing her computer back on the table, she set a stack of applications in front of her. They needed to hire three more servers. She would do the initial interviews before handing the best potentials over to Logan for finals. Kenna made notes, put a star on the ones she would call, and asked her brain one more time to stop thinking about what her dream meant.

She'd gone over it dozens of times and decided that it meant she needed to date. For a few months now, she had thought about "getting out among 'em" as her father would say, but if she was honest with herself, she was nervous, maybe even a little scared. She hadn't been on a date since her freshman year in college, hadn't been . . . intimate with a man since Adam. She'd been busy raising a little person and honestly had no interest in bringing anyone else into her life until a few months ago. She'd been sitting at a Rye family meeting and watching her father. He had been alone for as long as she could remember, and she wondered if he was ever lonely . . . if he ever wanted someone, even just to watch a movie with on Sunday nights after the busy week was over. It led her to think about her own life. She realized she didn't want to be alone forever. She had no idea to what extent she'd allow another person into her life—into their life—she only knew it was time to try. But, every time Kenna started thinking about dating in detail or tried to flirt, she found herself overwhelmed or embarrassed, and the urge passed.

Then she had the dream. Her mind had one opportunity to cast a new man in her life, and when it searched her dream database for a man other than Adam, all it came up with was Travis.

There was only one explanation: her mind simply didn't have enough data to pull from because there was no way Travis McNulty, Mr. Hookup and Bail, fit anywhere in her world. He didn't belong in her kitchen, shirt or no shirt, warm, hot smile, morning look or not . . . *Cut it out!*

Dating, it was time to start dating. She would talk to Sage.

Travis noticed Kenna leave around three, just after the late-lunch rush. She'd quickly waved to Logan before leaving out the back, but didn't wave to him. He knew it sounded juvenile, but she usually, at least, tossed her hand in a good-bye. This time, nothing.

Something was up. He wasn't sure what he'd done, but she was definitely acting weird. She'd even popped back around seven with her daughter in tow because Paige wanted to show her "Uncle Rogan" the new backpack they'd bought. Paige came into the kitchen to say hello to him and twirl around in her new pack, but Kenna called her to come up front without so much as a glance in his direction. Thinking she might be pissed at him, he found himself moving to the pizza counter to shave his fennel so he could eavesdrop. Pathetic? Probably, but the cold shoulder, her cold shoulder, was driving him batshit.

Travis used to find it interesting that his body responded every time he heard Kenna's name or her voice, but they'd known each other for years now and he'd simply accepted it. He probably had a little thing for her, but that was never going to happen. Women like Makenna were complicated enough; she'd also lost her husband a little over five years ago and seemed to be doing great raising her daughter on her own. A guy just didn't play with that kind of woman, at least, he didn't. So instead, he enjoyed her from his place and every now and then helped out in his own way. There was no harm in looking. That was, until she looked back and started messing with his clearly established boundaries.

"We've got three tables about ready to leave and two pizza orders up—actually four because two takeouts just called in." Logan walked back from the front and went into the walk-in. "I feel pretty good about bringing Todd back." He returned with a handful of arugula. "He's sticking with the promise to only wear one earphone and a belt. I think he's grown up since you fired him and he's only burned two things tonight. Progress."

"That is progress. He could turn out to be super apprentice after all." Travis laughed picturing Todd, their pain-in-the-ass apprentice, with a big gold star. "You look tired."

"Yeah well, I'm not getting a lot of sleep these days." Logan smirked, obviously referring to his new fiancée.

"Show-off," Travis said before Logan disappeared up front.

It was an hour before closing, so Travis checked the office and saw Paige's lunch box sitting next to the desk. He smiled—she'd forgotten it again. He had started making Paige's lunch a few months back when Kenna had forgotten the lunch box and he . . . well, he felt like doing something nice for her. She always seemed so busy, controlled busy, but he remembered wanting to help, so he did.

Travis picked up the soft Daniel Tiger lunch box and brought it to the counter. He unzipped the light blue zipper and found it clean. There were no bags or wrappers, no uneaten food, just a piece of construction paper. Travis unfolded the purple page. A happy face with buggy eyes and a tongue was drawn in crayon. Under the face, also in crayon, were the words, "Thank you," followed by several exclamation points and hearts and Xs and Os.

Travis felt his chest warm in a way he had not known before meeting Paige. He hadn't been around very many children, but he'd met Paige when she was just turning two and he lost a piece of his heart right then and there. Watching her grow up into such a smart and sassy little girl had secretly been one of the best things in his life. Not that he would share that with most people because, well, no one would believe him. Logan probably knew how Travis felt about both of the Rye family women, but he continued to keep things light by saying he admired the whole family. That seemed to work, but he was pretty sure Logan saw through his bullshit by now.

Travis turned the construction paper over and read the words, "mac and cheese. pretty pleez," with more hearts and kisses. He laughed. She was sending him requests now, and he instantly knew what he would be doing on his day off. He'd need to make mac and cheese on Sunday so Paige's lunch would be ready when Kenna came whirling through the restaurant on Monday morning looking for the forgotten lunch box. She didn't forget it all the time, but frequently enough that it had become sort of a game, one he looked forward to. There was something so simple about making a little girl's lunch, checking off one of what he assumed were the many check boxes in Makenna's world.

Chapter Four

Makenna and Sage sat on the dark yellow leather S-shaped couch at Lux Coffee the following Sunday morning. Paige sat with her legs crisscrossed, wearing jeans, daisy shirt, and green plastic clogs. Her earphones were on and she was staring at Makenna's phone, no doubt watching some shark attack or lions and hippos in a turf war. Those were her two current favorites.

The S couch was a coveted people-watching spot at Lux. They didn't always manage a seat, but when they did, it was a good Sunday morning. From the comfort of what they assumed was sixties-era upholstery, they watched the line of people moving single file past the fresh pastries laid out on mismatched plates and toward the register. That was where they picked up their coffee orders and paid Bri, the woman who sat behind a counter that looked like a converted altarpiece. Bri had long dreadlocks that were usually tied back in a bunch and a tattoo of a barcode on her wrist. She was studying philosophy at UCLA, Kenna learned one morning when she stopped to grab Paige a blueberry muffin on their way to school. Kenna rarely understood a word Bri said, but she loved to say things like "it's all crap," and "well, according to Nietzsche."

A few weeks after Adam's memorial, Sage decided Makenna needed to get out of the house, so they came to Lux. When Bri handed Kenna her Americano, she said, eyes averted as if looking at her was almost too painful, "That which does not kill us makes us stronger."

"Nietzsche?" Kenna had asked.

Bri met her eyes and smiled just a little, and then she nodded.

Makenna actually googled Nietzsche one afternoon and wondered how, with all of that swimming around in the girl's brain, she managed to give a damn whether morning commuters wanted extra foam or their scone warmed up.

"Third in line. Married?" Sage asked, after sipping her dirty chai latte.

Kenna tore her eyes away from Bri, who was simultaneously trying to explain to one kid in skinny jeans that he had, in fact, not paid for his drink while telling a very pregnant woman where she could find a bathroom.

"Um, third"—Kenna counted without pointing—"no ring. He's single."

"That doesn't mean anything. I think he carries himself like he's married." Sage set her cup down on the metal crate in front of them.

"What does that mean?"

"Oh, come on, you know, barely looks around. Seems perfectly content, like someone either rolled off of him this morning or made him an omelet or both."

Kenna leaned to the left to get a better look. She and Sage played this game every Sunday morning, so it was important to get things right. "Well, he just asked for one of those berry corn muffins and what looks like a side of bacon. No, correction, ham. Since he doesn't look overweight, I'm guessing no one made him breakfast this morning. Also, he's flirting with the new Tinker Bell-looking girl giving him his drink, so I don't think anyone rolled off him either. I'm going with single, lives alone, maybe recent breakup because some woman picked out those pants. Guys don't venture into royal-blue chinos on their own."

Sage nodded and gave her the customary victory high-five. "Well done."

"Thank you." Kenna crossed her legs, put a napkin across Paige's lap in an attempt to catch any bagel crumbs or cream cheese blobs, and took a bite of her own breakfast sandwich.

Sage broke off a piece of bran muffin and slouched back into the comfy couch, propping her boots, the ones with embroidered stars, out in front of her.

"Maybe we should start dating," Sage said on a huff.

"When I mentioned that a couple of months ago, you told me I was nuts and you were happy being single. You were leaving it to fate, remember?" Kenna brought her Americano to her lips and decided it was still too hot.

"Yes, I remember, but that was before—"

"Before what? Did Garrett piss you off again?"

Sage smacked her shoulder and looked around like she always did at the mention of Kenna's oldest brother. "Will you shut up."

"Oh yeah, this is definitely his kind of place."

"Someone could know him."

"I . . . highly doubt that. Not exactly his crowd."

"My desire to date has nothing do with your brother. He's not my type, we've already been over this. I get it. He's rude and doesn't know I'm alive. He seems friendly with everyone else, doesn't he?"

"No." Kenna now sipped her drink.

"He dates women, so he must be doing something."

"Eh, would we call it dating? More like he flirts and then never follows through. We've been over this, Sage. Garrett likes to be—"

"Liked. I know, he likes the game and that's it. I don't know why we are even talking about him again. I'm moving on. I have no interest in your sweaty farmer brother."

"Uh huh."

Sage sighed again and brought her muffin plate into her lap this time like a sulking child. Kenna always thought her best friend was more than beautiful. She was unexpected, sort of like an emerald compared to a diamond. Diamonds always got all the attention, but the emerald was special. She had golden brown hair cut short. She was sporting a pixie cut as of late, but Kenna had seen it with longer bangs and even what Sage had called an "uneven bob." This was the shortest her friend's hair had ever been, but she managed to look more feminine, more alluring, than most women with luscious locks. Her eyes were gray with twinkling spots of brown and her neck was long and porcelain. In fact, her whole body was porcelain, which she seemed perfectly fine with. Sage was the most comforta-ble-in-her-skin woman Kenna had ever met. She wore crazy earrings—like the big chandelier things she currently had on—and paired them with sweatpants and heels or boots. She wore whatever she wanted, and somehow, instead of looking ridiculous, she looked hip. She shopped at vintage stores, and Paige had recently started telling her she had Bally Harry hair. Sage quickly translated that to Halle Berry hair and took it as a huge compliment.

"I know we're done talking about him, but merciful Jesus, did you see the John Deer T-shirt he had on yesterday? I mean, that should really be outlawed. His eyes are green for hell's sake. He should be banned from green. To make it worse, there was a hole right by his neck." Sage brought her fingers to her own neckline.

Kenna threw the crust end of her English muffin right at her best friend's face. "Snap the hell out of it."

"Right, great, thank you. I needed that. Good. So, back to what I was saying, we should date. I'm ready and you said you wanted to, so let's commit."

"Okay. We should probably do an online thing because we don't want to date the customers and since we spend more time at The Yard than any single woman should, online is probably our best pool of potentials."

"Did you know there's an online dating site for people with pets now? And one based on your astrological sign." Sage finished her last bite of muffin and put her empty plate on the crate.

"Really?" Kenna took the plate with a mostly eaten bagel off of Paige's lap. Her daughter was still in a trance, and when Kenna glanced at the phone, she saw two hippos fighting. Paige was leaning forward as if she were about to jump into the screen.

Sage nodded, rubbing her neck and twisting her body like the yoga pro she was.

"Let's just start with a basic site. No animals or stars, just our profiles, and see what's out there. We don't even have to do anything yet because the thought of actually going on a date makes me want to heave."

"Then why are we doing this?"

"Because it's time. I've given it some thought, and that has to be what the dream was telling me."

"That you need to go on a date?"

"Yes. Well, sort of. That I need to expand my horizons. I need more male reference points, more data to pull from when I'm dreaming."

Sage stopped short of almost laughing her latte through her nose. "Reference points? A little cold, but good. That's funny. Speaking of, let's play a version of our game. If Travis were standing in line . . . what's his story?"

"That's silly, I already know his story."

"No, you don't. If you just saw the surface, tell me his deal. Unless you're too uncomfortable to go there with your new dream guy."

"Oh, you're cute. Fine." Kenna looked over at Paige, who had little curls of milk on her upper lip. She handed her daughter a napkin, eyes still on the video, Paige wiped her mouth. Kenna loved when her telepathic parenting worked. "Okay, Travis is in line on a Sunday."

Sage nodded.

"I'm at a bit of a disadvantage since I can't see the outfit, but I'll guess because I'm just that good."

Sage laughed and sipped her drink.

"He'd be in those cargo pants and some worn T-shirt with a motorcycle on it or even just a plain one. His hair would be all over the place and the beard would be trimmed."

"Even on a Sunday?"

"Yeah, because he was probably out the night before. He always trims it when he has a date."

"Huh, interesting. Go on."

"Slightly wrinkled clothes would tell me he's single and does his own laundry. Motorcycle reference, if it were there at all, would be subtle, so I'd assume he rides a bike. Usually, guys who actually ride go easy on the biker bling."

"True." Sage laughed again.

"He'd have his shades on his head and this early in the morning, he'd probably look hungover. I'd pin him as single party guy. Easy. Oh, and the body. We can't forget the body. I'd probably call boxing or some kind of alternative exercise because he doesn't look like a typical gym guy. There, like I said, he's easy."

"What about his job?"

"Probably wouldn't be able to pick up on that. Although have you ever noticed Travis when he watches food being prepared or even the way he looks at food?"

Sage smiled. "Can't say I have."

"It's like he's watching a movie, a love story even. His eyes get heavy but sort of playful and he watches every detail. I'm used to Logan's cooking eyes, but Travis is on another level. It's—" She looked up because she could feel Sage's silence. "What?"

"Nothing. He's easy huh? Just a surface party boy?"

"Oh, shut up. You asked about his job. I was just providing data. Game over. So, I shouldn't have judged before. Maybe dating will be fun."

"There's nothing fun about dating. And maybe that dream was trying to tell you—"

Kenna shot Sage a look that stopped her midsentence. "More data, that's all I need, and you need to date too because it's healthier than pining over John Deer."

Sage let out a sigh. "Do you think he knows?"

"No." Kenna was grateful for the change of subject.

"How did *you* figure it out?"

"Because you're my best friend. You're gorgeous, you dress like some urban fashion magazine, and for the past two years, you've dated absolutely no one. I began wondering why, and then I noticed that you lose yourself every time my brother walks into a room. I didn't need to be Bri or Nietzsche to figure it out."

"Is it that bad?"

"Well, he has no idea given that he's clueless on so many levels. I'm sure of that, but unless you're going to make your move, my dear friend, it is time to get over it."

"Right, I guess, I mean can you see the two of us together?"

"No."

"Oh, well, thanks."

"Garrett is his own man. Self-contained. He *is* that farm, Sage. I honestly wouldn't wish that on you and besides, you love the city and culture. He's . . . not that."

Right as Sage looked like she was gearing up to plead her case for continuing to ogle Garrett, Paige, whose blue eyes had finally left the screen of Kenna's phone, took her earphones out.

"Are we having another round, Auntie?"

"We sure are, and I'm buying." Sage took her niece-by-friendship's little hand and got in line for more caffeine.

Travis woke up Sunday morning with his customary headache. Last night had been a little out of hand, but fortunately, when he turned his head toward the side of the bed that wasn't his, there was no one there. Bad decisions may have been made, but he didn't bring any of them home. Progress. He'd gone out with Logan, Garrett, and a few of the other guys from the restaurant as a send-off of sorts. Logan was taking his first vacation since The Yard had opened. He and Kara were going on a road trip up Highway One, "until we run into Canada," as he'd put it. Logan and Garrett had called it a night early and Travis, of course, stayed to party with the boys. His throbbing head told him he was either getting too old or just plain tired of this shit. He dragged himself into and out of the shower. Dressed, he pulled on a sweatshirt and grabbed the keys to his bike, deciding on Egg Slut at the Grand

Central Market for breakfast. He'd pick up cheese there too before heading into The Yard to make the best mac and cheese a certain almost-six-year-old ever tasted.

The cool morning air helped with the headache. Travis had bought his BMW R nineT motorcycle last year. He'd had an older bike, but this one was a gift to himself for his thirty-second birthday. He liked bikes, the solitude of them. Sure, there was a tiny spot on the back if he wanted to bring anyone along, but that never really happened. He played but rarely paired.

Entering Grand Central Market, he stopped by to see Jarrod, who now had his own cheese shop in the market. Jarrod and Travis both went to the American Culinary Institute in Seattle, Washington. They had studied under renowned chef-turned-instructor Marjorie Frieze. It was a small school: there had only been twelve in their class. He and Jarrod had grown close through long hours in the kitchen and even longer hours at the clubs and bars around Seattle. Jarrod used to give Travis a run for his money. They were crazy back in those days, but then Jarrod met Sabrina and things quickly changed. Suddenly he was staying home, buying her flowers, and when they graduated, she was there cheering him on. Something shifted in Travis's chest thinking about it now. Jarrod had come from a really shitty family, and he seemed to have made his own way and found love.

"How's business?" Travis chomped into his egg sandwich and wiped his mouth.

"Good, crazy even." Jarrod was thirty-five, the father of two little boys and husband to Sabrina, who sang nights at the Peacock Lounge about four streets over from the market. He was tatted from shoulder to wrist on both arms, most of them having to do with his Nordic ancestry or his time spent in the army. Jarrod graduated from the academy and then moved on to apprentice with a cheese maker. His shop was always a source of fascination for Travis; there were so many cheeses he'd never heard of, and he tried something new every time he visited. He made a mental note that if Grady and Kate chose cheese plates for their wedding, he would ask Jarrod for suggestions.

"I'm glad to hear that. Did you put the new shelves up in the back?"

"I did. Well, Sabrina's brother did, but I helped. Got a new slicer too." Jarrod pointed to what looked like a slab of marble and a series of silver strings, four or five of them.

"Nice. How are the boys?"

"Growing up and mouthing off, you know, as expected. Sean's into skateboards now and Sabrina keeps trying to put kneepads on him. I tried to tell her she was lucky the kid agreed to a helmet." Jarrod laughed and, leaning on his display case, sipped his coffee from a brown paper cup. "So, you guys full of yourselves now after that *LA Times* feature?"

Travis laughed. "Tired, that's mainly what we are, but it's been great. Logan brought back your new manchego last week. That's more than a cheese, it's a statement, man."

"I've got to keep it interesting, ya know? It's taken me a few batches, but I think I've finally got the aging down. Logan was making something special. He seems happy. How about you?"

"Me? I'm good."

"Happy?"

"I, well . . . you know, I'm good. Not settled into wedded bliss and reproducing like you are just yet, but I'm doing my thing."

Jarrod laughed. "You better get on it, my man. You're missing out."

"Is that so?" Travis laughed, threw out his breakfast sandwich wrapper, and took the piece of cheese Jarrod handed him.

"Oh, yeah. The marriage thing is fun, but being a dad . . . it's over-the-top love, crazy."

"Crazy like we used to be?"

"Better." Jarrod's eyes were serious, caring even, Travis thought.

Hell, if love got someone like Jarrod, no man was safe.

"Great cheese, is that a Parmesan?"

Jarrod nodded. "Dodged the daddy talk like a true bachelor man. Well done."

Both men laughed.

"So what can I get you?"

"I need a good cheddar, the best one you have."

"What are you making?"

"Mac and cheese."

"You going with fontina? Or, a lot of guys are adding Gruyere too."

"No, I want classic. It's for a five-year-old girl."

Jarrod raised an eyebrow and Travis offered no explanation.

"Well, this is my best extra sharp. That's about ten pounds right there."

"Perfect, I'll take that and give me three or four pounds of that Parmesan."

"You got it." Jarrod wrapped the Parmesan in brown paper and put the cheddar in a box. After running Travis's credit card, he walked around the counter and handed him everything.

"Thanks, man. Give the family my love."

"Will do."

"See you next time. Come by when you can and I'll buy you lunch."

"Deal." Jarrod extended his fist, and Travis put the box under his arm and returned the bump.

By the time he reached The Yard, it was just past ten. Now that Logan was busy being in love, he no longer showed up on the day they were closed to catch up on his infamous yellow pad. Travis had the kitchen to himself. He flipped the lights, grabbed an apron, and turned the Red Hot Chili Peppers on over the sound system. *Jarrod had seemed happy*, he thought as he unwrapped his ingredients and pulled out a few bowls.

Travis didn't do marriage. He knew that made him a cliché, but there were far worse clichés he could imagine being. He didn't want family, at least not like the one he grew up with. He was content with what he had: his work and friends.

He needed to fix things with Makenna, figure it out because she was part of his life, he thought as he went into the walk-in for cream and butter. Pulling a food processor up from the cabinet beneath him, he hummed along to *Californication*, occasionally working his air drumming skills. Life was good, and he was good. Besides, he didn't have time to analyze, he had mac and cheese to make, a special request. Travis smiled at the thought of Paige's note and got to work.

Chapter Five

Monday morning had not gone according to plan. Makenna had been up late, obsessing about the millions of questions on the stupid dating profile link Sage emailed her to fill out. Good God, she didn't even know some of this stuff about herself, and she certainly didn't want to share it with complete strangers.

Complete strangers. Those words had struck her right around one in the morning because that's what she was really doing, right? Putting herself—her likes and dislikes—out there for Lord knows who to comb over and decide if she was worthy of coffee. She had started to freak out so she turned on *Sherlock*, whose blathering mind was much like her own. She didn't need more angst, so she clicked the remote and tried to sleep.

She must have fallen off sometime after three, so naturally she hit the snooze button past its limit and woke up late. She and Paige had raced around the house getting ready for school. Breakfast was a waffle wrapped in a paper towel to go. Kenna didn't have time for a shower, so she pulled her hair back, made sure she put deodorant on, and used one of those all-in-one face wash wipes right before she pulled up to The Yard and ran in to grab Paige's lunch box. It was full and sitting on the middle of the counter. He'd made her lunch again. Even though Makenna had been a complete lunatic without an explanation, he'd still made lunch. It was honestly one of the sweetest gestures. He made her daughter lunch, without fail. In that moment, she wanted to thank him, but he was nowhere to be found and she needed to go, so she left.

They pulled through the drop-off line at St. Christopher's with two minutes to spare, and Kenna could have sworn the teacher who helped Paige out of the car looked at her like she was a crazy, out-of-control mommy. *Maybe this stuff was in her head,* Kenna thought. Maybe she looked perfectly normal to people on the outside and only felt like a leper on the inside.

She drove through McDonald's for a Coke, put on some moisturizer, and kept one hand on the wheel while she hunted through her purse for lip gloss, ChapStick, something to keep her from looking just-out-of-bed by the time she pulled back up to The Yard.

She went in through the front door again. The fleeting warm and fuzzy moment over the lunch box was gone, and she was again hoping to avoid Travis. As she approached the hostess station, the specials board was off the wall and propped on the bar. The perfectly placed word *Ratatouille* and the little description below that Sage had worked on Saturday night before closing were wiped clean and in their place were the words, *Classic Mac and Cheese.*

Kenna threw her now-empty cup in the trash, frustrated that the bathtub of caffeine she'd slurped down on the drive in hadn't helped her frenzied, almost-late-for-school mood.

"Why has the special changed?" she asked, pushing through to the back kitchen, forgetting for a minute her whole plan to avoid the chef who was most likely responsible for the mac and cheese. That was her specials board, damn it—the one thing she had control over these days. "The specials board was done on Saturday. It was pretty. Why'd we have to mess with pretty on a Monday morning?"

Travis was the only one in the back kitchen, which seemed perfectly aligned with the rest of her crappy morning. He was already in his apron and, of course, his beard was trimmed close to that adorable cleft in his chin Makenna hadn't even realized existed until two weeks go. She stepped closer to him, determined to be brave, until he turned those eyes on her. Changing her mind, she stepped back.

"I did," Travis said, spreading pecan halves on two baking sheets.

"You prepped for the ratatouille and n—now you just changed it to mac and cheese? Do you even do a mac and cheese?" She was being ridiculous. It didn't matter that he'd changed the special. Well, it sort of mattered because that wasn't the plan, but she really should just turn around and get the hell out.

"Of course I do a mac and cheese. There's not a legit chef alive who can't pull off mac and cheese. I made extra yesterday, so it's the lunch special. I can change the special. It's allowed. Logan's gone for a couple more days. I set the menu. I made a cold salad with the prep work, so that's not a waste. Calm down, Ken."

"Why mac and cheese? Is it like a three cheese or something special?"

"Nope."

"You made plain old mac and cheese on your day off because you just got a wild hair up your ass and decided to do that?"

He said nothing, still adding pecans.

"Of course you did. Right, because why not? You probably rolled out of bed Sunday morning, still in your pajamas, and said, 'I think I'll show up somewhere, do something no one expects.' Fine!" She was tilting a little into crazy, which was normally manageable, but she was tired so that set her over into scary. She drew in a deep breath and finally turned to leave the kitchen.

"Hey, Ken."

Crap. She turned.

"I'm not sure what's gotten into you, but if you're going to play crazy lady this early, you need to get your facts straight."

Makenna scrunched her face in frustration. Her gaze was focused on the edge of the cutting board, so he naturally bent to catch her eyes. When he found them, he smiled.

39

"I don't wear pajamas."

Makenna felt her face flush, shook her head, and left. As the kitchen door swung closed, she could still feel the rumble of his laughter all the way in her toes.

Travis was relieved that things felt a little closer to normal. She was rambling and he was teasing, but something was still off. She wasn't gazing through him anymore or checking out his ass, but she seemed almost nervous. She normally blushed and dismissed him, but she rarely looked uncomfortable. *Shit, what did I do?*

Nothing. He didn't do anything. Whatever it was, she needed to spit it out. She was back to being all over him about "the plan" and her silly little details. He could hear her in the bar dragging what sounded like chairs around. He supposed that was a start back to normal.

Travis decided to put together the meatballs next, so he walked to the dishwasher to pick up two large stainless steel bowls he'd used earlier. When he turned, Sage was holding a rack of glasses and bumped right into him.

"Hey." He steadied her and the glasses.

"Hey, sorry. I've gotta get back to the bar." At first, she didn't meet his eyes either, but then she locked on to him. She knew something.

"So, wanna tell me what's up with Ken?"

"Umm . . . she hates it when you call her that?" Sage tried.

"Is that why she's either avoiding me or looking like she has a dirty secret?"

Sage huffed with phony indignation. "What? I have no idea what you're talking about. She's fine, she's good. Busy—maybe that's what you're sensing—she's really busy."

"No, that's not it." Travis tried not to laugh at her entirely laughable performance.

"Oh, well then I have no idea. Maybe you pissed her off."

"Do you think it was the Trixie thing? She seemed weird after that. Maybe—"

"Maybe what?"

"I don't know. She's never looked at me like that, and there was nothing on my jeans."

Sage seemed like a trapped animal with a fight-or-flight decision. "What are you trying to say, that she was upset or jealous of your . . . escapades?" She laughed. This time, it was a real laugh, and Travis knew she'd chosen fight.

"That's not what I was saying." Maybe he was because he had thought of it more than once. That day in the kitchen, it sort of felt like he should be embarrassed, which was weird because he didn't do embarrassed or ashamed anymore, but there was something about the look on her face. It felt personal.

Sage was hunching over a little bit. Were those tears of laughter now?

"Oh, forget it. She's acting weird and you're hiding something."

She stopped laughing. "Maybe you should ask *her*."

Travis said nothing, because why the hell hadn't he thought of that?

Sage smiled and left him standing there like an idiot.

"Travis, lunch is starting to pick up. I need some help up here, dude."

Crap, he'd left Todd up front alone? He really didn't need these distractions. Kenna was often a minor distraction in her sexy flannels or those muck boots that drove him a little nuts. He might even have a sexy farm girl fantasy starring a version of Makenna Rye, but that was no one's business. He knew who she was, she knew who he was, but that look she'd given him . . .

Why the hell did he care what she thought anyway? If she had a problem with his personal life, well, that was too bad. He supposed he did invite criticism with the phone call, but he didn't know they were standing there. Maybe he did. *Aw, shit!*

"Runner," he called, and placed the spinach salad in the window.

This was stupid. He had work to do.

❋

Garrett sat at the bar about a half hour into the lunch rush. He was wearing another green shirt. This one wasn't John Deer; it bore the name of some fertilizer, but Kenna just knew it would be a topic of discussion, or at the very least mentioned at coffee with Sage the following weekend. He took his baseball hat off, put it on the bar, and snagged a cherry out of her Coke.

"Hey!" She slapped his hand, but was too late.

"How's my favorite sister?"

"Only sister," she said, engrossed in her laptop.

"That too." Garrett took a seat next to her. "What're you working on there?" He leaned in and before she could turn her computer, Garrett began reading. "*Best date: A. Fancy Restaurant B. Intimate Bar C. Anything Outdoors or D. Moonlit Dive.*"

She closed her eyes and waited for the laughter.

"Moonlit dive. You think they're talking scuba or Jake's Rib Shack?" Garrett laughed. "What the hell is this?"

"It's a dating profile."

"Are you kidding me? You don't need one of those."

"I do. I can't date anyone here and I have Paige. I want to be able to screen people first."

Garrett shrugged and pulled her laptop in front of him. "Okay, well, let's see what you've got." He skimmed her answers.

"Well, I'm glad to see your ideal date is anything outdoors because the rest of that shit was lame. *Sexiest car, a truck.* Good choice again. *Are baseball caps worn backward ever sexy, yes or no?*" He looked up at Kenna. "That's a no-brainer. Again, you chose yes. Nice. *Sexiest job?* Who comes up with this stuff? Let's see what you put—a man who works with his hands. A farmer? Aww, isn't this cute, you're looking for your big brother. I'm flattered." He pushed the laptop back over to her.

Kenna shook her head. "Are you finished now?"

"Yeah, just be sure to meet in public places and let me or Logan know if you want us to go with and sit at a different table."

"Oh yes, that's a great idea. Thanks for that offer." She rolled her eyes.

Sage came out of the kitchen, her back facing them as she carried a rack of clean glasses. "Okay, so did you fix my profile?" Her back still to them, she didn't see Garrett.

"Garrett here has graciously volunteered to chaperone our dates if we need protection from the big bad world," Kenna said, hoping Sage wouldn't say anything more about her profile.

Sage's shoulders tensed and she slowly set the rack down on the bar, sort of like someone trying to avoid a bear attack. Kenna was sure at that moment Sage wanted to shrink into the floor, but she had no choice: she had to turn around and face the music. She looked quickly over her shoulder to confirm Garrett was actually sitting at her bar and immediately started hanging the clean glasses. Sage was suddenly all about keeping busy.

"Well, isn't that thoughtful of him, but we will be just fine."

Garrett was looking back at Kenna's computer, and she knew what was coming next. She wanted to warn Sage again, but there was no time.

"Wait, that's your profile?" Garrett asked.

Sage glanced at her, clearly looking for an explanation. There was nothing Kenna could do, so she scrunched her face in resignation.

"You think backwards baseball caps are sexy and you like trucks? You're looking for a guy that"—he looked at the screen again—"works with his hands, such as a farmer?"

"I . . ." She was still putting the glasses away, and Kenna recognized that look. Her friend was not going to find her way out, and there was no way in hell Garrett was going to win this.

Kenna slapped his arm and closed her laptop. "I never said it was my profile or hers, dumbass. That was a sample, showing us how to do it. You just assumed, as you always do."

Garrett gave her a look, as if thinking about this any longer was more than he was willing to do, and shrugged. Sage's shoulders dropped in relief.

"Do you want a beer, Garrett?" Sage asked, picking up the now-empty rack, still with her back to them and walking toward the kitchen.

"Sure. I'll take that new one."

"Give me a second." She disappeared into the kitchen and probably collapsed onto the floor, Kenna thought.

Garrett turned to Makenna. "The profile said Sage Jeffries at the top. When I looked over again, just then, it said her name."

"Huh, weird."

"Yeah," Garrett said with his eyes on Sage as she returned and poured him a Born Yesterday Pale Ale. "Really weird."

Paige sat in front of St. Christopher's toward the end of the U-shaped pickup line. On the adjacent sidewalk, a teacher wearing a striped wraparound dress seemed to be having trouble walking in the wedge heels she wore. Kenna wondered why, with everything else teachers had to deal with, they would choose to wear heels. The job seemed daunting enough from her perspective, making comfort a top priority. Hell, Kenna wasn't even a teacher and comfort was always her priority, she thought, looking down at her boots.

Two more cars to go before she arrived at the front of the line, so she reluctantly paused her audiobook, *The English Spy*, even though it was up to a really good part. Because her life tended to get busy, Kenna always bought an e-book or a print book and then the audio version. That way she achieved maximum reading time. When Paige was little, Kenna read all the time, but now she had school activities and things had gotten busier at the restaurant, plus there was always work at the farm. Makenna believed in covering all of her reading bases because fiction was her escape, probably her therapy too.

She grabbed a granola bar from the center console and pulled her navy-blue Jeep, correction, her muddy navy-blue Jeep, up behind a silver Jaguar. A teacher with a large stone necklace loaded two little girls into the clean, perfect car, and Kenna wondered if that mom had two pack rat traps in the back of her car. The thought made her laugh a little. Jaguar had probably never even seen a rat trap. Although, she thought as she pulled up next in line, she shouldn't judge a book by its cover. Her father was always telling her that Oprah said something like critiquing others only shows the weakness in ourselves. Since discovering Oprah, her father had become the most evolved farmer she'd ever met; he even starting reading her book club books. Kenna smiled at the thought, and then her smile grew as a vision of cuteness with pigtails climbed into her booster seat and pulled her seatbelt on. Kenna waved politely to the teacher and pulled forward.

"How was your day, Peach?" She handed her daughter the granola bar.

"Amazing." Paige ripped open the wrapper and took a big bite.

"Wow, really? What made it so amazing?"

"Well, we had extra circle time and I got to show everyone my penny collection. It was a hit."

Makenna smiled and tilted her rearview mirror down a little farther so she could see her daughter.

"That's great. Did you remember to bring them home?"

"Yup." She finished her bar and stuffed the wrapper into the seat pocket in front of her. Since becoming a mom, Makenna had purchased all the little trash bags and backseat systems for young children. When none of those worked, she finally asked Paige to hand up her trash when she was done, which hadn't worked either. Paige would be six in two months, and Kenna finally accepted the seat pocket as the trash bin.

"Can we put the top down?"

"No."

"Oh. My. God." Her sweet little hands were splayed out like a jazz dancer. "I forgot the bestest part of my day! He did it."

"Who did what?"

"My Travis, he made me mac and cheese. I left a note in my lunch box the last time with a picture and I asked with kisses and a heart. Mac and cheese was in my lunch box today."

Her daughter was practically bouncing with excitement, and Makenna felt that weird sweaty pressure in her chest again. That's where the mac and cheese had come from. He'd taken his Sunday and made her little girl's special request. Who did that? Certainly not the Travis McNulty she'd described to Sage over coffee. Things were growing more and more confusing.

"That was nice of him. Travis likes making your lunch. He told me." Kenna tried for perfectly together and calm mommy.

"My Travis is the best," she said, looking out the window.

"Honey, it's just Travis. His name is Travis."

"No, he's My Travis. Sierra at school says, 'My daddy makes my lunch every morning.' So I told her that My Travis makes my lunch. See, Mamma? He's My Travis."

Makenna did see. She spent the rest of the car ride home wondering whether she should worry about this as some kind of transference because her daughter's father had died or if she should just be happy that she had friends who cared about Paige and leave it at that. Not that Travis was exactly a friend; he was more of a coworker. He was her brother's friend, and just because she dreamed about him didn't mean that things were different, but maybe she should—*Oh for God's sake, shut up!*

Chapter Six

*T*ravis had just finished the cauliflower for their Friday happy hour special when Makenna, dressed in tight jeans and black leather riding boots, came through the back door. She'd done something different with her hair and her eyes looked more, well, more something, not that she was actually looking at him because the awkward thing was still going on.

"Morning," he said, because she was about to walk through the kitchen without even acknowledging he was standing right there.

She glanced back but kept moving toward the door to the bar. "Good morning. I've got quite a day today, so if you don't need anything—"

"Logan asked me to bring you up to date on our latest thoughts for Grady's wedding," he lied, but at least she stopped. "We were thinking since they're probably going to go with a fish and a red meat option, the salads need to be different because of the radicchio with the bass. So, we're adding a tomato salad with the fish option and this great endive, blue cheese, and bacon creation we came up with last night for the beef. Did they mention if they wanted family-style sides or the entire meal plated? I'm thinking since the reception is going to be right there on the grounds of the

Wayfarer, they might be going for something rustic, which would be awesome."

He was rambling like a child hopped up on one too many Tootsie Rolls, but he didn't care.

She met his eyes. "Sounds good."

"Which part?"

Kenna shook her head and moved to exit the kitchen, probably to run to her corner. "All of it. Sounds amazing."

Travis touched her arm and tried to stop her, but she seemed so uncomfortable that he let go. There it was again, the nervousness. Shit, he was starting to feel it too.

"Did you hear anything I just said?"

"Yes, I did, and I'm happy to discuss it later today, but I just got in. Right now, I need to set my stuff down and maybe eat something. I get that you're excited about the wedding. Logan is too, but I have about fifty other things on my list. So excuse me if I'm not jumping up and down over the endive."

He held his hands up in surrender and she kept talking.

"I just finished listening to Paige's latest plans for her nemesis, Sierra, all the way to school. Thank you for the mac and cheese, by the way. I haven't had a chance to thank you yet."

You mean you've been avoiding me for weeks, he thought but didn't say.

She met his eyes again, this time with a warmth he didn't recognize. "Paige loved it. Her exact words were 'Sierra's dad can suck it.'"

Travis laughed.

"Yeah, you're creating a monster, just so you know. I've been instructed to 'forget' her lunch box tonight so you can read the note she's going to make you during art class today. It promises to have lots of kisses and a drawing of you in your kitchen. So, stay tuned for that."

Travis started to say something, but Kenna still had more. He leaned up against the counter and tried not to look at her ass when she left to put a binder in Logan's office and walked back to finish telling him about her morning. Hell, at least she was talking to him.

"Then, I ran out of Coke yesterday, so I have nothing in my system. I may have been a little grumpy when some mother, selling Girl Scout cookies in the drop-off line, asked me how many boxes I wanted."

"How many did you get?"

"Six."

"Thin mints?"

"Four boxes."

"Nice."

"That's not the point. I still haven't washed my car and she sort of startled me, so I snapped and I might have tossed the twenty at her. I just wasn't very hospitable."

"No, you? I can't believe that."

She looked like she was going to laugh for just a moment, and then it was gone. Instead, she pointed at him.

"Damn it, is that a new shirt?"

"No, I just thought I'd shake it up a little today. Getting tired of the T-shirts. Looks like you did too. I like the boots. We must be on the same page, huh?"

"I—I guess, yes, maybe. Oh damn, I have work to do."

And with that, she practically flew out of the kitchen and then came bursting back in.

"Fine, you know what, this is stupid. It passed stupid a few days ago. I had a dream about you. You were there without your shirt on and now, now I keep looking at you and it's messed everything up. So, there you have it."

Travis attempted to ask a question but was silenced when she held up her hand, blew her hair out of her flushed face, and left the kitchen again.

A dream, huh? Well, thank Christ they finally got to the bottom of that, because he was beginning to think he'd lost her. He couldn't remember the last time he'd given two shits, but somehow the thought of offending or upsetting Kenna made him uneasy. Which was interesting. So was the dream. He wanted to know more, but he'd give her some time to work. He had mozzarella to pull before they opened for lunch but after the rush, they'd talk.

49

❋

There, it was out, she thought, sipping her second Coke of the morning. It wasn't that bad. Technically, she ran from the kitchen before he could even form a reaction, let alone speak, but it was fine. Now, things could go back to normal. Kenna read the same e-mail three times before she closed her computer. Oh, who was she kidding? The shirt, his smell, it was all still there. This feeling of uncertainty, the butterflies, could be a good thing, welcome even, but not for Travis. She was not his type, which was one of a few dozen reasons why she needed to stop... noticing him. Kenna checked the clock on her phone and walked out of the private dining room to see if the handyman service had arrived to hang the bigger specials board by the entrance. She plowed right into Travis before she even noticed he was there. Her hands immediately came up and were supposed to push away, but they clearly decided they liked where they were. Makenna stood, frozen, staring at his neck, well, more like the buttoned-up V at his neck, right below his Adam's apple.

Adam. Adam's apple. She'd never noticed that part of a man was named after her late husband. She had never even thought about it until now, standing between Travis's steadying arms, make that big steadying arms, looking at his... throat apple. Jesus, her mind had turned into a Dr. Seuss book, maybe that one Paige loved with the little blond guy in the yellow onesie standing on the big rainbow swirly thing. What was the name of that one? *Oh, the Places You'll Go!*—that was the one.

Travis's chest expanded in a deep breath, and she felt the stretch of his muscles. She couldn't stare at his throat apple named after her dead husband forever, so Kenna met his dark, dark chocolate eyes and for not the first time in her life, she cursed all things holy because even though she'd sort of told him about the dream, there was no relief. *It* was still there. The racing heart, flushed face, and attention to every single detail still floated all around her.

"What was the dream about?" His hands moved to her arms, up

and then down in what she was sure was supposed to be comforting, but the heat pulsing through her body felt nothing like comfort.

She closed her eyes, lowered her head, and thumped it a couple of times on his wall of a chest.

"Kenna?" His voice was lower than normal, a little husky and dead serious. There wasn't a trace of his usual wit.

"Okay, I have this recurring dream."

"I'm listening."

She stepped back from him and sat down on the green leather Carver chair she'd found at a neighbor's garage sale. It was narrow, but she held onto the wood sides anyway. She wasn't sure what to say. The dream suddenly felt incredibly personal, as if it meant so much more than just a bunch of nighttime illusions. She let out a slow breath as Travis lowered himself onto the cream-colored Farthingale, the latest addition to the dining table. That one she'd found at an antique store in Long Beach. *Focus, Kenna.*

She started with the white room, skimmed past petting the cat, and by the time she got to Paige sitting on the counter and grabbing her wedding bouquet, Travis looked like one of the kids at the library reading circle.

"Wow, have you ever had this analyzed?"

"No." She could tell he knew something good was coming, so he said nothing else.

"So, I tickle Paige and when I turn, Adam is standing by the stove, spoon in hand. He's in just pajama bottoms and smiling a really glorious smile. He says, 'Good morning,' pulls me in, kisses me, I touch his face, and then everything sort of fades into a soft light."

Travis was giving her the Poor Dead Husband look. She couldn't really blame him; it was a bittersweet dream.

"I—I'm sorry. How often do you have this dream?"

"The first time was a few weeks after Adam's memorial, and then a couple times a month for the two years following. By the time Paige was three, I was used to it and it became more sporadic. I had it right before we opened The Yard and then . . . two weeks ago."

Travis shook his head. "That's rough." He let out a breath.

"So, did I show up in the dream as some freaky shirtless neighbor?"

Kenna steadied herself. She owed him an explanation. "The dream is always the same, has been for years, until the last time. Until two weeks ago."

"Okay . . ."

"The last time I had the dream, when I turned in the kitchen,"—just rip it off like a Band-Aid, she told herself—"when I turned around, Adam wasn't standing there in his pajama bottoms."

Travis still looked confused.

"You were."

Oh, snap! David used that phrase all the time the gym, and it was the first thing that hit Travis's brain when he heard the plot twist in Kenna's dream. Her eyes settled on him with such weight that he tried to play it off by reminding her he didn't wear pajamas, which made her laugh. Thank God, because things were suddenly intense. A version of him was making Paige breakfast in her recurring dream. How did a guy respond to that?

"Have you ever, you know, substituted anyone else into this dream before?"

"No," she said, looking at him as if he might have some explanation to ease the awkwardness.

"Well, that's interesting."

"Yup."

"So that explains all the weirdness. This was *the* dream, and not just some sheet ripper we could laugh about and dismiss."

"Sheet ripper?"

"Yeah, you know." He saw the blank expression in Makenna's warm eyes and remembered how long she'd been out of the game. For some reason, that made him want to show her what a sheet ripper was rather than simply explaining it. *Yeah, that's a great idea, idiot.* "Huh, well, maybe you don't know. A ripper is a sex dream, you and me getting all hot—"

"Okay, that's good. I get it. No, there were no ripping sheets."

Travis smiled because her face flushed and she looked so uncomfortable that all he could think to do was make her laugh again. He had perfected the art of "it's no big deal," so even though he might like to explore why she had dropped him into her recurring dream, he went with his default—the easy way out.

Makenna was picking at the nail on her thumb.

"I think it's interesting and all, but it's just a dream, Ken."

She shot him a look that said she hated when he called her that, but he could also see her face ease a bit.

"I'm sure it's just because we work together and I'm one of the only guys you're around who's not a relative. I mean, there's Larry, but he's old enough to be your dad. The other guys are either gay or sporting some pretty serious beer gut."

She laughed. Mission accomplished.

"You're right," she said less than convincingly. "And I'm working on that, expanding my horizons, getting out there. So, I don't want you to feel weird about this."

"I don't."

"You don't?"

"No." Travis stood up before he said that he was flattered, a little bit intrigued, and a whole lot aware that if he wasn't drawn to his friend's sister before, he sure as hell was now. There was no point in saying any of that because that was just the stupid side of his brain or heart speaking. That side led to all kinds of things he didn't care to deal with.

"Okay, well . . . good. Me neither. Good. This was great. I'm glad we talked." Kenna opened her laptop.

Travis smiled. Damn, she really was something.

"I am too. Good talk. Now, stop being weird. It was a dream. We can't control our dreams. If we could, hell, there are a couple of Victoria's Secret models I would love to invite into my next one."

She shook her head and as he turned to leave, she was already back to working her mouse. She seemed lighter, relieved. That was good; she had enough crap on her plate.

Victoria's Secret models? Man, you're really an idiot.

Chapter Seven

Makenna woke up on her back, which was strange because she was a stomach sleeper and usually opened her eyes with her face smushed into her pillow. It was Wednesday, her still half-asleep mind told her, but then her eyes flew open as soon as she noticed the feel of Paige's little hand in hers. Her daughter was lying right next to her, awake and also looking at the ceiling.

"Are you okay, Peach?" Kenna said, softly squeezing her daughter's hand.

"Fine. Morning, Mama."

"Morning. Did you have a nightmare?" Kenna turned, head still on the pillow, to look at her.

"Nope."

"That's good. You going to tell me why you're in my bed and we're holding hands?"

"The otters." Paige's sweet face turned and they were now both looking at each other, still holding hands.

"Of course, the otters." Kenna gave her a silly confused face.

Paige giggled.

"Otters hold hands so they don't lose each other when they sleep. I didn't want to lose you, Mama. You would be sad if I dr—drif—"

"Drifted?"

"Yes, if I drifted way away, that would be bad. We have to hold hands at night so that never happens."

Kenna smiled and pulled her daughter close so they were spoons. Big spoon and little spoon. She kissed Paige's soft dark blonde hair, which smelled like her strawberry shampoo. Kenna tried not to cry. The love overwhelmed her sometimes and there were other days, usually when she cocked her brow in confusion, that Paige looked so much like Adam. It had been years; he had died when she was only five weeks old, but there were moments it still squeezed at Kenna's chest.

"We're not in water, so we are lucky that way. Not a lot of drifting on land." Kenna pulled her in closer.

Paige squirmed to face Kenna again and held her little finger to her mouth, as if she were figuring out a math problem. "Right, you're right. Those otters have it harder, don't you think?"

"Tough work being an otter." Kenna tickled her until she ran from the bedroom. She poked her head back.

"Rise and shine, silly boots. We need waffles and my hair is a nest of rats again."

Kenna laughed. "A rat's nest."

"Right." Paige spun on her slippers and headed to the kitchen. "We have a family meanie today."

"Meeting," Kenna said, getting out of bed. "It's a family meeting, not a meanie." She let out a breath, pushed her hair off her face, and quickly went into the bathroom so she could get to the kitchen before her daughter started making breakfast for herself, because she certainly would.

After rinsing and drying her face, Kenna noticed the unopened package of peanut butter crackers sitting on the basket next to her tub. She'd made Paige give them up last night in a trade-off that allowed her to have bubbles in Kenna's bigger tub—the "hacoozie" as Paige called it. After tub and bedtime book and e-mails, Kenna had forgotten to bring them back into the kitchen. She put some moisturizer on and picked up the crackers. The wrapper crinkled in her hand, and the memory hit her with such surprise that she leaned back against the bathroom counter for balance.

It was the morning she woke up in the hospital, the morning after Paige was born. Their baby girl had arrived at 3:30 in the middle of the night, so after the initial wonder and kisses, Kenna had collapsed in exhaustion. Early the next morning, she opened her eyes to Adam, all almost six feet of him, curled up on a couch that looked more like a chair. She was reaching for the peanut butter crackers on the side table and at the sound of the crinkle, Adam jumped to his feet.

"I'll get it," flew out of his mouth, his blond hair every which way. His shirt was wrinkled and his light blue eyes were foggy and bloodshot.

Makenna remembered smiling and despite being a little uncomfortable from the delivery, completely flooded with joy. She was only twenty-four when Paige was born. Adam was twenty-six and even though he came from money back in Rhode Island, they were both just getting started in their careers and had very little money of their own. Looking back, they probably had no business having a baby, but if anyone would have told them that at the time, they would have both rolled their eyes and laughed. There was nothing they couldn't do back then. Adam had held her hand, cut the cord, and cried while he kissed his daughter. The morning after, he was attentive and so gentle. When they left the hospital, it took twenty minutes for him to secure and recheck the elephant-print car seat. Before they pulled out of the hospital, he had looked at her and said, "Feels like we should at least get a manual or something, right?"

Kenna had laughed and touched his hand. "Can we stop for ice cream?"

"Still?"

"Oh, yeah. I think the little peach left me the cravings."

"She's totally a peach. Huh, she has a nickname now."

"Fuzzy." Makenna had reached behind her to touch the back of the car seat, needing contact with their new little person.

Adam had kissed her hand and later, while they sat in the car eating ice cream, he told her he was the happiest he'd ever been in his life, probably the happiest it was going to get. Told her that if it was all over tomorrow, he would be good, "all set with my girls," he'd said. Kenna would play that day, his words, over and over again in her heart for years after he was gone. Five short weeks later, she was cremating him and sprinkling him along the Divide Road on Catalina Island, baby Paige strapped to her chest in a big white sun hat. She had cried all the way up and all the way back down.

"Mama, the waffles are in the slots, but I need you to push the buttons because I'm not allowed."

Makenna shook herself free of the memory, swallowed back the ache, and walked toward the kitchen.

"That's right, Peach. No toaster buttons without me. Those listening ears *do* work."

"Sometimes." Paige was standing on the step stool, syrup in hand, hovering over the toaster when Kenna came into the kitchen.

"Okay, push them." Makenna took a Coke out of the refrigerator, kissed her daughter on the top of her head, and not for the first time, was so grateful for the magic Adam had left behind.

Kenna and Paige arrived at Libby's Little Breakfast Place at 5:45 that same morning. She wasn't sure how they'd managed to be early for the Rye family meeting, especially since it had taken them a good five minutes to find Fritters, the pig. He'd slipped between the bed and the wall last night. With Paige flat on her belly holding the flashlight, Kenna strained under the bed and reached Fritters with the tips of her fingers and rescued him from the dust bunnies. Kenna would need to move the bed out later and clean. *Where the hell did all the dust bunnies come from?* She barely gave it a thought because they were going to be late. Paige had chosen her striped tights and pink corduroy dress, and after a few hems and haws, she had let Kenna put her hair in two quick braids. She remembered her lunch box this time, made what Paige was now calling "the boring lunch," and strapped Paige into her booster seat by 5:30. It was remarkable timing for the morning routine, and as Kenna sipped her Coke on the ride to Libby's, she thought about him.

Every time she made lunch, she thought about him, which was ridiculous. He'd been making Paige's lunch for several months before the dream, and when she found out, he seemed embarrassed and dismissed it, but she thanked him and kissed his cheek. Maybe she started seeing him differently then. Maybe she still remembered her lips touching his cheek.

Trixie, she told herself, remember Trixie? Or how about the one named after the wine, yeah, remember Bordeaux? He invited her to The Yard's Christmas Eve dinner a few months earlier. Her dress, shirt, diaper, whatever she was wearing left little to the imagination. Right, stripper names and wine, that was the extent of Travis's type. So he made lunch on the side and had those biceps. It didn't matter because it would never work with someone like Travis. Besides, she would be dating soon. In fact, there were a few potentials to look over later this afternoon. She might even have a date by the weekend. Kenna let out a breath as she tied the apron Libby had given Paige to wear so she could play waitress while Kenna met with the men of the Rye family.

"Too tight, Mama." Paige squirmed and stuck out her belly. "I need to be able to work."

Kenna loosened the tie, made a bow, and flicked her daughter's braids as she marched over to join Libby, who was taking an order.

"You're early," her father said, taking off his cowboy hat as he walked past Paige and winked at her.

"So are you." Kenna put her bags down at the second booth, their booth, and took out her laptop.

"I know, but I'm always early. Peanut playing waitress again this morning?" Herbert Rye, her father, kissed Kenna on the cheek and she kissed him back, closing her eyes at the feel of his smooth cheek and the smell of Chaps cologne.

"I'm not sure how it happened, but we ended up early. Kind of nice not to be rushing for a change." Kenna took a sip of the Coke Libby had dropped off.

"I'll bet." Her dad looked over at Paige, his first and, so far, only grandchild. "She's getting so big. I can't even believe where the time goes. I'm making her a swing for her birthday. One of those Indian or Moroccan ones that hang."

Kenna glanced up from her computer.

"Heck, I don't know. She was showing me pictures a few months back and I told her I'd make her one. I'm actually having fun with it. Marrakech, that's what it's called. She said she wants to put it outside so she can 'be with her nature.' That's what she said."

Kenna smiled. "That's very sweet of you, Dad."

"She told me we could buy one, but I'd just as soon make it for her."

"It's a great idea. I'm sure she will love it even more."

"Hope so. Are we having her birthday at the farm or are you doing it at your place?"

"I haven't really thought about it yet. We've got a couple of months."

"Couple of months for what?" Garrett asked, bringing a cup of coffee over from the counter and taking his seat in the booth. "I hope we aren't waiting a couple of months to replace the blades on the number-two cultivator, because Ray says they're already shot."

Kenna shook her head. "Why do you always just barge in and assume your place in a conversation you know nothing about?"

"I'm just saying, we can't wait. And last time I checked"—Garrett looked at his watch—"this is the family meeting, so what the hell else would we be talking about?"

"Paige's birthday." Their father sipped his coffee.

"Oh, well, then I guess that's more important. I see you've put Paige the Magnificent to work again this morning. You're like the evil stepmother." He bumped Makenna's shoulder and she bumped him back while she pulled up her notes on the restaurant and the farm. She wanted to talk about catering the Malendar wedding and find out if Logan was going to expand the on-site garden next month or wait until next year.

When she looked up, Logan was heading toward the booth with Paige dangling from under his arm. Her brother looked fresh out the shower, and he was late.

"Put me down Uncle Rogan, I've got customers." Paige giggled, and Logan plopped his niece in Garrett's waiting arms.

"Uncle, now be re—son—" Paige furrowed her brow as she searched for the word well past her almost six-year-old vocabulary.

"Reasonable." Garrett set her down and kissed her forehead.

"Yes, reasonable. I'm a waitress and I don't have time for this." She put her chubby little hands on her hips, and Kenna watched her oldest brother melt into the booth.

"I get it, oh Magnificent One. Head on back to work."

Paige reached up and pinched his cheek, and Garrett laughed.

"I'm totally her favorite," Garrett said to Logan, who was now sitting next to their dad.

Logan shook his head. "You don't have a nickname, remember. Favorites always have a nickname. You're just . . . uncle." Logan exaggerated a wince. "Sorry, man. Firstborn but second-place uncle."

Before Garrett could continue the same stupid argument they had at least once a month, Kenna handed out copies of weekly financials for the farm and gave Logan the reports for The Yard. Libby took their orders with her sidekick and once the pancakes arrived, the family meeting was underway.

Kenna assured her brother that the cultivator replacement blades had already been ordered and that the guy he put her in touch with gave her such a deal they now had a backup. Garrett looked like a kid on Christmas morning, and Kenna moved on to the increase in feed costs and confirmed the dates of the Malendar wedding.

"This will be our first catering job and I guess we should hire someone, but I thought you could handle it, Kenna," Logan said.

Makenna clicked on the reminder to buy some foam balls for Paige's solar system diorama that was due next week and shot her brother a "don't I have enough to do?" look. "Is that in my job description?"

All three men laughed.

"Oh darlin', you tried that when you were little too. It's all right there under 'other duties as assigned,'" her father said.

"Plus, you're a woman. Isn't your kind all about overachieving?" Garrett popped his last bit of bacon into his mouth.

"My kind? Hey, have you guys discovered fire yet in the cave?"

Garrett laughed and ruffled the bun on top of her head. Kenna smacked his shoulder.

"All right, settle down," their dad said, as if they were all still kids around the breakfast table.

Come to think of it, when they got together, it usually felt that way.

"Kenna, if you're not up to it, we can look for someone. Maybe a part-time catering manager," Logan said, flipping through his report.

"No. Do you see those financials, all that black ink? We are finally looking so good. I don't want to mess with it. How hard can one wedding be?"

Logan smiled. He'd gotten his way, and Kenna would now need to create a new calendar. She really didn't mind a project. She liked being busy. Besides, it would be fun working with Kate and Grady. Since Grady's sister, Kara, was marrying Logan next year, they'd all become sort of close.

"Travis is all yours, I promise."

Kenna almost knocked her drink across the table. "Excuse me?"

Garrett steadied her glass.

"Travis. You can have him for the wedding. He's got some great ideas, and I'm still working with him while we put together the tasting menu. Kate and Grady are coming in a couple of weeks to taste test and pick their favorites, but since Kara's in the wedding, I need to be a guest that night. I'll leave the actual wedding to you and Travis."

Kenna focused on being grateful her laptop wasn't covered in Coke and nodded.

"Is there a problem?" Logan asked.

She said nothing but at least managed to shake her head the other way to indicate things were fine. More work, trying to date, Travis without his shirt on in her dream, an outspoken daughter . . . everything was just fine. She could work with Travis; she'd done it before. Granted, not on something as large as a wedding, but they worked together with Logan when the senator did his volunteer thing. This was a wedding and knowing Kate and Grady, it would be fun. Kenna wasn't sure she had time for fun, but she was turning over a new leaf, making time for things, important things. She was thirty, and a girl couldn't live on laptop screens, Littlest Pet Shop, and muddy boots alone. This project would keep her occupied, and working with Travis would be good. Wow, this was it, that delirious talking to herself moment right before she slid into complete meltdown.

"Ken." Garrett touched her shoulder. "You all right?"

"It would be great if everyone stopped asking me that. I was just thinking of ideas. Yes, of course I'm fine."

"I was just giving you crap. If it's too much, with Paige and all, I get it. We can hire a coordinator, even just for this one project." Logan's face grew serious.

"No." She added a new calendar to her list—Malendar-Galloway Wedding.

"You sure?"

"I am. Done. I'll set up some meetings for you, me, and Travis to sit down and make sure we're on the same page. I'll also call Grady and Kate to see if there's anything we are missing or other things we can contribute. I've got this."

Logan smiled. On some level she'd probably never understand, seeing either of her brothers smile was worth any backflip. She supposed she could blame her need to keep everything together, especially when it came to money and their security, on her mother. More like her lack of a mother. She left when Kenna was five, right about Paige's age. The thought of it made her sick to her stomach ever since she became a mother herself. What kind of woman left her children? She had no idea and had probably spent most of her life working to make up for something lacking. She took another sip of her Coke and moved on to asking Garrett for the new-hire paperwork for the two new farm hands he'd hired. There was no point in dwelling on the past. Makenna never dwelled. Ever. It didn't help the sun rise any faster and it never made anyone rest easy. That's what her father always used to say when any of them started to get sappy.

"It's somewhere in my truck," Garrett said, finishing his coffee and standing.

"Yeah? Well, let's go find it because your new guys won't get paid without it."

The Rye family exchanged kisses and pats on the back. All the men took turns snuggling their favorite little waitress, and Kenna thanked Libby once again.

"Pleasure's all mine. Anytime." Libby smiled, winked at their father as she always did, and then blended into her morning breakfast rush.

Sometimes when Kenna tucked Paige in and the house was quiet, she felt alone. Left behind. But most days, such as this one, she realized that she and Paige had people who loved them. They were their tribe, or her pack as Paige liked to call them. Was it possible for a little girl to watch too much National Geographic? Kenna would have to worry about that some other time.

Chapter Eight

The polka-dot weekend bag was all packed and sitting on Paige's bed. She and Kenna were collecting an assortment of books from the bookshelf while Fritters took a few more spins in the dryer. Paige would be gone for four days with Adam's parents on Coronado. It wasn't far, but Kenna was still buzzing around making sure she had everything. They had stopped at Walgreens last night to pick up a new elephant-shaped toothbrush and a pack of colored pencils. The latest issue of *National Geographic Kids* had arrived in the mail on Monday, so Paige would have plenty to discuss with her Nino and Gigi, as she called them. More nicknames, which pissed Garrett off to no end and made Kenna smile.

Karen and Bill Conroy had arrived in LA on the 9:15 from JFK. According to a text Kenna received, their driver had hit some traffic and they were due at her house in about an hour. That was a half hour ago and her pulse was starting to quicken. They came to visit twice a year, and every year Kenna felt as if a piece of a life she'd barely started popped in to say hello. Bill looked so much like Adam, well, what Adam might have looked like as an older man; Karen had her son's blue-sky-on-a-Saturday-afternoon eyes. Kenna thought about Adam from time to time, but she missed him every time she saw his parents. Missed him for her own selfish reasons and missed him for them. She could never imagine what it had been like for them to lose a child. At the time, she was too absorbed in her own grief to even notice, but time had a way of sorting through pain, and now she was able to see. She was able to be there for them and share her daughter.

"Fritters smells yummy." Paige held her fresh-out-of-the-dryer pig up to Kenna's nose.

"He sure does. Okay, I think we're all set. Anything else you think you'll need?"

Paige shook her head, so Kenna put her favorite blanket on top and zipped up her bag.

The doorbell rang.

Paige ran to the door, and Kenna heard happy greetings along with oohs and ahhs as Paige got an early start on what'd been happening in her life. Kenna took a deep breath, picked up the polka-dot bag, and went out to greet Adam's parents.

"There she is," his father exclaimed and pulled her in for a hug.

Kenna hugged him back and then leaned in to kiss Karen on the cheek.

"You look wonderful." Karen Conroy was clearly being generous, as always.

"Thank you. You guys do too," Kenna said, handing Paige's bag to Bill.

"So, anything we need to know about Little Miss here?" Bill ruffled Paige's hair and she grabbed his hand.

"Oh, I'm sure she'll give you an earful, but no medicines; she's great and very excited to spend time with you guys."

"Yes, I am," Paige exclaimed.

"What will you do with yourself for four days without her? Sleep probably." Karen laughed.

"Mama's going to start dating."

Makenna thought she'd experienced awkwardness with Travis these past few weeks, but this topped it.

"Oh," escaped her in-laws' mouths in unison.

Makenna crouched down next to Paige. "Honey, where did you hear that?"

"Mama, sometimes I use my earphones to trick you." She giggled, and so did Makenna.

"Okay, good to know." She stood and tried to soften the concern in Adam's parents' eyes, but before she had a chance, Bill put his hand on her shoulder.

"There's no need to explain to us."

"Of course not. You're a young, beautiful woman, and it's been a long time."

"Frankly, we were surprised it didn't happen sooner."

"You were?" Kenna was relieved.

"Honey, we want you to be happy, and he . . . Adam would want that too. You know that, right?" Karen seemed to be forcing herself to say her son's name as if it was some coping exercise, but Makenna still saw the same raw pain in her eyes. She was pretty sure she always would.

Kenna swallowed back things she thought had gone away. "I do. Thank you."

"We don't need to get all crybaby," Paige said. "Let's go so Mama can meet someone like My Travis."

Kenna was sure shock was all over her face.

"Okay, that's enough. You can tell Nino and Gigi all about your lunches and your Travis during the car ride." Kenna rolled her eyes and moved her daughter and her dead husband's parents out to their waiting car. Her life had never been a sitcom and hadn't quite reached reality show crazy yet, but sometimes it felt pretty close.

After Paige was safely tucked away with her grandparents, Makenna went to work. She checked off a little more than half her to-do list, which included meeting with the handyman again to explain why the hand sanitizers needed to be installed right side up. His assistant had installed them upside down and when he first arrived to observe what Kenna thought was a clear mistake, he looked at her and said, "Looks kind of cool like that, no?"

It often amazed Kenna that something so simple, which seemed obvious to her, was lost on some people. "No, it's not cool," she had responded, and they spent a good part of the morning making things right. She'd earned a lunch, so she sat with Sage to tell her about Paige sharing her new dating status.

"Oh wow, so they were cool with it?" Sage asked, after serving burgers to the couple two stools down.

"I don't know why I thought they wouldn't be. It's not like I was hiding anything from them, but when she blurted it out, I felt like I was going to fall over. I'm going to talk with her when she gets back. She's obviously smarter than I'm giving her credit for. She seemed to joke about it, but the idea has to be weird for her too. It's just change, more change."

"Speaking of change, it's been a few days since you told Travis about the dream. How are things? Back to normal?"

Makenna wasn't sure she knew what normal was anymore.

"Things are good. I haven't really seen him that much, but things are fine."

"Back to normal?"

"What does that mean?"

"By normal, I mean not just good. I mean he's back to annoying the holy hell out of you. That you couldn't possibly ever imagine stripping him out of those cargo pants he wears all the time and running your tongue up his—"

"Okay, okay. I understand the question." Kenna sipped the new tea Kara was making her try for her nerves. She would have killed for a Coke.

"And the answer?"

Kenna looked at her and even though she was still running her hands up Travis's chest in her mind, she was trying to get back to normal.

"The answer is, damn it, I don't know. I still see him differently. He doesn't drive me nuts. I mean he does, but in a different way. I don't get it. It's like that dream gave me permission or opened a door." Kenna shook her head. "It doesn't make any sense. You don't just do a one-eighty with someone because of a dream. That's why I need to date."

"Maybe you've always had feelings for him."

"What?"

"Yeah, you know, the love-hate thing. Lots of people start off that way. There's tension that leads to passion."

"Aren't those called dysfunctional relationships?"

"Not always. Sometimes, they're just windy roads. Were you immediately attracted to Adam?"

"Yes."

"You guys got along instantly?"

"Yes. I met him in class, he made me laugh, and I thought he was gorgeous. He asked me out two weeks later."

Sage blinked as if she'd turned down the wrong way and was trying to find her way back.

"Okay, so that was a bad example. Well, sometimes the rest of the world has a more complicated time finding love."

"What's going on with Travis has nothing to do with finding love. It's purely physical, some kind of reaction I'm having because he's maybe the most sexual guy I know, so that's why I put him in my kitchen."

Sage went to interject, but Kenna finished up. She was sick of thinking about this.

"Anyway, it doesn't matter because I got it out. I told him and we're moving on now. Have you looked at any of the profiles Match sent? How are things going on your dating front?"

"Kenna, the man is your brother's best friend. He makes your daughter lunch."

"Yeah, what's with that? He made her mac and cheese last week. Came in on his day off to make her lunch."

"Right, so there's a detail you overlooked in that party boy story you gave me a couple of weeks ago. I don't really think it's just physical for you. Don't you think you should at least—"

"No, no I don't. I'm a single mother. My idea of a good time is reading and planting flowers. I own a bunny, Sage. I'm not his type and he's not mine. It was a fluke, so please," she pleaded, "let's drop this and move on."

Sage sighed. "Fine. I'm not really seeing anything so far in the profiles. I told you I had a couple of coffee dates, but nothing really."

"What about the guy with the tattoos? Seemed like you were talking with him a lot."

"Yeah, we finally met yesterday at Starbucks. He designs bikes, hotter in person, but his favorite movie is *Princess Bride*."

"So?"

"So? I can't do that. I mean he's all man on the outside and then you hit me with that? I overlooked that he ordered a Frappuccino, but *Princess Bride*? He even took my hand and said, 'as you wish.'" Sage mocked a shiver, or maybe it was a real shiver.

"You know most women would love that combination: tough yet sensitive. Not you, huh?"

"No. I mean, figure out who you are. I'm not really interested in the new modern man. I'd rather have genuine. I'm meeting the cowboy, bull rider I think, tomorrow."

"A real bull rider, or one of those candy asses in the sparkly jeans who hang around Sharky's pretending to be bull riders?" Garrett walked into the bar, nodding as he let two women who were getting up from their stools pass him before he took a seat.

"Do you lurk around corners waiting for your cue?" Sage asked, eyes locked and drifting from Garrett's face to his chest. He was wearing a button-up work shirt and looked surprisingly clean, maybe even right out of the shower. Kenna was sure Sage noticed all of that and more. She cleared her throat, hoping her friend would snap to before her chin hit the bar.

Garrett smiled. "I'm all about timing." He winked.

Makenna laughed. "Oh please, do you practice this garbage in the mirror?"

"Don't have to. I'm the real deal." Kenna wondered how much

of Sage's speech he'd heard and if he had heard the whole thing, what game was he playing?

"You certainly are," Sage whispered as she bent across the bar to take Kenna's lunch plate.

"Stop it." Kenna almost laughed, and her friend simply smiled.

"Beer, Garrett?" Sage asked as she put their plates into a dishwasher bin.

"Nah, I'm thinking of having one of your creations."

Sage stopped cold.

"Are you for real?" Kenna asked.

"Didn't we just cover that when I walked in?"

Kenna could see Sage pulling herself together.

"Okay, what did you have in mind?" Sage asked, leaning one hand on the bar.

"Oh, wow. Now, if anyone practices in the mirror, little sister, it's your friend here."

"What are you talking about? I'm a bartender. That's my line. You said you wanted one of my creations, and I'm simply asking you what you want. I need more than just make me something."

"Why? I'm not the drink master, you are."

"Mistress, it would be drink mistress, and actually, I prefer the gender neutral, mixologist."

Garrett laughed, and Kenna enjoyed the show. Sage was handling her brother like a pro.

"Got it. Okay, well, what do you recommend?"

"Let's do this. Give me a base—gin, whiskey, tequila?"

"I've been in here enough. You tell me."

"Oh, come on, this is too easy." Sage smiled, and it was like she and Garrett were the only two people in the bar. She was focused and he was intrigued. Kenna had rarely seen her brother intrigued by anything that wasn't growing or mechanical. It was a treat.

"I've gotta go with your last name, Rye. Yeah, we'll start with rye whiskey, that's your base," Sage said without hesitation.

Garrett had no idea who he was dealing with. Sage Jeffries was an expert on all things booze and Garrett.

"Okay, now what?" he asked.

"Well, I usually ask for a flavor or an essence someone is looking for. I once had a guy tell me he was from Seattle and wanted me to describe Seattle in drink form."

Garrett smiled. "What did you make him?"

"It was my own creation, but when I was done, it looked like a cloudy sky."

"Huh, so you want me to give you a flavor? I'm kind of a—"

"Classic, you're a classic."

"I am?"

"Yes, you are."

"Okay, so I'm a classic and the base of my drink is rye."

"Right. Got it."

Garrett looked over at Kenna as Sage grabbed a crystal mixing glass, added rye, and what Kenna thought looked like vermouth. She dropped in a couple of ice cubes and stirred with a rhythm all her own. Eyes on her creation, Sage was in her groove and Kenna recognized a strength that was pretty damn sexy. Her brother seemed to notice it too. Sage took her long metal straw, tasted it, threw the straw in the sink, and strained the chilled liquid into a martini glass. Deftly fishing a cherry out of a jar, she dropped it into the glass and added a few drops of something from what appeared to be a tiny soy sauce bottle. Then, she twisted a piece of orange rind over the drink, balancing the peel on the glass. She glanced up at Garrett, who was glued to her movements, and slowly pushed the drink toward him. Kenna thought maybe she needed to have her hormones checked because she was pretty sure she'd just watched her best friend seduce her brother without even touching him.

"Sip, it's not a gulp drink."

"What is it?"

"A Manhattan."

"Ah, I've been there once. Here's hoping your drink is better than my trip." Garrett sipped and his eyes warmed. He looked at Kenna again as if to say, "get a load of her, will ya?"

"It's good, really good." He smiled, his voice deep and rich.

Sage instantly went from hot sexy bartender to girl in high school who trips, dropping her books on the way to the library. Her hand slipped off the mixing glass and it almost fell to the floor. Garrett reached over and steadied the glass, his hand over hers, and Sage turned bright red.

"Are you okay?"

"Yeah." She pulled her hand away and put the glass in the sink. "I'm good. Fine. I'm glad you liked it. I need to . . . I've got an order to get in the back." Her pleading eyes quickly darted to Kenna and she disappeared behind the door. Kenna was sure her friend was on the other side of the back kitchen door desperately trying to catch her breath. The woman had it bad. Kenna's clueless brother finished his drink, popped the cherry into his mouth, and smiled. When he left a twenty on the bar, leaned in to kiss her on the cheek, and turned to leave, Kenna thought about saying something, giving him a hint, but Sage would kill her, so she kissed her brother back and let him go.

Sage returned to the bar, delivering two grinder sandwiches to the balding man and his female companion who'd placed her gorgeous gray coat on the stool next to them. Sage handed them two silverware rolls and refilled their drinks; then she took the twenty Garrett had left on the bar and removed his glass.

"Was I a complete loser?"

"Not at all. You were pretty badass there for a while, and then he smiled at you and you clearly didn't notice his bottom two teeth are stupid crooked because you about melted into a puddle."

Sage shook her head. "I don't know what it is. It's not like I haven't been around my share of intimidating guys. He's just different. Not intimidating actually, but this force that messes with me. I swear I lose my balance, physically, when he's around."

"It's because you don't really know him. See, same with me when it comes to Travis. I'm weird because of what he represents in the dream, but I don't really know him. If you knew Garrett, not the dream you've conjured up in your mind, you'd be out of love with him."

73

"I'm not in love with him."

"Right. What is it Oprah says? You're in love with the 'idea of him.'"

Travis lived at The Gas Company Loft on Flower Street in downtown Los Angeles. It was next to the Staples Center, which meant he was surrounded by a dozen cookie-cutter sports bars that served crap food, most of it in a pocket or covered in cheese. Somehow, he'd managed to find a great Ethiopian place, and there was always the Grand Central Market.

His apartment was on the ninth floor and his furniture was from Crate and Barrel, all of it. He remembered the day he bought it, all in one day. He'd arrived in the morning, bought everything he thought he would need, and made Amber the saleslady's day. She even gave him her number. They slept together and two weeks later, she texted him her thanks and asked if he wanted an invite to her wedding. Women could be so strange. Not that he wanted to marry her. He hadn't even thought of it actually, but it seemed lately, most women weren't interested in marrying him, either. Well, Trixie would probably marry him, but the few times they'd slept together, he awoke to her crying or staring at him, playing with his hair. Yeah, Trixie had to go and fast. But there were women in his life he'd thought about spending more time with, and they didn't want him. Maybe it was a vibe he gave off or he had some sign on his back that read "temporary." Not that he was complaining, but sometimes he wondered where this was all going. He wasn't a kid anymore and if he was honest with himself, he did think about having a family. He just wasn't sure how to do that without becoming the family he came from. Yeah, he'd stay single forever before he'd end up in some minivan, bullying his kids into cracking helmets every Saturday until it was the only way they knew how to define themselves.

Travis didn't allow much time for thinking and didn't spend much time at home. In fact, his place wasn't really a home; it was more like a display. Sure, he'd hung a few pictures of his family and friends around his place, but he'd recently started thinking he should buy a home and set up something permanent for a change. He had still been in Seattle working with Benji when Logan called him and said he was opening his own place and wanted to do it with him. That's how he'd said it, not that he "wanted to give him a job" or "come work for me." He'd said, "I'm opening a place and I can't do it without you. Get down here and let's do this together." There was no way he could resist. Logan had become his best friend, and his ideas for the not-yet-named Yard were inspired.

Travis had pissed Benji off when he gave notice, and a little over three weeks after Logan's call, he moved into the apartment where he now stood drinking two shots of espresso. The weekend he arrived in Los Angeles, he had dinner at the Rye farm. He'd previously met Garrett and Logan's dad when they came up to visit him in Seattle, but until that night, he'd only heard of Makenna. He'd been with Logan the night she called about Adam and had taken him to the airport so he could wait on standby and get the last flight out that night. He didn't know her back then, but watching his friend try to get to his sister's side broke his heart.

The night he met Makenna, Paige had just celebrated her second birthday and her husband had been gone for almost as long. Travis thought she was beautiful even back then. Long dark hair, freckles, and sun-kissed skin, Makenna Rye looked like a farm girl. Her cheeks were always pink because she was usually outside or coming in from outside, and the way she carried herself was refreshing. She almost didn't seem aware of her body. He was pretty sure she knew she was a woman, but she must not have received the gender memo that her body was a weapon. She was a bit of a tomboy, which was expected because her mother had run out on the family when she was only five and she was surrounded by men. Yet, Travis thought that brought out her moments of softness even more. He had been drawn to that, intrigued by the way the light played on her face, the way she laughed in spite of her pain, and how she clearly loved her family.

When he saw her with her daughter, it was apparent she was strength and loyalty and completely off-limits. Not because she was his best friend's sister, but because she was way out of his league. The weeks following meeting Makenna Rye, Travis had decided she was sort of like a painting in a museum. He could appreciate her, look at her all he wanted, but if he tried to touch her, make her his, alarms would sound and he would break his own heart all over again. She was a bring-a-man-to-his-knees kind of woman, which was fine because she was also in this sort of grief limbo. He didn't need to watch other men date her because she didn't date. He knew someday things would change, but for the time being, Travis loved their friendly banter and teasing.

He walked to his kitchen, made another espresso, and when his phone vibrated, he almost let it go to voicemail. He'd ignored the last group text when UCS beat Cal, however, so he needed to answer this. They'd be on top of him eventually. After all, it was football season, so he might as well get it over with. Travis downed his espresso and tapped his phone.

"Morning, Dad."

"Trav, it's your dad."

Travis rolled his eyes because he'd just said hello. Two sentences in and already his father might as well be talking to himself.

"Hey, Dad."

"We'll be there on Wednesday. You coming to the game?"

"No." Travis had learned a long time ago that short answers worked best with his father. If they kept things simple, then they avoided arguments and Travis didn't end up saying things that he wouldn't be able to take back.

There was silence on the other line. He waited.

"You working?"

"Yes."

"You can't get the day off?"

"No."

"All right, well, your brother and Avery are coming too, so that's good. I'm sure we'll see ya. Call your mother. She's . . . she misses you."

"Will do. I'll see you guys next week."

"Sounds good."

Travis hung up and collapsed into the chair. Hell, Brick was easier than his father. There was so much unspoken, controlled tension that sometimes he wondered why they even bothered.

Chapter Nine

Kenna had just finished reading the fifteen-page profile of some guy who sent her a winky face on the dating website. She knew every little stupid detail about him and really nothing at all. Just as she was going back to look at his pictures, Travis came around the corner. She quickly closed her laptop, but it was too late. He saw her panic and true to form, he pounced.

"Watching porn again at work, are we?"

"Why are you always . . . here?"

"Hey, someone has to work. Whatcha got there, Ken?"

"None of your damn business."

"You know normally, I wouldn't care about your spreadsheets, but that was a really quick laptop close. Someone's hiding something again."

"Do you know how annoying you are?"

Travis nodded and took the seat next to her. He smelled good. *What? What the hell do you mean he smells good? Stop it!*

"Come on. We've known each other forever now. I've been in *the* dream. You can tell me things."

"Um, three years is hardly forever and no, I can't tell you things. And we don't need to talk about the dream. Besides, it's not a big deal. You just startled me."

"Uh huh. I made Paige hand-cut fries yesterday." He looked at her with his puppy eyes and Kenna shook her head.

"Fine. I'll try this. I'll tell you and if you so much as smirk, I'm going to kick you in the balls."

Travis winced. "Seems a tad harsh, but okay."

"I'm serious. I am way out of my comfort zone here already, but it might be nice to have a male perspective."

He was still waiting like a kid at an ice cream truck. Kenna let out a slow breath.

"I'm thinking about, well, Sage and I are going to start dating."

"Huh. Well, you two do have a lot in common and actually would make a lovely couple, but is she responsible enough to be a co-parent? She's a bartender, after all."

Makenna just shook her head and returned to her laptop. "See, you're incapable of being normal."

"Sorry, I couldn't resist." Travis laughed and Makenna made a point of not meeting his eyes because they were pretty incredible when he laughed. She didn't need incredible Travis right now when she was trying desperately to focus on anything but him.

"Seriously, though, this is news. So you're . . . on the market now?"

"Wow, what an evolved and sensitive way to put it, Travis."

"What? I could have said, 'So, I hear your rack shack is open for business.'"

Kenna felt a laugh bubbling up now, but she clamped down on that quickly because laughing at Travis was a guilty pleasure. The man was funny, but it was wrong to laugh at him. Every fiber of her female self told her not to entertain his knuckle-dragging humor.

"I stand corrected. That is, in fact, worse."

Travis nodded. "See? So, you're dating. Is this all part of your plan to—how did you put it again—'expand your horizons'? You know, so I'm not the only guy you dream about."

She shot him a warning look, but his smile was wicked and sexy. She couldn't be sure, but he seemed different, more playful maybe?

"Yes, I'm looking into dating."

He laughed. "Only you, Ken, could make something as simple as dating seem like it has multiple parts and requires a manual."

"First of all, there is nothing simple about dating. I mean, just the thought of it makes my hands sweat. And . . . I have a complicated life. I have history and Paige and . . . Oh God, why am I even bothering to share this with you?"

"Because I asked and you know I'll be honest with you."

Kenna gave him a questioning look.

"It's true. You may not always like what comes out of my mouth, but I'm usually honest. For example, I'm sure this is tough for you. I get that you have history. I'm not meaning to minimize that, but at the same time, I'm sure you get the 'Oh honey, do you miss your husband?' stuff all the time. I'm sad you lost him, but I think it's great you are, er, 'looking into' dating again."

That was pretty close to what she was thinking. She wasn't looking forward to the looks when she explained she was a widow or explaining herself at all for that matter. Dating seemed like tons of marketing, and Kenna was beginning to think she wasn't up for it at all.

As Travis looked at her, his eyes softened. "So, what's your plan?"

Kenna opened her laptop. "I'm trying to go through some of these profiles."

"Wait, you're online dating?"

"Yeah." She rolled her mouse and clicked on another profile.

Travis leaned in. *Holy smokes, is that cologne or his soap?* Whatever it was, her body woke up.

"Are you kidding me? Match.com? Ken, this isn't for you."

"What the hell does that mean?"

"I just, Match is for people with . . . experience. You haven't dated for years. Why don't you ease into it, date some people in your life or friends of friends, you know?"

"No, I don't know. I don't want to date someone from work and I thought, well—experience? That's ridiculous. There are people on here who are recently divorced. Hopefully they've been out of practice too. I'm being very selective. Like, look at this guy." She turned the laptop to him. "Clayton, he's thirty-five and there are a few great pictures of him hiking."

"His name is Clayton? No, that's not a good one."

"Why?"

"Well, that name for one, and you don't hike."

"I know. Well, I have hiked, I just don't take the time now. I was thinking that's something he could bring to the table."

"Eh, I don't think it's a good idea to try and change who you are when you start out. What does he do?"

"Well, it says here"—she scrolled down—"he works in marketing and he has a dog. She's a labradoodle and her name is Sadie. She's in his profile picture."

Travis said nothing.

"What?"

"Oh, I'm sorry. I just fell asleep. Are you serious? Clayton from marketing and his super special puppy? This is what you're coming out of the gate with?"

"He seems nice. All I'm really looking for is nice."

"What's the endgame here, Ken? Sex? Marriage? Dog park membership?"

She smacked his shoulder. *Don't touch. What's wrong with you?*

"I have no idea what I'm looking for. I just think it's time I got out there. I'm thirty, and sure, sex would be good. I . . . I don't know. Forget it."

Travis looked at her, puppy dog eyes again.

"Don't."

"What?"

"You're giving me the Dead Husband Look again. Cut it out."

Travis laughed and ran his hand over his face as if erasing the look. "Sorry. I would never intentionally give you that look." He stood. "Listen, you do what you need to do. I'm sure Clarence—"

"Clayton."

"Yeah, whatever, I'm sure you'll have a great time."

"You're being a smart-ass."

"Probably." He patted her on the shoulder, and she felt the warmth of his hand through her sweater. Damn, that dream had messed her up.

"Hey."

Travis turned back.

"Do you use Match.com?"

Travis gave her a smile that felt more intimate than she'd ever experienced before with him. Maybe it was because she was asking a personal question, which she often avoided with him because she assumed his personal was X-rated, but the smile he was giving her now was super close to deadly.

"Only when the dating pool gets shallow, Ken." He turned and walked back to the kitchen.

"How often does that happen?" she yelled, hoping to catch him before he pushed through the doors.

"Let's just say it's been a while."

She heard the kitchen doors swing closed and took a sip of her Coke. She'd bet it had been a long while. He was probably never without a date or whatever else he wanted.

Travis met Logan at the Grand Central Market so they could do their usual tour through Valeria's for dried chilies, pine nuts, and some salted cod for the light stew they were featuring on the summer-spring menu. They would probably spend the morning hitting the rest of the vendors too before ending with La Tostadaria, which had the best tostadas they'd ever tasted.

Travis had made countless dishes over the years and because of it, he'd grown and learned what he was good at. He knew he could create good food. He had a natural sense of what went together and was brave enough to risk those flavors that went right to the edge. Despite all of that knowledge, he also knew his limits. Many would say that's what made him a good chef, knowing how far to push. The title of chef encompassed many different varieties, which amazed him. It wasn't just an apron or a white hat; chefs came in all different shapes and sizes. He finished up his morning coffee, threw the cup away, and watched Logan load up on chilies and negotiate a bulk order for half a dozen kinds of lentils. The construction on The Yard's new dry-storage pantry would be done next week, and his friend was clearly having a good time stocking up.

"How'd it go?" Travis asked when Logan joined him, checking off things on his list.

"Good. They'll deliver next week. I got the salt cod and they had black-eyed peas."

Travis nodded, knowing exactly where he was going.

"I was thinking we could do that cold bean salad we talked about last summer." Logan looked up from his list.

"Good idea. That and the gazpacho should round out the summer menu."

"Done," they both said.

Logan folded the pieces of his yellow pad and put them in the back pocket of his jeans. "Time for tostadas?"

"Always time. Lead the way."

"Kenna's dating." Logan looked back at him.

Travis looked over his own shoulder and then around in a mocking "where the hell did that come from?" gesture. "I know."

Logan kept walking. "Any thoughts on that?"

"On Kenna dating? Um, no. She's been alone for a long time. Lots of people date. I date and no one makes a big deal out of it."

"I thought we already established that what you do is not dating."

"I took a woman out last night, and I'll have you know that I woke up alone this morning."

"What? Did she have to get to work early?"

"I may have mentioned that I had an early day."

Logan shook his head and ordered their usual, ceviche and Peruvian octopus, while Travis found two seats along the counter.

"I'm just saying"—Logan put the tray down, followed by a stack of napkins and two beers—"she seems like she's ready and there's no way she's going to find someone online. Not Kenna. She's too . . ."

"Kenna?"

Logan laughed, took a bite of his tostada, and washed it down with a sip of beer.

"I think you have a thing for her, or the beginnings of a thing."

"I do not have a thing." Well, maybe he had something, but he was doing a great job ignoring that because Makenna was not for him.

"Yeah, you do. What's the holdup? Is it Paige?"

"I love Paige." He tried not to sound offended, but just the idea that Logan would think he didn't want Makenna's daughter in his life was insulting.

"See! You see that response? You feel that way for Kenna too, but you transfer all of it onto Paige."

"That sounds creepy. Why don't you go ahead and clarify what the hell you're talking about."

"Sure. You care about Makenna, but for some reason I haven't quite figured out, you don't do anything. You're not shy, that's for sure. I think it goes back to your mess with Avery or your family or both." Logan took another bite and while he was still chewing, he said, "I'm guessing it's something about not being good enough or not wanting to be like your parents crap. Am I right?"

"Holy shit, is this like an intervention? I thought we were just stocking up and eating. If I'd known we were going to dissect my life, I would have showered."

"That's not going to work." Logan wiped his hands and took another pull of his beer. "You've been avoiding this."

"It has nothing to do with Avery. I don't even think about . . . that, whatever the hell that was, anymore. As far as not wanting to be my parents, I'm thinking that's a given. Does anyone want to be their parents?"

Logan shook his head and said nothing. Travis knew he was waiting him out, hoping he'd talk more. *Shit!*

"Why are you bringing this up?" He could feel his chest tighten at the mention of his ex. He should probably start calling her his sister-in-law, but it still felt reality TV-level screwed up. In fact, his whole family situation was a screwup he was never interested in dissecting.

"Because you're holding back. You can only roll on and off so many women, man."

"Oh God, it's finally happened. You're all warm and fuzzy with Kara and now you think the rest of us are just sad fuck monkeys." Travis slowly shook his head back and forth. "Thank you, steady, boring, settled guy, but I'm fine."

"You do have a thing for her, though."

Travis laughed him off, finished his beer, and stood, giving up their counter space to a waiting couple. They walked out of the market in silence. When they got to Logan's truck, his friend gave it one more shot.

"Fine, forget your past heartbreak."

"It was not heartbreak."

Logan wrinkled his brow.

"Maybe it was, but it was more like heart stomping or like a chewed-up-and-spit-out heart. Break makes me sound weak, like some pussy who was dumped by his high school sweetheart once she realized he was never going play college ball. I'm not that guy, so let's call it my heart chewing—that's got a better ring."

Logan laughed and started the truck.

"Okay, I've sort of forgotten what the hell we were even talking about."

Travis was silent. He sure as hell wasn't going to remind him.

"Oh, right, you being into Kenna. She's ready to date and you've had this weird energy thing with her for a while. You wanna talk about that?"

"No."

Logan sighed.

"Why would anyone want me near their sister?" Travis asked.

"Oh, don't give me that bullshit. You make her daughter lunch. You're coming out of this phase. I can see it even if you can't."

"Phase? What phase is that?" he asked when they pulled into The Yard's parking lot.

"I like to call it the 'oh poor me' phase." Logan smiled as he loaded up their hands with bags.

"Huh, so it's sort of like the phase you were in before Kara decided to rescue your sad ass."

Logan appeared to think about that last comment and then said, "Sure, that phase. Your sad ass is next, my friend."

Chapter Ten

Makenna got out of her Jeep on Friday night and immediately felt overdressed, which was odd because she usually felt just the opposite. Her heels sank into the gravel of the parking lot of Rock Brewery. Kenna put her weight onto her toes in an effort to keep from ruining her only decent pair of black pumps. It was a beautiful night. Sage had blown out her hair and she wore a silk blouse. The material felt wonderful on her skin, and Kenna tried to breathe past the shallow gasps that had started as she parked the car. She could do this; it was just a date. The familiar sound of football spilled from the televisions lighting up the night sky around the restaurant. She made her way to the concrete walkway and through the front door.

The place had a casual vibe. She could have worn her jeans. Damn it.

It didn't matter. None of what was spinning through her head mattered. She was putting herself out there, as Sage had said. She took a deep breath, and as she walked into the restaurant, she was greeted by a peppy woman, younger than she was, and dressed-up Kenna felt like she could be the girl's mother. She gave the woman her name, the hostess nodded and gestured for Kenna to follow her.

This was ridiculous. Her feet hurt already and even though blind Date Number One seemed like a decent guy online, she wasn't sure he was worth all this. Rolling her shoulders back, Kenna followed the hostess to a tall, handsome man in jeans and a checkered button-up. She still felt overdressed, but when she got closer, he stood and for the first time since she'd created the stupid dating profile, she didn't feel ridiculous. Maybe this would work, maybe she just needed to put herself out there and be friendly. Kenna stopped talking to herself and smiled as Date Number One, aka Clayton, took her hand.

"Makenna, so nice to meet you. Wow, you look great."

"Thank you. You do too."

He laughed—good laugh. Makenna took the seat across from him and set the absurdly tiny purse Sage had lent her on the table. She let out a breath, noticing the pseudo picnic tables placed around the half-in/half-out patio. The evening air calmed her nerves and she was feeling downright optimistic.

"Do you like wine?" He gestured to menu on the table.

"I do. This is a great place. Do you come here a lot?"

"I have to confess that I do. It's sort of a local haunt for me. Oh, where are my manners, I almost forgot. Up." Clayton patted the seat next to him, and an enormous, beautiful dog hopped into the seat.

She tried not to look shocked, but Date Number One introduced her to Sadie as if she was another person who had just joined them on the date. Strange. It wasn't quite the "lock the door and call the cops" moment of a horror movie, but it felt like "look out the front blinds and maybe lock the door" time.

"Sadie, can you say 'hello' to the lovely Makenna?" As if she spoke English, Sadie lifted her paw and let out a quiet ruff.

Makenna grinned because it was impressive. She'd never seen a dog so well behaved, and Sadie was beautiful. So the man liked his dog. So he brought her on the date. Maybe she was being picky. This was fine. The waitress poured their wine, a merlot Clayton chose.

"Do you want to have your chicken or a burger tonight?"

Kenna looked up from her menu to say that she was actually looking at the fish tacos when she realized Date Number One wasn't talking to her. Sadie tapped her paw on his menu twice.

"Burger it is, but no cheese this time." He stroked the top of the dog's head.

Okay, maybe that was weird.

"This is great. I'm surprised they let you have Sadie in the restaurant. I mean we are almost on the patio, but it's still really great that they allow dogs, right?"

Makenna smiled. Clayton met her eyes and went from happy to crazy in seconds.

"Why does that surprise you?" he asked with a chill that told Kenna there was no right answer.

"I, well, usually restaurants don't allow—"

"Do you have a problem with dogs, Makenna?" He glanced over at Sadie as if he wanted to cover her ears in case the big bad dog hater said something mean.

Makenna shook her head. This was past ridiculous, but she didn't want to be known as Cruella de Vil. "I love dogs. I was just saying it was nice."

Clayton huffed, glanced at his menu one more time, and set it aside. He then poured some of the water from the glass bottle on the table into a white bowl in front of Sadie. She was still sitting eerily human-like at the table.

"I'm sorry I was a bit abrupt, but sometimes the discrimination gets to me. I'm not saying you were discriminating, I'm just really sensitive to the human privilege that's rampant in this country."

Kenna was in the middle of sipping her own water. Managing not to spit it across the table, she swallowed and took a deep breath. She had no idea what to say. Dog discrimination—he was serious. She truly did love dogs and cats, even rabbits and goats. Hell, she was a farm girl; she loved all animals, but when she thought of discrimination, privilege of any kind, animals never really entered her mind. Her head already hurt and just when it seemed like the waitress had forgotten them, she arrived.

"Hi, guys. What's it going to be tonight?"

Clayton straightened up like a Boy Scout. "Hi Liz, we're going to start with the chips and guacamole. Not too spicy, please. Yesterday, it was a little much for our tummies."

"Oh, sure thing. And how about for entrées?"

"I think we'll split the spinach salad and then she's going to have the burger, no cheese, no bun, and I'll have the roasted chicken."

The waitress finished writing and Makenna was certain her jaw was on the table. *That really just happened*, her mind attempted to process. She never even had a chance to decide if she was going to be pleasant before things escalated to "bar the door, change your number, and call the cops because the boogie man is in the house" kind of crazy. She stood up and put her napkin on the table while the waitress watched in confusion. Clayton looked up, not bothering to stand. Kenna had a feeling he'd been to this part of a date before. She picked up her purse and extended her hand to Sadie first, who put her sweet paw in the center of Kenna's palm for a shake. Turning to Clayton, she really wasn't sure if she should bother with a lie because it probably didn't matter.

"Well, I'm going to go. This has been interesting and it was a pleasure meeting both of you, but I need to leave."

"Do you want to order and take a doggie bag to go?" Clayton asked, wide-eyed.

Makenna couldn't hold it back for one more minute. Laughter spilled from her and she simply turned and walked out.

They'd been slammed all night. Travis sent an order out to the floor and went into the bar to refill his water when he noticed the brunette. Corner bar table and shoes off, dangling from one finger, while her other hand was rubbing her foot. She had on black slacks and a silk blouse that was some sort of blue and cut low to show off whatever that French word was for the skin at the end of a woman's neck down and between her breasts. Travis knew what it was because that and the lower back were his two favorite parts of most women, but he always forgot the proper name. Whatever it was called, the woman sitting at the bar had a beautiful one. Her hair was dark, but the light of the bar tables picked up bits of red, making him want to run his fingers through it.

She crossed her legs and moved to the other foot. Her movements were fluid and he knew it was weird, but she looked like she smelled delicious. It was strange because other than her décolletage—that was the word, he knew it would come to him—there wasn't much skin showing, and yet he found himself staring. He wanted to run over there and see if he could help her rub her feet, but he didn't really do the sophisticated A-list girls these days. They were too much work and usually a letdown.

He needed to get back to work, but he allowed himself one more look, really wanting to see her face. His eyes traveled from her painted toes, up her legs, and as she uncrossed her legs, her long dark waves shifted from one shoulder to the other. Travis still couldn't see her face, but he recognized the bracelet. It was one of Paige's friendship bracelets, like the one on his own wrist, but hers was purple instead of green. Just as he was trying to figure out why he'd never met or noticed any of Makenna's friends, the woman flipped her hair out of her face in frustration. She beamed at Logan, who approached the table, and Travis dropped his water glass. It shattered and most of the bar barely noticed, but she did. She looked over and Travis couldn't breathe. Her hair was long and silky, lips moist, and whatever makeup was around her already gorgeous eyes made her look different, dangerous. Travis dropped his head and walked into the back room. He needed a minute because holy crap, Makenna got him going lately with mud on her boots, but this Makenna was several degrees past comfortable. Not in just a cocktail party, nice-to-meet-you way; the woman out there rubbing her feet was a take-me-home-and-spend-the-weekend-in-my-bed beautiful. Travis held onto the counter and closed his eyes. He needed to get a damn grip. He was tired, sleep deprived. That had to be it. He quickly opened his eyes because his mind filled with images of sliding her blouse open and kissing her skin until she was purring—

"You making a mess, man?"

"What?" Travis spun around to face Logan.

"You broke the glass out there. I was . . . are you all right?"

Travis let out a slow, steadying breath. "Me? Yeah, I'm great. I don't know what happened out there. Just slipped."

"I'll take over for a while. You should probably eat something. It looks like we're going to be like this until closing. Why don't you go sit in the bar? Kenna's out there. Bad date, so maybe you can console her." Logan laughed.

"What?"

"You consoling Makenna, that's what."

"I can, I mean, I'm a consoler. Sure, no big deal at all." *Shut up, idiot!*

Logan stopped laughing. "Are you sure you're okay?"

"Yeah, I'm good. Why was it a bad date?"

"I'm sure she'll fill you in. Let's just say the guy brought his dog."

"Sadie? Oh man, she went out with Clayton?"

Logan looked confused. "You know her date?"

"Yeah, well, not really, but I saw him on Kenna's computer. Shit, I told her Clayton was a bad idea."

"So you're a dating counselor now, or just for women you secretly want to date yourself?"

"Don't start. We've been over this. Not going to happen."

"So you keep saying."

"I'm taking a break."

"Good idea."

Travis grabbed a pizza and a piece of chocolate cake and asked Sage for two Cokes.

"I'll add some rum to hers." Sage slid the drinks to him.

"Hey." Travis put everything on the table and took a seat across from the beautiful woman sitting alone at a bar table.

"Hey." She looked up at him, smiled a half smile, and Travis felt his heart jump. She was the same Kenna: tiny scar over her left eye, full lips, and a bulb to her chin that usually called on him to grab it like she was his kid sister. The kid sister part was gone. He felt the urge to grab her, but there was nothing familial about it.

"Bad date?"

"I'm not even sure we should call it that. It was honestly unbelievable. Can we share this? I'm starving."

"Sure." He handed her a plate and a rolled napkin. He knew he didn't have to say a word; she was raring to vent and he was hoping he didn't have "Damn, you're gorgeous!" plastered all over his stupid face.

"I honestly don't know where to begin. Remember Sadie from the profile?"

Travis chewed and nodded.

"She's not his dog, oh no, she's his wife. His canine wife, and don't you dare say a word because that would be canine discrimination." She laughed, took a bite of his pizza, and followed it with a large sip of rum and Coke.

Travis listened as Kenna shared the hilarious story of her first online date complete with flailing arms and the occasional snort of laughter. He'd never seen this version of her before: she was free of her details and defenses. It was almost as if the total disaster of her date had liberated her, torn away something unknown. He had always thought his best friend's sister was pretty, smart-ass, and bossy, but when she leaned on her elbows with the sleeves of her silk blouse rolled up and dark hair dancing around her face, Travis was gone. The dim light of the bar, the glint in her green eyes—for a moment it felt as if they were on a date and those eyes were dancing for him.

After much laughter and a little consoling, he had to get back to work. Back to reality.

"So, what now?" he asked, stacking their plates on the empty pizza tray.

Makenna puckered her perfect lips in thought and shook her head. "I guess I just have to keep trying. You know, just because I had one 'ruff' date, doesn't mean I give up, right?" She grinned, pure mischief, and he got the pun.

"True, but you might want to . . . 'paws' a minute before heading out there." They both laughed and as Travis turned to leave, he could tell she was trying to think of another pun. Just as he was pushing through the kitchen door, he heard her gravelly, sexy, touch-of-rum voice say, "I know, I know, but the whole thing really ticks me off, get it? Ticks?" He looked back, shook his head, and watched her nearly fall off the stool in laughter. Catching his gaze, she stopped and mouthed, "Thank you." He nodded quickly, because that was all he was capable of at that moment, and went back to work.

Chapter Eleven

Since the day they opened, The Yard had needed a bigger dry-storage pantry. Once they expanded the menu, space was even tighter. Logan wanted things organized, and the new space was finally finished.

Makenna walked in Saturday morning ready to "help stock and take inventory," she said. Travis agreed to help since Logan had texted that he was running late—big surprise. He didn't mind. His friend was happy and Travis wondered if there would ever come a day that he wouldn't be anxious to get away from the woman in his bed. He looked at Makenna, hair now pulled back, black long-sleeve T-shirt clinging to all the right places. She had a hole in her jeans at the knee, and his eyes fixed on that patch of skin.

"Cleaner and inventory queen at your service." Kenna reached into the bags she brought in and held up rags and wood polish.

Travis managed to pull his eyes away from her knee, dismissed his stupidity, and went back to thinking about the voicemail his mother had left him last night saying that everyone would be in town for the USC game next week. John and Avery were coming too, and "it would be great if the whole family could get together." He'd deleted the message. He would call her back, just not today.

"Where's Logan?" Kenna asked.

"Where's Paige?"

"You go first." She took a sip from the plastic cup she'd brought with her.

"He's late; slept in." Travis wiggled his eyebrows.

"Wow, thanks for that visual."

"Your turn, where's Paige?"

"Grandparents."

Travis tripped a little at the term. He kept forgetting Makenna had in-laws. That she'd been married before.

"Do you like them?"

"Adam's parents? Yes, they're good people."

Adam, another word, another name he didn't often hear. Paige's father, Makenna's husband. She loved him, Travis could tell, even though the twisted pain of what she had lost had all but faded from her eyes.

"Is it weird?" fell out of his mouth before he had a chance to think about being sensitive. "Sorry, that was a stupid question. You don't need to answer that."

"Is what weird?"

"Being around his parents without him."

Tilting her head in thought, she set down the dust cloths and polish. "I don't know that weird is the right word. They take Paige twice a year and have since Adam died, so I'm used to it now. But it's always a little . . . sore. His father looks like him so that can be a bit . . . weird. Yeah, I guess it is weird." Kenna looked down and opened her laptop.

"Does Paige look like him?" *What's with the twenty questions, genius?*

Kenna seemed to jump at little at the question, but then beamed at the mention of her daughter. "She does. Haven't you ever seen a picture of Adam?"

Travis shook his head and wondered why he was suddenly so curious. They'd finally made their way back to normal. All he needed now was to ask the wrong questions and make her uncomfortable again.

Makenna took out her phone, tapped the screen a few times, and her face softened into an odd mix of light and sadness. She was so beautiful in all her complications. She turned the phone to him and there he was—Adam. Tall, tan, and sporting longer blond hair. He sort of looked like a surfer—like Mr. California. He was holding a bundle in a pink blanket and smiling for the camera. Travis felt a punch to his chest and found himself staring at the man's eyes, the look on his face as he held a daughter he only knew for five weeks. It struck Travis that he knew more about that pink bundle, about the man's daughter, than he ever would. Life was so screwed up sometimes. He was glued to the picture.

Makenna cleared her throat and Travis forced himself to look at her, completely surprised to see her smiling, the sadness gone. "So, that's Adam. Mystery uncovered. That was a few days before he was gone. Strange, huh?"

"You have no idea. I mean, I guess you do. It's . . . you've been through more than most, Kenna."

"I know." She glanced at the picture one last time and put the phone back into the pocket of her jeans.

She looked up at him and their eyes held. Travis reached out and touched the side of her face. He needed to touch her; it was almost as if his heart was confirming that she was real and not part of the picture she'd just put away. She was. Her cheek was soft and he felt her tense at his touch.

"I'm sorry."

"For what?"

"For what happened."

"It was a long time ago."

"I know, but sometimes when we are teasing or I'm giving you a hard time, I forget."

"I like it that way, thank you. I'm not sure I could bear it if you treated me like I'm some kind of—"

He touched her face again, this time moving his hand past her jaw and just onto her neck. Her chest pulled in a quick breath.

"Soft, so soft. You wouldn't want me to treat you like you were soft?"

99

"Right." She stepped back from him.

Travis could have laughed and shrugged the awkward intimacy of the moment off, but he honestly couldn't move. He found himself wanting her in a way that felt so foreign because it had absolutely nothing to do with getting her naked. He wanted to pull her into him, touch her, and make her laugh.

Makenna cleared her throat again and Travis finally snapped out of it.

"Damn, I'm sorry."

"It's fine."

"How's the dating going?" *Great transition, idiot.* He could see her physically recoil at the abrupt change.

"It . . . it's not. I had a couple of what we daters now call a 'coffee trail,' but I'm starting to figure out that it's not them. I mean, sure, my first date was a nightmare—"

Travis barked, and Kenna smiled and they were back to normal.

"He really was, but some of these other guys are fine. Great even, but I don't want to get to know them. I don't care about their stories and for the life of me, I can't imagine ever telling them any of mine, let alone introducing them to my life, my daughter. See, it's me. I never realized it until I got out there a little, but I'd much rather be here, working or hanging out with my family or Sage. I'm sure some single women get excited about dinners or learning about a new man, but I just feel awkward. I'd much rather stay home and read a good book."

"That can be fun, but pretty solitary."

"Do you read, Travis?"

"I do."

"What kind of books?"

He could tell she fully expected him to say something like *Playboy* or James Bond, and he could have, but this was the first real conversation he'd had with a woman in a while. Actually, since his last conversation with Makenna, and he wanted to keep it going for just a little longer.

"I like mysteries, crime or spy stuff. It needs to be fast moving, because I have a short attention span. I'm sure you're shocked."

Makenna laughed and was now picking at the edges of the white dust cloth she held.

"I like Patterson," he continued. "Although I'm really into Daniel Silva lately. I always feel like I've been on a really cool vacation after I read one of his."

Kenna's mouth was almost open. He enjoyed the response he got when he was honest and genuine with her. She never expected him to be human; it threw her for a loop, which was added fun.

"Daniel Silva? I love Daniel Silva. I've read them all. I just finished *The English Spy,* which wasn't my favorite but still brilliant. I honestly don't know why Ciara puts up with him. That scene where he paints over her clouds, what was that? Oh, wait, have you read it yet?"

She wasn't like any woman he'd ever known, had sex with, or otherwise. He wasn't sure if it came from being raised by a single father and two brothers or living on the farm or having a daughter on her own. He had no idea what made her who she was, but he offered up thanks for whatever created Makenna Rye Conroy and put her in his life. She was full of feeling. Unafraid to show she was trying new things. Maybe that's why his eyes refused to look away. He shook his head indicating that he had yet to read *The English Spy.*

"Oh, sorry, I'll shut up then because I hate when people spoil it for me. Logan and Garrett both do that. I'll just say that Gabriel Allon is one of my favorite book boyfriends. He's a close second to Roark from the In Death Series, which is really saying something."

"Ken?"

"Stop calling me that!"

"Fine, Makenna."

The sound of her name, her full name, sent a chill up his neck. He was sure he'd said her name before, hadn't he? Whenever he thought of her, which was more and more frequently these days, he always thought—Makenna. From the look in her eyes, it seemed like she was savoring warm coffee, maybe with a little Bailey's in it. Based on her expression, he was sure he'd never said her full name before. She was hearing him say it for the first time.

"Makenna," he said again just for fun.

"Yes, what?"

"I like the way that sounds. It's a nice name."

"Thank you. Yours is nice too, although I hate it when people call you Trav. It makes you sound, I don't know, like you have a big gold chain around your neck and you wear sweatbands."

"Tube socks too."

"Yup, throw those in. Trav is like a Will Ferrell character, but Travis is more . . . Paul Newman. I like it."

"*Cat on a Hot Tin Roof*, Newman, or *The Hustler*, Newman?"

Makenna appeared to mentally scroll through her catalogue of Paul Newman films. "No, I'm thinking more *Cool Hand Luke*, Newman." She met his eyes and he felt the neck shiver thing again. *Cool Hand Luke* was his favorite Newman movie. Did she know that?

Travis laughed off his feelings. "Great. I'll let my mother know you approve. Give me those cans of tomatoes, will you?"

She handed up the four cans. "Huh."

"What?" He stacked the cans and turned to her for four more.

"I've never thought of your mother. What's she like?"

"She's a mom."

"Well, of course she is. I meant what's she like."

"That is what she's like. She was born to be a mom and she does it really well. Carpools, cookies, PTA, all of our football games with a cooler. She's that kind of mom. Her name is even Mary."

"Wow, I think I know some Marys at Paige's school. Does she wear great clothes too?"

"Always." He took the last of the cans and climbed down the step stool.

"Monogrammed towels?"

Travis nodded.

"Summer camp every year."

"Spring and Christmas family portraits," he added.

"She's the works. Do you like her?"

Travis skipped a beat. "I'm not sure anyone has ever asked me that. Yes, I do like her. Well, let's put it this way, I love her. She's a great mom and has always been there for me, so long as I stayed in line. Do I like her, who she is, and what she represents? I'm not sure."

"Huh," she said as they moved down the wall to the rice and grains.

"What?"

"Oh, nothing. I'm too nosy."

"I'm an open book."

"You are certainly not." Kenna typed figures into her laptop.

"Um, yes I am. Nothing to hide."

"That's not true. We all have things we hide."

"Ask me anything. Right after you hand me those bags of lentils."

She handed several bags to him.

"Fine. Are your brothers nice?"

Travis laughed. "Nice? Why, are you thinking of dating one?"

She swatted him with the last two bags of lentils. "See, you're avoiding with humor. It's okay. I do that too."

"I'm not avoiding anything. My brothers are competitive. That's how we were raised. John is successful and he wins. He always wins."

"He's the older one, right?"

"Yeah, he's a coach at USC. He played college ball, quarterback, and two years with the 49ers until his rotator cuff gave out for good. Surgeries and lots of PT. When he healed, schools were falling over themselves for him. He's the second in command at USC football. He'll probably be a head coach before he's forty-five."

There was an awkward silence, but Travis found himself screwed up just thinking about his brother. The guy didn't even need to be in the room to rattle his cage. Travis moved bags and boxes around on the shelves with pinpoint focus. Yes, he was angry—filled with it sometimes. That's why he'd taken up boxing, but it clearly wasn't working.

"Oh," she finally said.

Travis glanced over his shoulder. "What?"

She shook her head. "Nothing. I've just never heard such a . . . rote description. You should do his PR."

He could tell she was trying to lighten things up, but his shit—the energy spilling off of him at the thought of his brother—was probably freaking her out. Apparently, his open book was a scary one. He pulled in a deep breath, let it go slowly, and turned to her, leaning up against the section of shelving he'd just whipped into shape as if it were a Little League team. "Sorry, but that's John. He's the golden boy. Family hero."

"I see. What is Andrew?" It was interesting that she assumed everyone in his family had a part. They did. Very perceptive, but he guessed every family had players. He'd told her he was honest, an open book, but as the tension crawled into his shoulders, he decided that was a stupid reveal. He continued. No turning back now.

"Drew is the prodigy. He was their midlife baby. Nine years after me. Three-sport all-star athlete. Third draft pick. He's a halfback for the 49ers. Second string, but still my father's wet dream. Finally."

Yeah, the look on her face told him she had never seen this side of him, and she probably didn't want to because most people preferred fun, flirty Travis. Needing to break the awkwardness again, he grabbed the bags of flour and stacked them under the shelves.

"And you are?" She touched his back, and Travis froze.

He wondered if he could pretend he hadn't heard her. He turned and wiped his forearm across his forehead. She wanted to know the role he played. Yeah, it was time to close the family album. How the hell did they end up on this subject in the first place? Oh right, he had nothing to hide. *Stupid ass.*

"Okay, well, this looks great. Much better." He crossed his arms and pivoted around the large space. "Did you record all of the inventory you needed?"

Makenna nodded, saying nothing. He could feel the questions circling in her mind.

"They'll all be here next week, so I'm sure you'll get to meet 'the fam.' It's a treat, believe me."

"They sound pretty perfect. What's the problem?"

"Oh, they are perfect. That is the problem. All the pieces fit together. Hell, last summer they even vacationed together."

"They? Aren't you part of 'they'? A piece?"

Travis laughed. *A piece of shit,* he thought but didn't say. "There's nothing perfect about me. We all know that."

The slightest spark flashed in her eyes and then it was gone. Makenna finished her inventory on her laptop and packed it into her bag. They both walked back toward the kitchen and Travis hit the light. Makenna turned to him in the doorway, the glow from the kitchen highlighting her expression. She touched his face, looked at his lips, but leaned in to kiss his cheek instead. He thought about turning so she'd kiss his lips, but when he kissed Makenna for the first time, allowed himself to taste her, he didn't want it to be an accident. *When* he kissed her? Christ, he was in trouble.

"Travis?"

Her endless green eyes met his as she remained standing in the doorway. He couldn't speak, so he raised his eyebrows in acknowledgment.

"Perfect is boring."

He grinned. "Unless we're talking spreadsheets," he joked, because he was about to drag her back into dry storage and lock the door.

Makenna laughed and walked through the door. "Yes, but only in the case of spreadsheets."

By the time Logan arrived with a stupid grin on his face, the inventory was done. He and Travis spent the rest of the morning and most of the afternoon finishing up the tasting menu they were going to serve to Grady and Kate next week. Kenna had all of the options, and she was formatting a card they would print so the happy couple could check their preferences. The Malendar wedding was still a couple of months out and so far things were going smoothly. She had emailed the wedding cake baker, and he agreed to send over samples for the tasting next week so they could present Kate and Grady with a taste of the full wedding dinner. Kenna had to admit it was fun putting together a couple's wedding, at least from the catering perspective. The wedding planner handled other things like seating and the wedding party. That didn't seem to be quite so much fun, but the food had proved a pretty interesting experience.

Logan sat next to her, peeking over her shoulder as she finished typing up the selections.

"That's confit, not condit."

"Thank you," Kenna said through the pen she was holding in her mouth. She made a few other corrections and saved her document. "Done. Okay, so Sloan, aka perfect hair, is the wedding planner and she just emailed me that she will be handling the wine."

"Why? If we're doing the food, wouldn't it make sense that we'd have our guy do the pairings?"

"It would make sense, but that's not how they want to do it. At least, that's not how Sloan wants to do it."

"That's stupid. Why do I feel like this is some kind of weird wedding team power struggle?"

"Oh get ready, my dear brother, you're next. I spoke to Kara last week and she said you guys were getting married on the beach?"

"Well, we're just in the early stages and she wants the beach. I just want her. So as long as the food is good and she's there, I honestly couldn't care less." Logan's face was warm. "Oh, and you guys, I'd need you there too."

"Thanks. I think the beach is a beautiful idea."

"Yeah, well, back to reality. I'm a little pissed about the wine, so I might talk to Grady about that when they come in because it makes no sense. The wedding planner probably has some connection to a big distributor that can buy and sell our guys up the river, and I don't think that's what Grady wants."

"You don't think that's what he wants, or it's not what you want?" Kenna smiled.

"Both. I'll talk to him."

"Sounds good. I'm still emailing this to the big bad wedding planner though and then you can look at their selections."

"Great. How's your life going? I saw Paige at Dad's yesterday. Things go all right with Adam's parents?"

"They did. It seemed like they had a great time and Paige came home with lots of new clothes and extra sand, so that usually means a successful trip."

"And the dating thing?"

"Subtle, Lo, very subtle."

"Kara wanted me to ask. She said you seemed pretty discouraged."

"I'm finding my way. It's a little artificial for me, you know?"

"I do. Maybe the online thing isn't a good idea."

"Maybe not, but I don't exactly have time to hang out in bars and my life doesn't put me in contact with a lot of single people. It's fine. I'm good single. I was thinking I needed to get out there, but that feeling is starting to pass. I'm meeting some guy this weekend, so we'll see."

"What about Travis?"

Kenna almost fell off her seat. "What about him?"

"Have you ever thought of dating him?"

She'd thought of Travis more than she wanted to admit in the last few weeks; couldn't stop actually. Was it that obvious?

"No," she lied.

"Huh, well, maybe you should."

"Why? Travis is . . . we work together and he has a pretty substantial reputation."

"He just hides behind all that stuff."

"Oh, okay. Where is this coming from?"

"Kenna, you're open to letting someone in your life. Travis is obviously interested."

"He is not obviously anything. I'm not his type."

"What is his type?"

"Tiny dresses, big boobs, not much talking. Trixie came in a few days ago in a sad attempt to see Travis. She looked like a damn supermodel. I'm not that."

Her brother looked genuinely puzzled. "You dress up for dates. I don't see the difference. And I'm going to pretend you didn't just bring up Trixie as a viable option for Travis."

"A viable option? I know he's your friend, but I don't get the impression that Travis needs options. He seems perfectly happy with what he's doing."

"Oh, come on Kenna, that's all a game. Why do you think the guy makes lunch for Paige?"

"Because he, because she's his . . . He's being nice. I'm sure he feels bad that I'm rushing around, or . . . I have no idea why he makes her lunch."

"I do. He cares about you."

Kenna said nothing. She felt like she'd slipped down some rabbit hole where everything she used to understand no longer applied. Her brother was telling her Travis had feelings for her as if it was the most natural, expected thing in the world. As if it was so obvious and she was ridiculous for not seeing it.

"Am I ridiculous?"

She hadn't realized she'd said it out loud, but Logan laughed.

"I wouldn't go that far, but it's pretty obvious, at least to me. Ask him."

"Ask him what?"

"Why he makes Paige's lunch."

"No, that's such an odd question. I mean what if he doesn't know?"

"Or, more likely, what if you're afraid to hear the answer?" Logan stood, patted his sister on the back, and returned to the kitchen.

Well, thanks for that, big brother. As if she needed anything more to think about.

Chapter Twelve

*T*ravis showered after a few rounds with Brick. The last round, he had really "held his own," according to David. That was progress. He'd pushed hard this morning to get some of his crap out because he knew there would be a text on his phone by the time he got to work.

Good morning! Sorry you couldn't meet us last night for dinner. We are thinking of stopping by the restaurant tonight after the game. Too bad you're going to miss the game too. Your brothers are really bummed.

"Oh yeah, I bet," Travis said out loud to an empty kitchen.

We can't stay long, though, maybe just drinks, because Drew needs to get to the airport.

"And God knows where Drew goes, so go the rest of you." He was talking to himself again. He hadn't even seen them yet and they were already making him crazy. He slipped the phone into his pocket and tied his apron at his waist. He didn't reply; he didn't need to. They'd show up tonight either way. It was as if he orbited around them, occasionally bumped into them, but never really connected. He wasn't sure when that had happened, but he was pretty sure it was around the time they stopped having anything in common. They'd have drinks, probably not eat any food just to spite him, and then go back to their lives until the next time they found themselves in his "neck of the woods," as his father liked to say. John lived fifteen minutes away from him, and the only time they spoke to one another was when the family got together. That was to be expected, considering he was now married to Travis's ex, but every now and then Travis realized just how messed up it all was. None of it really mattered right now though because he had a tasting menu to finish. Grady and Kara would be in around two, the wedding cake guy was bringing his samples by one, and there was work to be done. His kitchen, his life, his work.

Makenna had managed to get the linens and dishes from the wedding planner. It was like pulling teeth, but Sloan finally gave it up. Kenna set two places in the private dining area for Grady Malendar and Kate Galloway. Grady ran the Roads Foundation and was the son of US Senator Patrick Malendar. More importantly, Grady was Kara's brother and Logan's soon-to-be brother-in-law. *Lots of coupling and love*, Makenna thought as she placed three wineglasses at each seat. Logan had won the wine battle against Sloan's large distributor, and Grady wanted to see what Twisted Tree, a local vineyard, had to offer.

Makenna stood back, admired the table, and felt a calm sense of satisfaction. It seemed so much of her life was a hurried frenzy that she never really took the time to step back and look. Adjusting the flowers on the table, she decided to add calm reflection to her list of things to work on. She walked toward the hostess station and along the way, bussed a table because Summer still had a bit of a lunch rush. Entering the back kitchen, she dropped off the dishes and stood watching her brother and Travis do what they did best: create.

Small plates covered the large stainless steel counter, each of them white with perfect bites of food in the center. Travis was placing two roasted kalamata olives gently next to each baby lamb chop while Logan stood waiting to hand him the basil oil. The only reason Kenna knew any of this was because she had seen the menu, studied the details, checked for typos, and wondered what the hell most of it was. Watching the meal come to life was something special. When Logan had asked her to be part of his restaurant, Kenna never realized what a journey it would be. At the time, she assumed he did it to take her mind off the tailspin of Adam's death, but now she saw it. Kenna was always about the pieces, the numbers, the pennies. She wasn't particularly creative; she liked reading and had become a master at Play-Doh thanks to her daughter's tutelage, but her brain didn't work in a creative way. When she'd said that to Logan once, he'd pointed out the chairs in the private dining room.

"Everyone has a creative part, Kenna," he'd said.

"Those are just chairs that I found on sale. I liked the colors and the price. You're the one who came up with the idea for your place. I'm simply following the design."

"Okay, and I just pull things out of the dirt and cook them in a pan."

She'd laughed.

God, she loved him. She loved both her brothers, but Logan had saved her. Garrett had held her, fixed her in his own way, but Logan gave her purpose without making her feel weak. Kenna hoped he knew what that had meant to her, but maybe she needed to tell him more. It was such a strange thing becoming the "tragedy" of a family. For a time, everything swirled around her axis until she became strong enough to stop it and look around. Kenna felt like she was only recently doing that: looking and appreciating. She let out a slow breath.

"Are we good? Is everything ready?" Logan asked, looking up.

"Everything looks great. Summer had a couple more tables to sit last time I walked by, but we look good, busy but not crazy."

"Great. Okay, well, I think we're ready in here. Travis?"

Logan rubbed the back of his neck and Makenna recognized the tension. Neck rub was always Logan's stress tell. Travis didn't look nervous at all. She wasn't familiar enough to know his signs, but she was sure somewhere on the inside he had to be nervous . . . or maybe not. Either way, his calm was good for Logan. They complemented one another.

"As ready as we're ever going to be." Travis patted his friend on the shoulder and Logan seemed to instantly relax. "Shall we change into our we-never-spill-anything aprons now?"

Makenna laughed and left them to it. Sage had her hands full with a group of young executives who were asking her what it was like being a female bartender. Kenna caught her gaze and rolled her eyes as she passed. The woman had infinite patience.

Like magic, Summer sat the last couple waiting for a table and was returning to her post as Grady and Kate walked through the door. Makenna loved when things worked out. She felt that calm again, shook hands, and led the couple back to the private dining area.

"What was on that shrimp?" Grady asked after the formal tasting was over and Travis and Logan joined them at the table.

"Green peppercorns." Travis sipped his water.

"I don't think I've ever had better food." Kate wiped her mouth and looked at Kenna. "I see Sloan finally caved and got you the linens. Do you like these? I mean, I like the look of them, but they're sort of scratchy."

"I think they're pretty, but you may want to go with flax. I didn't dare say anything to Sloan, but I think the ones you have are a burlap-linen blend. We use burlap feed bags on the farm, so the rustic is there, but I don't know that I'd want to put that to my face."

Kate and Grady both laughed.

"Logan picked out flax napkins when we opened. Here, feel." Makenna grabbed two napkins from a server station.

Kate put the napkin to her mouth. "Yes, much better. Thank you."

"Okay, napkins solved. The wine is excellent too. Let's let Sloan handle the champagne, but have Logan's guy do the wine?" Grady looked at Kate, she nodded in agreement, and then as if they were sitting at a cozy little table for two, he kissed her. It was simple but felt so human for two public figures. Grady pulled his eyes back to the rest of them. "Sorry for that, but we've spent so much time sneaking around that I kiss her every chance I get. I can't seem to help myself."

Kate shook her head. "I think we're finished and we indicated everything on the card. Thank you so much for this. It made it really easy." Kate handed their selections to Makenna.

"You're welcome. So, all we have now is the wedding cake samples and coffee. Your cake guy is in the kitchen and we have two local coffee roasters I'd like you to try," Logan said, standing.

Travis stood after him and looked like he was going to add something when Summer came into the dining room.

"Travis, I'm sorry to disturb, but your family is here. I sat them in the bar." She flashed him her hostess grin and then quickly vanished.

Makenna watched Travis go from casual and thriving in his element to visibly uncomfortable. He looked to Logan, who reluctantly nodded.

"They're early," Logan said.

"Does that surprise you?" Travis shook his head.

"Not really."

Travis found his smile as he turned to Grady and Kate to shake hands and again extend his congratulations. His eyes swept past Makenna, and she saw what looked like armor fall into place. He appeared ready for battle, and then he was gone.

Chapter Thirteen

While the happy couple tasted cake and sipped coffee with Logan, Makenna excused herself and went through the kitchen to the bar. She'd never seen Travis's family and she had to admit she was curious. The picture he'd painted in the stockroom wasn't particularly flattering, but families were complicated—she was sure they weren't all that bad. Sneaking behind the bar, she waited as Sage cashed out a couple of suits and ties.

"How's it going?" Kenna asked, leaning in to catch a glimpse of the bar table closest to the front door.

Sage exhaled. "Jeez Louise, those guys asked me to do a hand-muddled old-fashioned, which is a pain in the ass. The one in the bow tie said he read about it in *Men's Journal*. Who the hell came up with lifestyle magazines for men? Now every guy anywhere close to the corner office thinks he's Don Draper."

Makenna was still leaning, her eyes focused ahead.

"Oh, that's why you're here." Sage looked over Kenna's shoulder. "Yeah, I've had my ears on them. Poor Travis."

Makenna stopped leaning and looked at Sage. "Why poor Travis?"

She held up her finger, smiled as she turned to deliver a credit card slip, and then said, "Look at the poor bastard. His dad seems like a real blowhard, as my Uncle Mikey would have put it."

"I didn't know you had an Uncle Mikey."

"He's dead. Heart attack. You didn't miss much. Anyway, Travis's dad is the one standing even though there's a seat, kind of loud like maybe he's on the sidelines coaching the Super Bowl, but without the bad polyester coach pants. Travis's older brother, I think his name is John, is wearing those. Yikes, it's a little hard to believe our Travis, well, your Travis, from the looks you've been giving him lately, was raised by the Cleaver family over there."

Makenna laughed and then went around to stand at the bar so she could hear.

"This is a nice place, Trav. Seems real urban. What was this, like a garage?" The "blowhard," according to Uncle Mikey, said right as Kenna turned her back to the group.

"Lumberyard," Travis said, barely above a mumble.

"Huh, well, it's cool, but they don't have nachos."

Kenna heard Travis laugh. "Yeah, well, you're not eating anyway, so I'm sure you'll find those at the airport bar. I should probably get back to work."

"They can't spare you for a few more minutes? I hope they've got other cooks back there."

"Yeah, do you punch one of those time cards in the back? Like are you 'on the clock' as they say in the movies?" a different, younger male voice asked.

The table laughed and Makenna found herself squeezing the edge of the bar.

"No," was all Travis said.

"Huh, well, that's good, and you don't have to wear a hairnet, so that's a bonus, right?" Blowhard added.

"Okay, that's enough, guys. There's certainly nothing wrong with food service work," an older woman's voice chimed in. Makenna was certain she was the mother.

"Yeah, but I always thought of food service as a transition job. You know, something you do on the way to somewhere else, or something bigger. Trav, did you work in a restaurant when you were in high school?"

Makenna was pretty sure it was time to punch Blowhard, or at least ask him to sit his ass down.

"Yes." Again one word from Travis.

"I thought so. Like I said, transition. He's still doing the same job he did in high school."

"Easy, Dad. It's not Trav's fault he got injured. He's doing the best he can with his shitty knee, right Trav?"

"Right."

Holy cow, isn't he going to say something, anything?

"Well, anyway, let's not waste our time on this crap anymore. Your brother here has some big news..." Makenna rolled her shoulders back. She was filled with something that felt like protectiveness or affection, she wasn't sure, but whatever it was coursed through her like one of those five-hour energy drinks. As Blowhard was rambling on about some endorsement his son with the good knee just "scored," she walked over to the table with her best interview smile and stood next to Travis, who still smelled delicious.

"Excuse me, Travis." Kenna put her hand on his shoulder. "I'm sorry to interrupt, but Logan needs you to approve the changes to the menu, and if you have time, the senator's son and his fiancée would like to say good-bye."

Travis looked at her dumbstruck, as if waking up from a self-induced coma and surprised someone was stepping in to help him.

"I . . . sure. I'll be right over. Makenna, these are my parents, Tom and Trisha, my older brother John, and his wife."

"Avery, nice to meet you." The blonde with the high cheekbones and the huge ring extended her manicured hand, which Kenna quickly shook.

"And I'm sure you already know who this is," Blowhard said, putting his hand on the shoulder of the young man sitting. He looked at Makenna as if she was about to break out in some sort of fan frenzy. Whoever the superstar was, he looked like Travis, but with a different nose and no facial hair.

Kenna politely looked to Travis for direction.

He let out a huff of frustration. "Dad, not everyone follows football. Kenna, this is my youngest brother Drew."

Drew managed to pull his face from his phone long enough to deliver a toothpaste commercial smile and shake Makenna's hand. It was one of those greeting-a-weak-girl handshakes, and Makenna wanted to puke.

"Okay, well, it's very nice to meet all of you, and again, I'm sorry to pull him away, but we have some pretty important guests here today and they always love to hobnob with the chef."

"Oh, well, Trav, you go on. We don't want to keep you." Trisha McNulty was now wide-eyed and almost as shiny as the blonde with the big rock on her finger. Her hair was cut into a short bob and reddish like the lightest parts of Travis's beard. She was exactly as her son had described her: a mom.

"Please tell Mr. Malendar and the soon-to-be Mrs. Malendar that I will be right over." Travis played along.

Kenna nodded and when she turned her back to the table, she smiled, a big cheek-hurting smile. That felt good, really good, and the look on Travis's face was priceless.

She heard his mother say, "You know a senator?"

Kenna grinned all the way back to the kitchen. Grady and Kate had already left, but Makenna guessed unless they were in football jerseys Travis's family wouldn't even notice. She knew that sounded mean, even in her mind, but she didn't have a high tolerance for bullies. At least from what she heard, the McNultys seemed like bullies. Kenna sat down in the back kitchen and opened her laptop. She remembered in the fourth grade her friend Marty used to get really winded because of her asthma, and anytime she used her inhaler, this group of kids in their class made fun of her. Kenna eventually learned that people picked apart other people to make themselves feel better, but her fourth-grade self was pissed that her friend was always crying, so she kicked Timmy Britton's ass and ended up in detention. Bullies made Kenna mad—maybe that was the farm girl in her. She grew up with teasing brothers. Teasing was one thing, but what happened to Marty, and out there with Travis, was cruel. There was a difference.

A few minutes later, Travis came into the back kitchen. "What was that?" he asked on a laugh. "Yes, chef. No, chef. Did that really happen?"

"It did." Kenna opened the box containing their latest liquor order and tried to focus on the invoice. She needed to restock the wine rack and add the new inventory to her master spreadsheet.

Travis ducked down to catch her eyes. "Where did that performance come from?"

"I was curious, so I went to the bar to spy and your father asked, 'How many cooks does this place have?' I lost it." She clicked her mouse with one hand and then added the bottle she'd pulled from the box to the concrete and steel rack. When she turned back, Travis's gaze seemed puzzled.

"You were sticking up for me, Ken."

Makenna raised the next wine bottle like she was going to swing it at him if he called her Ken one more time.

"Sorry, Makenna. Is that what that was?"

Her face was warm. She hadn't meant to get involved, but she felt something: a need to protect him and the brilliance of his work. She couldn't allow them to make him feel—how had they made him feel?—less than. In the past, she had always been first in line to help knock down Travis's inflated ego, but what happened out there wasn't fun bantering between friends. It was ugly and rooted in something Kenna couldn't begin to understand. Family wasn't supposed to act like that.

As Paige liked to put it, Travis was part of their pack. He was one of theirs, and the likes of the football contingent, family or not, wasn't going to mess with him.

"Yeah, I guess I was sticking up for you. They were rude." She added two more bottles and stared a bit longer than necessary at her computer screen. She glanced up and Travis had pulled himself up onto the counter next to her, his legs swinging, like a little boy with a secret.

"You like me."

Kenna blew out a puff of air and turned back to the wine rack. "Hardly." *Two more merlot, and what the hell was the one I just added?* Damn it, she could feel the weight of his eyes. When she turned to figure out if it was rosé or pinot noir she had just added, he jumped off the counter.

"Makenna." He was standing next to her.

Holy smokes!

"Yes." She tried to look over his shoulder, anywhere but his eyes, but he was too damn tall, so she lowered her eyes and focused on his neck. Not helping. It was a pretty great neck.

"I'm not sure anyone's ever stuck up for me, except maybe Logan, but never a woman."

"Yeah, well, that doesn't surprise me considering the women you associate with." Kenna closed her laptop; the rest of the wine could wait until tomorrow. She needed air, needed to go pick up her daughter.

Travis laughed. "Well, thanks, but I'm used to dealing with my family."

"I know you're used to it. I could tell, but it pissed me off. It's not a big deal." Goodness, he was still so close and she wasn't used to this new soft, thankful Travis voice. It sounded lethal. "I just wanted to rub a little bit of your success in their faces."

He laughed again and, this time, put his hand to his stomach, sort of like he was feeling his abs or he was hungry. Kenna wasn't sure what he was doing, but her mind wandered and her face grew even warmer. "That you did. My mother will probably be talking about the senator for months now, so thanks for that."

She grinned and backed toward the door. He took her arm, clearly not aware that lately the simple touch of him rushed through her body.

"Thank you."

"You're welcome," she said quickly and made her escape through the back door. The air was cool, the sky was blue, and she hoped to God her keys were in her bag because she wasn't sure she could take one more minute of him.

✺

Travis didn't get home that night until almost one, but he was on such a high, he didn't care. The tasting had gone well, they were busy until closing, and when Makenna had swung back around six because she forgot to leave a check for the new after-hours cleaning service they'd hired, Paige had run back into the kitchen and handed him her lunch box herself. She hadn't had time for a note, so she looked up at him and said, "Surprise me," and pulled him down so she could kiss him on the cheek.

"What'd Sierra bring today?"

"Bacon and bread and tomatoes. It was brown like from the toaster."

"BLT?"

Paige nodded. "That's it."

Travis rolled his eyes dramatically. "Any amateur can do a BLT."

Paige giggled and then Makenna's voice called her to come up front. Her eyes widened and she waved as she ran off.

He'd stayed late after closing and made her a club sandwich with toothpicks through each piece, topped with tiny little pickles. He also made a quick potato salad from the leftover fingerlings that were part of the pork special. The lunch box was packed and in the walk-in. He'd pull it out right before they came through tomorrow morning and watch that sense of relief fill Makenna's eyes. One less thing for her to worry about. Shit, maybe Logan was right and he was caring for her through her daughter's lunch box. That was screwed up, but as Travis unlocked his front door and threw his bag in the entryway, he didn't care.

Grabbing a beer out of the fridge, he plopped his tired ass down on his leather couch and turned on *The Walking Dead* he'd DVRd last week. After a few sips, he felt a second wind coming on so he opened the Vietnamese food he'd grabbed on the way home. He took a few bites and a smile spread across his face.

The McNulty clan was probably already back in San Francisco where they belonged, and Makenna Rye definitely liked him. Life was good. Of course, he still had to figure out what to do about his feelings, which were quickly moving past like, but for right now, he was good. Happy even.

Chapter Fourteen

*W*hen Adam died, he left Kenna and his daughter rather well-off by most standards. Adam Joseph Conroy was the oldest son of the Rhode Island Conroys. His father was a "bigwig," as Adam had described him once, with MetLife. His parents were part of the pastel-wearing country club set, but they were good people. Probably similar to Logan's fiancée's parents, the senator and Mrs. Malendar, but with nowhere near the media coverage.

Makenna liked her in-laws even though they were not thrilled when their son chose UCLA and graduated with an engineering degree. On the few visits the Conroys made while she and Adam were in college, Kenna always got the feeling they wanted their son to follow in the family business. When he asked Makenna to marry him during the end of their junior year at UCLA, his parents flew out and took them to dinner. They were warm and welcoming, and Kenna could see they were hoping Adam would move with his new wife back to Rhode Island. His mother wanted a big wedding, but they ran off to Vegas on a whim one weekend. Adam was big into whims. After his parents recovered from the disappointment, Adam told them over Thanksgiving back at their family compound that he wanted to be a boat builder-designer and he had taken an internship with Frank Green's prestigious design company, starting at the bottom. His father was visibly displeased, but it was short-lived because less than a year later, Kenna was pregnant and all was forgiven. The Conroys were doting grandparents and even stayed a few nights on the farm getting to know the crazy men in Makenna's life. Things were zooming along, and then Adam was gone.

Every time she pulled up to St. Christopher's, she was reminded of the money. Stone buildings and plaid skirts weren't exactly her scene, nor had they been Adam's, but when he left her all that money, she thought Paige should have the best school and St. Christopher's was the best. So there she was in the parking lot, putting a mint in her mouth and preparing to meet with Mrs. Moritz, Paige's kindergarten teacher. She'd called early that morning while Kenna was still at the farm and wanted to "chat." It wasn't "anything urgent," she had said, but she wanted to talk to Makenna in person. Kenna knew from growing up with her brothers that teachers didn't call parents in to talk face-to-face unless something was wrong. She looked at the clock on her phone and, with only a couple of minutes left before her meeting with Mrs. Mortiz, she checked her reflection in the rearview mirror and got out of her car. As she walked the long brick entryway to the school, she tried not to notice that despite her best efforts with the baby wipes, her clogs were still smeared with mud.

Makenna stopped by the front office and was given her visitor's badge. Letting out a slow breath, she willed herself into a less-frazzled mommy as she walked to building B and down the hall to room 210. The door was open and Mrs. Moritz was at her desk. Kenna knocked lightly on the doorframe, and the teacher's bespectacled eyes met hers.

"Mrs. Conroy." The petite woman, wearing a cardigan the color of Easter eggs, stood up from her desk.

"Please, call me Makenna." She walked forward, extending her hand.

"Well, thank you for coming in. I hope it wasn't too difficult for you to leave work." Mrs. Moritz gave Kenna a look she'd become

quite used to. It was a popular look at St. Christopher's once anyone realized Paige's mom was a "working" mom. Kenna found this
odd since most of the teachers or administrators giving her the oh-
poor-dear-juggling-all-of-that look were, in fact, working mothers
themselves. Kenna guessed it was because most of the students'
moms didn't have jobs outside their homes. Working dad, stay-at-
home mom seemed to be the standard at St. Christopher's Private
School.

"No, it was no trouble at all."

Mrs. Moritz's small, pink-lipsticked mouth curved. "Here, let's
sit." She gestured to a small round table with kindergarten-size
chairs. They sat, and Paige's teacher rested her folded hands on the
brown linoleum table. She looked a bit like an overgrown student.
Kenna felt like she did when she sat down with Paige and her animals for a tea party, but this probably wouldn't be as much fun. No
Doritos.

"Well, first I want to say that I just love little Paige." A re-
hearsed laugh followed, and Makenna found herself wondering if
Mrs. Moritz spoke to everyone in her life like a kindergartner.
That would be super annoying, she thought and then realized she
needed to respond.

"Thank you. She loves your class."

"She's so . . . creative and beyond her years, if you know what I
mean."

Oh boy, here we go.

"I'm not sure I do, Mrs. Moritz." Kenna tried for the same
pink-lipped smile but wasn't as successful. She was growing annoyed, needed to eat lunch, and wasn't much in the mood for the
condescending chitchat she was sensing would follow. Why the
hell couldn't people just get to the point? "Is something wrong?"

"Well, not really wrong, just . . . concerning. Maybe trouble-
some would be the right word. We had an incident yesterday that
was, just between you and me, sort of funny." More fake laughter.
"But it happened in the classroom, and I need little Paige to understand we can't just blurt things like that out."

Damn it, what'd she say this time, and why did this woman keep calling her little Paige? It made her daughter sound like some plastic doll. Kenna's mind was sifting and sorting through what Paige may have said. They'd been talking about global warming this morning, nothing controversial there. Maybe it was a bad word or even something sassy she'd recently picked up from watching the *Iron Chef*. They should probably stop watching that show, but it was one of their favorites, next to *Cupcake Wars*.

Kenna felt her head throb. "Okay. What exactly did she say?"

Mrs. Moritz seemed a little flustered by what Kenna had always been told was her candor. She probably wanted to continue meandering along with the story, but Kenna's stomach was growling and she really wanted to apologize for whatever bad word her daughter had said and be on her way.

"Little Cali is one of our other students, and she had exciting news to share with the class this morning." Mrs. Moritz's eyes widened and reminded Kenna of Snow White, or maybe Cinderella. She was never a fan of the princesses. Mulan, the one that kicked ass without the doe-like eyes, had always been her favorite. But Mulan wasn't speaking; this was definitely Snow White.

"She was explaining that the stork was going to bring her family a baby sister. The class was overjoyed and clapping, until little Paige told her that wasn't true, that the baby would need to travel through the birth canal and come out of her mother's vagina."

It took what little discipline Kenna had to keep from laughing her ass off and slapping the brown linoleum kiddy table. "I see." She tried to look "concerned" and "troubled," not sure if any of it was working.

"So, you can see why little Paige saying that babies really come out of the vagina could be . . . distressing to other children."

Makenna tuned back in to hear the tail end of Mrs. Moritz's comments. Her daughter's mind was always curious and she was eager to set people right, so Makenna wasn't surprised. And she was right. The stork? Who the hell still thought kids were that dumb?

Mrs. Moritz was looking to her for a response.

Makenna folded and unfolded her hands and refrained from giving the response clamoring to get past her lips, "Well, that is where they come from." Instead, she went with the standard controlled-mommy response she'd practiced since she was old enough to know she was different from most mothers.

"Of course, I understand, and I certainly apologize. I will have a talk with Paige and explain to her what is appropriate to discuss in class."

Mrs. Moritz let out a sigh, more Snow White, and stood from the tiny table. "I just knew you would understand. Well, I'm glad that's done."

Makenna stood and smiled. "Thank you for letting me know."

"Absolutely, that's my job. We are partners after all." She extended her hand. Kenna shook it and once she was standing in the green-and-white tiled hallway, she took a normal breath.

After driving through McDonald's on her way to The Yard, she sat in the parking lot to politely leave a voicemail for Date Number Two explaining that she had to cancel. She would not be dating. She didn't have time to meet anyone. Clearly everything in the universe was telling her she needed to focus on raising her daughter and holding their life together.

"Why are there only single flowers on all the tables? Are we trying to depress people? Can't we put a little green in there or maybe two flowers? This just seems sad."

Travis looked up from filling a large pot with water at the sound of Makenna's questions. She was walking around the empty tables as Summer followed close behind.

"They're Gerber daisies. That's a happy flower." Summer was bubbly, which struck a dramatic contrast to Kenna's scrunched-up brow. She was clearly pissed about something. He shut the water off and moved the pot to the stove.

"Not by itself it's not. Why the hell is it so hard to put another flower in there? It's not like the daisy isn't making room—it clearly is. It's trying, it wants to have a friend, right?"

"I . . . sure?" Summer nodded, and her curly blonde hair bobbed almost like a cartoon character.

The bits of the conversation he could hear sounded a little nutty, but it was obvious there was no way Summer was going to say a word. He was struck by how different the two women were as they weaved in and out of the tables. Summer was younger, but that wasn't it; she'd lived less life. Even Makenna's movements spoke to her need for efficiency, her constant thinking. Travis would normally be drawn to the wide-eyed stroll of a Summer, but at that moment, he couldn't take his eyes off the queen of complication as she stomped around nagging about the flowers.

"I've got some greens in the back. I will give each one a friend," Summer said in as friendly a manner as her name implied.

"Good." Kenna turned and threw herself into a seat at the pizza counter.

Travis pretended to watch his water boil so he could eavesdrop.

"What was that about?" Logan asked while starting the pizza oven.

Kenna began moving books and the sausage grinder they had on display. She was doing that thing she did when she was pissy. Travis had once heard Sage call it "stress cleaning."

"Nothing. I was just saying that we need more flowers on the tables."

"We do?" Logan stacked the last dough box and looked at his sister.

"Yes, they look lonely. There's just one on each table."

"I know."

"Right, well, I want that changed. I do the taxes here, and I say the flowers need company."

"Okay."

Travis quickly glanced over, and Logan looked a little scared. He turned around and tried to be the comic relief.

"Did I hear something about poor lonely flowers?"

Kenna shot up her hand in a gesture Travis recognized.

"Got it." He turned back to his water.

"Do you want to talk about anything?" Logan asked as he followed her into the back kitchen.

Travis felt a little stupid, but he moved away from the stove to wipe the already clean pass-through that connected the front and back kitchens.

"I have no idea what I'm doing," he heard Makenna say in a strained voice. "I'm trying to move forward and it feels like every step I take isn't working. I'm trying to make the best decisions for Paige—"

"Which you are," Logan said.

"Right, but I don't fit in, and Paige is . . . well, she's advanced, and I'm sure that has something to do with the fact that it's just the two of us."

"Is advanced a bad thing?"

"No, but now I'm adding this dating thing and I'm not sure how that's affecting her. You know how she is."

"I do, and I love every bit of her."

"I do too, but you're not raising her alone and when you're called to a teacher conference in the middle of helping your father clean up because raccoons got into his composter, it's . . . hard."

Travis kept wiping. Logan didn't seem fazed by his sister's rant.

"Why did you have to go to meet with her teacher?" Logan asked.

"Because Paige corrected some girl in class and told her babies come out of a vagina instead of from the damn stork!"

Even out of the corner of his eye, Travis saw her hands flailing as he tried to hold in his laughter.

"Then, to make matters worse, when the little perfect lily-white Disney character girl told her she was wrong, my daughter gave her a couple of websites where she could look stuff up."

Logan laughed and Travis lost it too, but he covered his mouth and walked back to check on his water. He glanced up again and saw Makenna through the pass-through. She was smiling the really great smile she normally saved for her family. He was staring and, of course, she looked up.

"Travis, I'm sure you've heard the whole damn conversation, so you might as well join in the laughter."

"I mean, there's certainly nothing wrong with vaginas," he said, throwing some salt into his pot and joining them in the back.

Makenna laughed and Logan was almost crying by this point.

"See, now this makes me feel better. When I'm here or on the farm, I'm me. It's when I have to go out into the real world that I usually feel awkward and stupid. I just need to stay in my bubble."

"Does this have anything to do with the dating thing?" Logan asked.

Makenna looked at Travis. He should have left, given her time to talk alone with her brother, but he found himself wanting to know the answer.

"No. Probably. I have no idea. I mean, maybe that's part of it. I just canceled Date Number Two, so all I really have to go on is a couple coffee dates and the dog guy." She held her hand up to Travis again because she must have thought he was going to bark. She was right, but he refrained.

"Oh, and I have yet to tell you about the super classy guy a couple of nights ago who wanted me to send more pictures. I understood that to mean more pictures about my life, you know, me on vacations."

Travis ran his hand across his face because he already knew where this was going.

"Oh no," she continued, "he meant pictures with more skin showing. Yuck!"

Logan looked at Travis, neither of them laughing anymore. "You need to be careful, Kenna," Logan said while Travis stood there trying not to think about pictures of Makenna.

"I know. You don't need to worry about me. I was just giving you a glimpse into the creepy online dating world. You don't need to get all big brother on me. Besides, I'm done. Experiment over. I'm back on track. Paige and I are perfectly fine on our own."

"That is true, you are, but you never know. You might—" Logan looked up at Travis.

Seriously?

Travis turned to leave, but not before he heard Makenna's parting words: "Please, can we be done talking about this, because I'm pretty sure I'm going to smack you if you tell me I'll meet someone. I already did that. I met him, married him, and we had a beautiful child. That was my happily-ever-after. Except it wasn't. I'm pretty sure most women only get one shot at the prince and the horse thing, so I'm done."

As he lowered a basketful of linguini into the boiling water, Travis tried to clamp down on the want. Not for himself, although that was in there too, but this was more wanting for her. She deserved someone, another happily-ever-after, and for the first time, he wanted to be that guy. It was too bad Travis was nowhere near a prince and he'd never even been on a horse.

Chapter Fifteen

Kenna was tucked away in the private dining area all morning and through most of lunch. At around one o'clock, Travis peeked his head around the corner.

"Hey, Todd was confused."

"That's not exactly news, is it?" She hit send on an e-mail.

He laughed. "He got confused and made an extra burger. Did you want it for lunch?"

Makenna looked up from her laptop.

"With fries. I'll even get you a Coke." He smiled, and she did too. His heart picked up more than it already had when he was making the burger in the kitchen, realizing he wanted to help her out of her bad mood.

"You joining me?" came right out of her mouth, and Travis could tell she was just as surprised as he was.

"Yeah, be right back."

When he returned, Kenna closed her laptop and they sat eating in silence for a few beats.

"So, sports. You come from a big, sort of huge, sports family."

He offered lunch to help, see if she needed to talk, and of course now she wanted to discuss his damn family again. What was it with her needing to know? Too late to change his mind now, so he unrolled his napkin and answered.

"I do."

"That's two words. You tend to do that when things get personal."

"Personal? Is that what this is?" Travis flashed her a halfhearted grin and took a bite out of his sandwich.

"Is that the new grinder?" She was trying to change the subject, to make him comfortable so he'd open up. He'd played this game with women before, so he simply nodded.

"Do you like what you do?" she asked.

He was thrown by the random question, but it was an easy one. "Yes, I love what I do."

"Why?"

He put the sandwich down. "What's this about, Makenna?"

"I'm just asking a question. We can talk about things, remember? You said that a while back. Or does that only apply to my . . . things?"

"No. Fine. I played football all through high school. Football and baseball actually, but I was pretty useless at bat, so mainly football."

"That's still impressive."

Travis laughed. "Yeah, well, I was recruited by USC for football, full ride, and then I blew out my knee senior year of high school before I even arrived on campus."

Kenna said nothing.

"It was the weirdest thing. I knew I was going down. I was wide open for a sack, but I sort of tried to move and ended up twisting the crap out of my leading leg. I went down and my ACL was shot. By the time it healed completely, I was finished."

"Were you devastated?"

"No. Best thing that ever happened to me. Sometimes I wonder if I subconsciously moved—if I knew. Training says if you're going down, you let it happen, fall, and go with it. Stay loose. Why the hell did I move? I pushed off. I guess I'll never know why, but once I got my knee back, I honestly didn't care. My dad, my brothers, they all left me the hell alone. I was no longer a commodity for the McNulty name. It was freeing."

"Oh well, good."

"What was the question?" He tried to smile. "My job, cooking, right. I tried college through my sophomore year, but I wasn't into it. So I left and went to work at a restaurant. I'd done busser and prep cook stuff in high school, but once I started cooking, I fell in love. The energy, the flow, I was hooked. I went to culinary school."

"Realized you were brilliant?" She grinned and continued eating her fries.

"Something like that."

"Logan says you're brilliant. Hey, so does Paige, and she's a tough customer."

Travis laughed and when she joined him, all he heard was her laughter. It filled the room. He decided she didn't do it enough.

"I love what I do, so I'm always working at it. I think it's like that with anything. Logan's passionate about this place, about growing things fresh and being responsible. It's who he is, so it's easy. I mean, I guess it's not easy, but it's where he wants to be all the time. I'm that way when I'm in a kitchen. It's all mine and yes, I guess it's something I do well."

"Did your family support you?"

It was such a simple question, but Travis found the pain of the answer caught in his throat, so he opted for silence.

"Okay, well, having met them, I'm guessing they didn't. That they stopped supporting you after you lost your knee?"

Travis nodded. He never talked about this anymore.

"Sorry, I ask a lot of questions."

Travis shook it off. "Do you like your job, Makenna?" It wasn't exactly subtle, but he needed to move on.

"I do. I get to use all those accounting classes, but I'm not stuck in an office. The restaurant is flexible; so is the farm. Flexible is a gift, especially with Paige."

"Long hours, though."

"I don't mind working. I was raised on hard work, so it's really all I know."

"Seems that way. Is it difficult being a single mom?"

Kenna raised her eyebrows as she finished chewing. "Apparently I'm not the only one who knows how to ask the questions."

Travis took another bite of his sandwich.

"I don't like calling our life, my . . . situation, I guess is the right word, difficult. Life isn't easy for anyone. My set of circumstances may be unique, but struggle touches everyone in some form or another, don't you think?"

"I do, but losing your husband when your daughter was only—what?"

"Five weeks and three days."

"That seems like a pretty extreme situation to come back from."

Kenna glanced up at him and let out a steady breath. She was thinking about her answer and he found himself dying to know.

"I suppose it is. Being a mom is challenging, single or not single. It's about as far from accounting as I could have gone. There's nothing but gray area, and there's rarely a right or wrong answer. Some days I'm sure she's going to win the Nobel Peace Prize and then the next day I convince myself she'll become hooked on drugs or air dusters. There are lots of monsters under the mommy bed."

They both laughed.

"I guess not having someone, a partner to bounce things off of, is tough," Kenna continued. "All of the decisions are on me and each one moves me a little closer to the nuthouse. But, with all of that, being her mom is the most important thing I will ever do. I need to get it right."

Travis wasn't sure he fully understood, not yet, but sitting there with her, he was certain she was what he liked to call an A-plus. Major effort, maximum return. She was brilliantly herself and watching her search his face with uncomfortable eyes, he realized she had absolutely no idea.

136

✻

Makenna knew he needed to start prepping for dinner, but there he was, as cool as if it were Sunday afternoon. He sat laughing with her and even when she asked him personal questions and tried to get him to run, he stayed. In the privacy of her favorite space, the whole thing felt a whole lot like a date, except if it were a date she probably would not have just flicked a chunk of dried mud off the side of her shoe.

"So, rough morning and the dating's not going well?"

"I meant what I said, I'm done. I'm better off without it and I have plenty of things to keep me busy. I'm fine."

"Yeah, me too. I'm fine too."

"Oh yeah? Again, we're just in sync, huh?" She rolled her eyes at the absurdity that they had anything in common. Travis nodded.

"Did you have to chase a bunny around your backyard this morning and then listen to a lecture from your five-year-old about how we need to change out all of our lightbulbs to save the polar bears while you drove her to school?"

The look on his face told her this was what he was waiting for from the moment he sat down. He wanted her to vent. Travis shook his head.

"No? Did you forget your breakfast and, because you ran out of the shower and threw your jeans on when your daughter yelled that Popcorn was running away, did you forget to then go back in and put your underwear on? Did you realize you'd forgotten un-dergarments when you were sitting in the drop-off line sandwiched between the BMWs and the Range Rovers? Did you start your day feeling completely out of control?"

"Well, I did realize I was dangerously low on toothpaste this morning. I need to get some more. Wait, so you're commando to-day?"

Kenna tilted her head and felt like they were standing on oppo-site sides of a canyon. She was beginning to wonder if there was anyone who could relate to her insanity. "I . . . that's all you got out

of what I just said? All that happened before the teacher conference and you're on my underwear?"

Travis stood, walked around the table, and pulled her to her
feet. "Makenna."

"What, no Ken today?" She looked up at him with bravery she
wasn't feeling.

"No, no Ken." He pulled her into his arms and hugged her. She
had no idea why—maybe it was the release of someone taking hold of
her or the simple warmth of him—but she started to cry. It wasn't a
hysterical cry; she felt a shudder and a few tears sink into the cotton
of his shirt.

"You're fine."

"I know," she whispered.

He brought one hand to her face and wiped away her tears with
his thumb. "Just remember to breathe, okay?"

They were suspended, standing there in the rainbow light of the
private dining room, surrounded by her collection of chairs, and she
didn't want to let go. In fact, for a second before she remembered it
was Travis she was clinging to, she wanted him to pull her into his
lap, make her pancakes, and share the Sunday paper. She wanted to
drag him out into their backyard garden with his coffee cup so they
could watch Paige chase Popcorn around. It smacked her in the
chest and for a moment, she couldn't possibly take his advice.

"Breathing, right. I will try to remember that." Kenna went to
step back, but Travis brought both hands to her face, held her, and
then kissed her forehead. *Holy smokes!* She saw the same Sunday
morning right there on his face, too, but then it was gone and
Travis reverted to his default—humor.

"Now, I'll let you get back to that laptop before I offer to help
you find your panties." With a smile that wasn't helping her find
breath, he turned to leave.

She wasn't sure if they would ever be in this same place
again . . . if their guard or sarcasm would ever be this far down, so
she needed to get one more thing out.

"Why do you make lunch for Paige?"

✹

"I—I make her lunch because it started off just, and now it's—I don't know, I just do." It was again a simple question and yet he couldn't answer. His heart was pounding in his chest.

"Is it like a pity thing and you don't want to say that, so you're tripping over your words?"

"You think I make your daughter lunch out of pity?"

"I don't know. That's why I'm asking. Maybe it's 'oh, poor single mom, always rushing around, clearly a train wreck in the dating world, let me help her out because I'm Mr. Smooth and nothing ruffles me.'"

Travis smiled. She actually thought that's why he could barely speak? That it had nothing to do with the fact that she was standing so close to him or that as each day went by, he wanted her more? It didn't occur to her that she was sexy and beautiful or that her daughter's lunch was sometimes the highlight of his day. All Kenna could see was that he was smooth and she was a pity case.

"Mr. Smooth?" He stepped into her even though he already felt like he'd gone a couple rounds in the ring with Brick. "Nothing ruffles me?"

Kenna huffed and put her hands on her hips. "See, right there, the way you slow everything down. You're worse than the damn yoga teacher Sage made me try. I felt stupid and awkward around her too."

"You feel stupid and awkward around me?"

"Stop it! Stop sexifying everything. Yes, I feel flustered and even more out of control than I normally do when you are around. I know that you have little or no responsibility, but it's your energy, your flow."

He stepped closer and she stepped back. Of course she did.

"Makenna."

"Are you mocking me right now with this prowling cat thing? Because I'm trying to keep myself together and I don't need you mocking me. I'm simply asking why you make Paige's lunch. A simple answer would work. Do you do simple answers?"

He took two steps this time and unless she was going to step out onto the main floor, she had nowhere to go. They were inches from one another. He could smell her, feel her breath mix with his.

"I get flustered," he told her.

"Oh, yeah. I bet. When does that ever ha—"

He took her arms gently, pulled her in another inch or so, and held. Her lips were right there, and if he leaned in just a centimeter, he would finally know what Makenna Rye tasted like, the feel of her lips, whether she drove the kiss or rested on a moan. And that was the problem, wasn't it? What if once he knew, he couldn't stop? He let out a shuddering breath and went to ease her back, but then he thought about what Logan had said, thought that maybe it was time, time to go after something more than what he'd learned to settle for. Makenna almost looked scared, but then her eyes softened as if she understood something he hadn't even said yet. She reached up, touched the side of his face, and he was a goner. She'd figured out why he made Paige's lunch, why he teased her. She knew—it was right there in her eyes, her touch, and suddenly nothing else mattered. He'd figure everything else out later.

"See? This is what I look like flustered," he said softly, and then he kissed her.

Chapter Sixteen

*I*t was so unexpected, she almost fell back, but he had her. His big warm arms tightened, and Kenna relaxed into a kiss she could never have dreamed up. She'd been prepared for heat. Honestly, there wasn't a conscious female who wouldn't notice the heat of Travis McNulty and wow, the man had a mouth. The heat was expected.

What she hadn't expected, what was currently liquefying her bones, was the tenderness. The way his fingers played with her hair and teased her face. The gentle caress of his lips or the slow dip of his tongue. She and Travis were famous for their banter, but this was more like a whisper. A soft, easy murmur. A sharing of feeling, not just lust. Kenna was lost in the tenderness. His flattened palm smoothed down her spine, and she felt like she was on one of those rides at the fair where the bottom dropped out. Her heart was in her throat just like that. She should have stopped, pulled away, but he was such a surprise that she didn't want to move. Instead, she wanted to learn more, get a closer look.

"I—I'm sorry about that." He slowly pulled away and appeared to be searching her eyes.

It was not possible that the man didn't know the voltage of a kiss like that. Could he possibly need to check for impact?

"Oh, don't be, but just to be clear, what exactly was that?"

"Huh, maybe I did it wrong." He pulled her back in.

"No, no, I'm pretty sure you did it right," she said, laughing.

Travis grinned, still holding her.

"Where did that come from?"

"I wanted to kiss you. You didn't pull away or smack me, so I kissed you."

"Right, why?"

"Now that's a more complicated question."

"Sort of like the lunch box?"

"Yeah."

"And you're not about complicated, right?"

"Right. Well, maybe. What was the question again?"

Makenna stepped back. She needed to get her head on straight because this was real. It wasn't some dream or a date with some dog guy from online. This was Travis, her brother's best friend, a guy she worked with. Oh crap, wasn't she just saying she had enough to keep her busy? Okay, it was okay, she could fix this. "It was just a kiss."

"I'm not sure I'd call that *just* a kiss," Travis said.

Damn it, why did she keep saying things out loud? Was that one of the first signs of insanity? Maybe Paige could Google that for her when they got home. Paige . . . she needed to leave, now. Makenna grabbed her laptop, threw her purse over her shoulder, and quickly looked at her phone. "Listen, I was super weird today and I'm sorry. I'm sure you do this help-the-damsel-in-distress thing all the time and you were . . . being nice."

"Actually, I definitely do not do *that* all the time and nice? Are you telling me that was nice?"

Kenna held her laptop to her chest, begging for something to magically transport her to her car. "No, it was, that kiss was, not nice. It was sort of the opposite, maybe like an explosion."

Travis smiled and she blushed. Damn it, some things never changed.

"I have to go. I have to get Paige."

"Uh huh." He was leaning up against the wall now, just leaning there like he was waiting in line. Probably waiting for the next unsuspecting basket case to come along with her weird-ass dream and—*Oh brother. Leave, Kenna!*

"I have to go. Bye." She didn't wait for him to respond this time and walked as fast as she could without running. She must have looked like the seniors who power walked through her neighborhood every morning. Yes, that's what she was doing, power walking away from Travis, that kiss, and a whole flood of feelings she didn't have time to sort out.

Travis knew he had a stupid grin on his face. He couldn't help it. The kiss played in his mind. Even as he pummeled chicken breasts for the piccata dinner special, he couldn't shake her. He'd known what he was doing; it hadn't been just some rash rush of lust, although the rush had almost knocked him over. It was exactly what he'd told her: he wanted to kiss her and he did, but he wasn't ready for the after. He happily fell into the kiss, but the flood of questions he saw in her eyes, her reaction... He knew how she was with something as simple as changing the lunch special. He should have known the questions would be there, but he fell into her and almost forgot his own damn name. She ran away so fast that he didn't even have a chance to come up with answers, which was probably just as well—he didn't have a clue what his next move should be.

"You done with those?" Logan asked as Travis breaded the last cutlet and added it to the wax paper.

"Yup." He handed him the tray, caught his eyes, and smiled. Makenna's eyes were similar to her brother's, but where his were green and gold, hers were mostly green. Shit, he was standing in the kitchen waxing on about his best friend's eyes like one of those poets in a flowing white shirt. If his father were there, there was no question he'd be called a pansy.

"What's up with you? Why are you staring at me?"

Travis kept smiling but looked away. Everything felt different. It was sort of like being drunk, but without the stupid. It was more of a recharge as if everything was clear, almost raw.

"Sorry, I'm just a little wired." He wanted to tell his best friend, but how did a guy go about telling his friend he couldn't stop thinking about a hot kiss with a beautiful woman when that woman was the friend's sister? Yeah, you didn't. You kept your mouth closed and sliced lemons, so that's what he started to do as Logan turned and walked to the front kitchen with the cutlets.

"Okay, I've never seen that stupid look on your face, so I'm guessing my sister has something to do with it," Logan said, pushing back through the door a few minutes later. "Now, if that's the case, I really don't want the details. At the same time, you're my friend and I want to know, so let's talk about this but on neutral terms. Like . . . food. Let's use food."

Travis wasn't sure this was such a good idea, but he agreed.

"Okay, I need to make this quick before Todd burns the hell out of your cutlets, so . . . I've got it. Remember those really great strawberries we saw when we were at the market last week?"

"The ones you said we should do something special with, like shortcake?"

"Yes, those are the ones."

"Yeah, I remember."

"If I were to go back to the market and get those berries, would there be a reason to celebrate? Like something out of the ordinary that would warrant making strawberry shortcake?"

Travis laughed. It probably would have been easier to just tell him that yes, he'd kissed Makenna and watch him squirm, but this game was sort of fun, too.

"Yeah, I'd say we could use them today. Something out of the ordinary did happen that would call for special strawberries."

Logan nodded. "Good." That was all he said. Before he got to the door, he turned back. "Just make sure you don't waste the strawberries, or I'll kick your ass."

Travis shook his head because that made absolutely no sense, but he understood the warning.

"I'll do my best."

"That's all I ask. We need more lemons."

"I'm on it."

They sold out of the dinner special and closed just after ten. Travis was walking out to the parking lot when his phone vibrated with a text from Makenna. He read it and realized it was coming from Makenna's phone, but Paige had sent it. He had a stupid grin on his face all the way home.

Chapter Seventeen

Sundays were normally set aside for coffee with Aunt Sage and then the library, although last Sunday they'd given up library time for a *Jack and the Beanstalk* puppet show. This Sunday, they were supposed to get back on track because they had lots of books to return and not much left to read. Their library, or "libary" as Paige often called it, time was way overdue. Last night, when they'd arrived home, Makenna had ordered pizza while Paige took a bath. Once they were snuggled in their pajamas, Paige asked if they could skip coffee and the library because she wanted to leave plenty of time to make cookies for her school bake sale.

"These need to be super duper," she'd said, biting into her giant slice of pizza. Makenna had a feeling this had to do with Sierra, but she didn't say. Instead, she called Sage, who was exhausted from a long night and fine with skipping coffee. Kenna managed to get the scoop on how things went at The Yard the rest of the night and Sage's brief online dating update, which wasn't much; her heart didn't seem to be in it either. Kenna somehow avoided mentioning the kiss. Part of that was because Paige was sitting right next to her and the other part was she wanted to see the look on her friend's face in person.

Now that Makenna was home, she wasn't sure if the kiss had actually happened or if she'd simply dreamed the whole thing up again. No, it was as real as that vertigo feeling she had every time she thought about it. With no plans for their Sunday, other than cookie making, Kenna agreed to let Paige stay up, and they watched *Brave* for probably the hundredth time.

The doorbell rang a little after eight on Sunday morning. Paige was on the couch watching a documentary on the Galapagos tortoise, or at least she was when Makenna fell back into bed at around six. Who the hell was at the door on a Sunday?

"I've got it, Mama."

Yeah okay, Peach, thank you—Wait, what? Makenna flew out of the bed. "Paige, don't answer that—" Too late. Her daughter was standing next to Travis, who was crouched down hugging Paige with one arm and holding a paper bag in the other. He looked up, the corner of his mouth barely turning up, and slowly stood.

"Looking good, Makenna."

Holy smokes! She brought her hands to her hair and tried to pat and fluff, but it was no use. She blew the strands she could see out of her face and for the gazillionth time in her life, attempted to look normal. This time was a particular challenge because she looked down and realized she was in her red-and-white-striped pajama bottoms and a white tank top. No bra. *Great.* She crossed her arms, but he'd already noticed. Damn it!

Travis, on the other hand, appeared to be freshly showered, wearing cargo pants that looked like he had been born in them. She had cargo pants and tried to sport that look, but they never looked like that. She looked more like G.I. Jane, and not the Demi Moore version. Maybe it was his bike. Maybe a motorcycle did something to a guy, relaxed him and made him so damn Sunday perfect. His born-in-these pants were paired with a dark gray T-shirt that had the same worn and tumbled sexy look. There was some logo across it, but Kenna couldn't read it. He was delicious, all "bright-eyed and bushy-tailed," as her father used to say when she was in high school and perfecting her not-a-morning-person attitude.

Paige held Travis's hand and pulled him toward the kitchen. "Did you bring everything?"

"I've got it all." He set the bag down on the counter of their small kitchen. "Everything we need for emergency school bake sale cookies."

"What?" Kenna said, her voice barely awake.

Paige curved her lips into her little "uh oh" face and froze in place. Travis looked down at Paige, then at Kenna, and back at Paige.

"You, oh no, you . . . didn't know I was coming over?" He shot Paige a pleading look and held out his hands in exaggeration. "Paige, you texted me that your mom needed help."

"She does." Paige nodded and swung her nightgown back and forth, as if trying to up her cuteness factor.

"I do not need help. We are perfectly capable of making cookies for a bake sale. Paige, we make cookies all the time and you've never needed to call in . . . reinforcements."

Kenna needed a Coke. She went into her bedroom, grabbed her favorite sweater off the chair, and covered the peepshow tank top she was wearing because it was bad enough he was in her house now. The last thing she needed to worry about was whether her nipples decided to show their appreciation. Again, holy smokes. She walked back into the kitchen to find Travis and Paige still standing there like kids in detention. Kenna opened the refrigerator, cracked open a Coke, and welcomed the morning caffeine.

"You know that stuff can eat a whole steak?" Travis said.

Brave guy, Kenna thought, but said nothing and took another sip.

"I say that all the time to Mama. Did you see that video on YouTube? They put Coke on batteries, the ones for your car too. It ate everything off there. Coke is bisgusting."

"Disgusting," Kenna and Travis corrected in concert, and just like that, the awkward became super awkward.

"Okay. First of all, you, missy, are in big trouble. This is Travis's only day off and I'm sure he has far better things to do with his time than drive all the way over here to make cookies. There's a whole book of cookie recipes. We do not need a professional chef for crying out loud."

"I know you're mad because you came out here without covering your boobies, but Travis didn't see, did you?"

Travis covered a laugh and shook his head with a grin so wide, it put the cat from *Alice in Wonderland* to shame. Makenna was grateful for the sweater because her entire body started to hum.

"See," Paige continued, "so you don't need to be mad. And you're wrong—these cookies need to be extra yummy. We need him. Sierra said her dad has a family cookie recipe." She raised her eyebrows and paused as if she'd just revealed the most devastating news.

"Is this that same girl with the lunches?"

Paige nodded.

"Honey, you can't keep running Travis around. This is crazy."

She dropped her head. "She said she would sell more cookies than me, so I thought if I called My Travis, then we could show her. Didn't mean to be mean."

"You're not being mean, but Uncle Rogan is a chef too. Maybe you could ask him."

Paige huffed. "He's too busy playing kissy-face, and I asked him last time and he told me he sucked at baking."

Travis laughed. "He really does."

Paige pointed at Travis. "See! So, I called My Travis." She wrapped her arm around his leg.

Makenna finally met Travis's eyes. They were smiling and comfortable. She let out a slow breath. "I'm sorry about this."

"Don't be. I'm happy to help, and I do happen to have a chocolate chip and pecan cookie recipe that's going to make Sierra and her father cry."

Paige clapped and jumped up and down until she noticed Kenna was giving her "the look."

"You are still in trouble for using my phone. I'm assuming she used my phone?"

Travis gave Paige an apologetic look and showed Kenna the text: *mama and i need help with cookies bring eggs and stuff meet at our house sun at 8* ♥

She shook her head. "When did you get this?"

"Last night at around 10:30."

"Paige Eliza Conroy."

Travis winced in empathy for Paige. Looking at both of them, Kenna couldn't hold up the pissed mother tone anymore and started to laugh.

Travis reached out, and pulled something from her nest of morning hair. Kenna did her best not to be startled, but he was standing in her kitchen and her heart felt like it was ready to leap out of her chest again.

"Feather." He smiled, showing her the white fuzz.

"My pillows are down."

"Is that so? Mine too."

She couldn't look away. It was like a weird movie scene when everything around the main character goes fuzzy. Where had this connection come from? Kenna had tried, but she could not seem to find her way back to thinking of Travis as her brother's annoying manwhore friend. He was now that man who made lunch for her daughter, had insecurities and a family of his own, and had kissed her silly in her favorite dining room . . . and she'd kissed him back.

And if all of that wasn't enough, now he'd woken up early on a Sunday morning to help her daughter bake cookies. Kenna's head was swimming and her heart was still trying to escape. Travis held her gaze, and then they both heard a huff from the little person below and looked down.

"I'll put some music on. You two can get started, but I need to brush my teeth," Kenna said.

Travis clapped his hands together and made a show of removing his ingredients from the bag. "Do we need to eat breakfast first?" he asked.

Paige stared up at her, a look of pleading in her eyes. Kenna shook her head in surrender. "Sure, let's have breakfast. Ask your Travis to make you an omelet. He's good at that." *He's good at a lot of things*, some sexy part of her brain said, completely oblivious to the fact that her daughter was right there. As if she'd said it out loud again, Travis crossed his arms and grinned at her.

Kenna turned and heard him laugh before she closed her bedroom door.

Teeth brushed, she washed her face and pulled her hair into a bun. While she was changing into jeans, she could hear giggling and clanking pans. Travis's laughter mixed with her daughter's, and again Kenna felt the ground shift. She touched the walls and let out a slow breath at the realization that they were still blue.

By sunset, they had packed up the "super duper" chocolate chip and pecan cookies, as well as the double chocolate chip cookies for the kids who didn't like nuts. Paige had taken Travis on a tour of their cool little house and he even met Popcorn, who was in his hutch in the backyard. The dishwasher hummed as the three of them lay on the couch, coming down from a sugar rush and watching Animal Planet. He'd known Makenna for a few years now, had been over to her house a couple of times with Logan, but he had never actually been part of her house, not like this. She was an incredible woman in her own right, but this home she'd created for herself and her daughter was another layer. It felt deeper than anything he'd ever experienced, even growing up as a child in his own home. They were a unit—Makenna and her daughter—and as much as Travis wanted her and loved hanging out with Paige, the magnitude of what he was potentially messing with hit him.

"I need to get going," he said, standing up and stretching because he hadn't been so relaxed in years.

Paige ran to the kitchen and brought him back a Ziploc bag packed with cookies.

"Ugh"—Travis patted his stomach—"I'm not sure I can eat one more cookie."

Paige nodded and handed him the bag. "Have them for breakfast. That's what I'm gonna do when I'm a grown-up."

"Eat cookies for breakfast?"

"Yup."

Travis looked at Makenna, who had gotten up off the couch and wrapped her sweater around her body like she was giving herself a hug. Smiling, she shook her head at her daughter's big plans.

"Paige, did you thank your Travis?"

"I did."

He bent to hug her, and Paige reached her arms up to pull his head closer. She kissed his cheek. "Thank you, My Travis. I will let you know if we sell more than stinky Sierra."

"That's not very nice," Makenna said while Paige released him and they turned to the door.

"I'm going to walk Travis out to his bike. Please go into your room and get ready for tub. Make sure you don't—"

"Start the tub, I know, I know." Paige huffed off to her room, making a show that she was not happy things couldn't always be cookies and Animal Planet.

Makenna shook her head, held her sweater tighter, and walked out the door in front of him.

He closed it behind them, and Makenna barely got out a "thank you" before he pulled her in and kissed her. It was urgent and searching as if he'd been holding his breath all day and needed her to keep going. That's what it felt like, his next breath. The cool evening air crept under his shirt, making him even more aware of the warmth of her body. When they eased away, she looked flushed and gorgeous under the night sky.

"I still don't have an explanation for what that was, so please don't ask me." Travis touched her face.

"I won't. I think it's pretty obvious what we're dealing with now."

He gave an exaggerated look at her professional investigator tone. "What do you think it is?"

"Well, you clearly have a crush on me—you want me actually—and you're using my daughter to get to me. I don't know why I didn't see it before," Kenna said while he moved into her until she was pressed against her car in the driveway.

"You have part of that right. I do have a crush on you and do want you, but I think your daughter is using me as her own personal chef."

She laughed and he kissed her again. When he slowly pulled back, she kept her eyes closed.

"I'm not sure what I'm doing," she whispered.

"It's just a kiss, Kenna. Please don't freak yourself out worrying about this. Nothing has changed, your life is fine, and I won't mess with that."

She opened her eyes. "How can you say that? Nothing has changed? I can't look at you anymore without wanting to either sniff your neck or tear your clothes off. And when I'm not doing that, I'm watching you work or you're making me laugh. Everything has changed, and what if we can't find our way back? What is that damage going to look like?"

He touched the side of her neck and, still holding her close, tried to think of something to say that she hadn't already put perfectly. "Okay, things have changed, but maybe we won't have to go back. Maybe we can move this forward and different will be better."

"Maybe." Kenna put her head against his chest before she turned to walk back into the house. Realizing he had nothing else to say, yet wanting to be with her for a minute more, he held onto her hand before slowly letting her fingers slip through his.

"Goodnight, Makenna."

"Goodnight, My Travis."

After tub, Makenna dried Paige's hair, read a quick story, and tucked her in.

"Burrito, burrito, please," Paige begged, bouncing on her bed.

"I don't have time for burrito tonight." Makenna handed her a glass of water.

Paige declined the water and flashed her sulking face.

"Hey listen, missy, you're the one who bombarded me with your Travis before I even got out of bed. After that little stunt, you should be banned from burrito and bedtime stories for like . . . a century."

Paige pulled the covers over her head and laughed. "A century is a super duper long time. I think dinosaurs lived that long ago."

Makenna laughed and took a deep breath, inhaling the fresh smell of her just-out-of-the-tub daughter, and found her patience.

She raised one eyebrow as if surveying the bed and put her hands on her hips. "I'm not sure how I'm supposed to make a burrito out of this mess," she said in her best chef voice. "Look at this. How can I work like this?" She threw a few of Paige's stuffed animals around the bed and fluffed her pillows as Paige giggled and rolled from side to side getting ready. Kenna went to the end of the bed and flipped the bedspread into the air. She loved the look on Paige's face as the colorful material fluttered down over her.

"Okay, yes, this is looking better. Now, we need to prepare." She smoothed the bedspread dramatically and folded the top down to reveal her daughter's smile. Her eyes were closed and she was doing her best to look like the meat in a burrito. That was the game. When Kenna had her all tucked on every side, she stood with her hands on her hips, Paige watching her from a tiny cracked eyelid.

"What do I want to put on this burrito?"

"Cheese," came a little voice.

"Yes! Lots of cheese." Kenna then pretended to sprinkle shredded cheese down Paige's body, being sure to tickle her along the way. "That looks perfect. Now let's add some salsa."

Paige squealed but tried to hold still as the game progressed. They added a few more things, including guacamole, Paige's favorite, and then with as much dramatic flair as she could muster, Kenna did a gobble, gobble, kiss, tickle that would have made Cookie Monster proud. Paige laughed herself exhausted and then, with a big sigh, wrapped her little arms around Kenna's neck.

"That was a good burrito." She kissed Kenna's cheek.

"It sure was."

"See, aren't you glad you didn't stay grumpy and miss out?"

"I am, Peach, I am." She kissed her daughter on her nose and clicked off the daisy lamp on her nightstand.

"Mama?"

"Huh." Makenna picked up her towel off the floor.

"You like My Travis, I can tell."

Makenna was so grateful she'd already turned off the light so her daughter couldn't see the shock. It was hard to believe she was only going to be six next month.

"Of course I like your Travis. He's Uncle Rogan's best friend and I work with him. He's a nice man."

"No, I mean you *like* like him. You want to hold his hand and play kissy-face with him." Paige was now hugging herself and rolling back and forth in her bed, giggling.

Makenna picked up one of her pillows and gently hit her daughter on the head. "You are silly. There will be no kissy-face. Now go to sleep, silly pants."

"Night, Mama."

"Sweet dreams."

"You too."

Makenna walked out of her daughter's room, closed the door to just a crack, and leaned up against the wall of their small hallway. It was true, she did want to play kissy-face with Travis and hold his hand. Kenna had always thought bringing a man into their world would be work, but Travis was sort of always there. He'd snuck up on her, and now she wasn't sure she wanted him to leave. At the same time, she knew Travis and couldn't help but wonder if this was another phase of his, sort of like scuba diving or when he decided he wanted to hike all seven peaks. She would like to think he would never involve himself if he wasn't willing to stick around, but it all felt too easy. As her father had said a million times when they were growing up, "Nothing worth having is easy."

Chapter Eighteen

"Is that a Ring Pop?" Travis asked the following Thursday morning as they gathered to discuss the Malendar wedding, which was now less than three weeks away.

"Sure is." Kenna sucked it between her lips, then licked her bottom lip and wrinkled her nose.

Travis was finding it next to impossible to maintain a professional working relationship with Makenna sucking on a bright red Ring Pop, but just as he was about to suggest they share, Logan saved the day with his professional purpose.

"Okay, Kenna spoke with Twisted Tree and they're all set to provide the wine." Logan flipped to a page on his yellow pad and sat next to both of them at the corner table of the bar.

Travis looked at Makenna when she shifted and her leg bumped his. Her face was in her laptop, but he could have sworn she was doing all of this on purpose. She sucked the Ring Pop again.

"We are doing the roasted vegetables with a choice of the sea bass or the filet?" Logan looked to Travis for confirmation.

"No, the ham, remember?" Travis said, finally moving his eyes off the Ring Pop.

"Right, and the smashed potatoes. I spoke with Lacey about

the ham and she's all set to deliver. They'll smoke them, too."

Travis nodded, and Makenna scrolled through the menu on her laptop.

"I'm a little bummed they didn't pick the wild mushroom confit because that word looked great on the menu," she said.

Logan shook his head. "Kate doesn't like mushrooms."

"Oh, well, that explains it." Makenna had the nerve to look relaxed. He was now the one with the racing heart and crazy eyes. *Damn, how long do Ring Pops last?*

"Okay, so cheeses—goat, some kind of double crème, the Comté, and"—Logan flipped the page—"and a blue, probably that bold one from Jordan's shop."

"Is the Comté the one that tastes like it was dipped in toilet water?" Makenna scrunched her face as if she could smell it.

Add playful, Travis thought. She was downright playful.

"No." Logan was not amused and moved on. "Warm bread, those seeded crackers we made for Restaurant Week, some roasted grapes, and maybe like an apricot spread?"

"Fig," Travis said, eyes still on Makenna.

Logan nodded and made notes. "Okay, that's it for now. Did you order the flax linens and email the invoice to—what's her name again?"

"Sloan," Makenna added, finally looking up from her laptop.

"That's really a perfect name for her. She came in yesterday to 'observe' and she's very wedding planner-ish, don't you think?" Logan asked.

"Yeah, not the Jennifer Lopez movie version, more like *The Devil Wears Prada* Meryl Streep version, if she were a wedding planner instead of a magazine editor."

Logan nodded, and Travis sat there enjoying watching the two of them play off one another. There was a rhythm to their relationship that worked well professionally and connected them personally. Logan always seemed to know where Makenna was at with just one look, and she had a way of getting into his head better than anyone. They were siblings, but not in any way that was

160

familiar to Travis. The connection was enviable and probably the result of years of caring and hard work. He felt a longing but let it go. As much as he had enjoyed kissing and would probably continue kissing Makenna, he had little experience with that kind of connection.

"Did you get that, Travis?" Logan asked.

Travis tried to search his mind for what had been said while he was thinking about things that had nothing to do with work or weddings, but he drew a blank.

"Sorry, what did you say?"

"The cheese, I ordered it and they'll deliver two days before the wedding. I want to make sure it doesn't end up in the refrigerator."

"Oh yeah, room temperature. That's a given."

He glanced up and Logan shook his head at him.

"What?"

"Nothing. Just fun watching you figure things out. Strawberries or no strawberries." Logan laughed, tore off a piece of paper from his pad, and handed it to Kenna. He turned to leave and then turned back.

"Oh, I almost forgot. They're using Grady's Nana's Depression glass for nonalcoholic drinks and Kate's grandmother's red punch bowl. Both have sentimental value, not to mention they're probably worth a fortune, so Grady wants us handling those as part of food. He's having someone drop them off next week."

Makenna added it to her list, closed her laptop, and the dueling Rye family cyclones left Travis sitting at the table, wondering whether Ring Pops came in strawberry.

Makenna picked Paige up at school and drove her up to the farm for the night, as agreed. One of the goats, or does, as Paige kept correcting her, was going to have her babies soon. Makenna had spoken with her father, who was thrilled at the prospect of having sleepovers with his granddaughter until the big day. Donk, as Paige called him, agreed to drop her off at school in the mornings. They were on day one of goat watch, and Makenna was hoping it didn't take Gracie too long to have her babies.

With the evening free, she arrived back at work right in time to see Vinnie.

"Vinnie is at table six. This time with a new redhead," Makenna whispered through the service window about twenty minutes after arriving.

"Has she gone to the bathroom yet?" Travis asked, still tossing the Brussels sprouts in his pan.

"Not yet, but they're halfway through the main course, so it should be any minute now."

"Let us know when the show starts," Logan said as he added chicken to a spinach salad and put it up in the window.

Vincent Pastorelli, as he always introduced himself, was one of their first regulars. He'd divorced three wives and had more money than any of them would ever see. He came in for dinner every Thursday night, in some version of his Adidas tracksuit, white socks, and brown dress shoes. His hair was black with the help of Grecian Formula. He had a tan—its origin was the subject of much debate among the pizza guys. Some thought it was natural; some swore it came from a bottle. Vinnie was a nice man, a horrible tipper, and a character. He always had a date for dinner and she was usually much younger. There were a few repeat dates, but most of the time he had a different woman each week. Makenna was sure he must use a dating service—probably online, she thought as she rolled silverware and waited for the show. It wasn't lost on her that Vinnie seemed to be more skilled at dating than she would ever be.

"Showtime," she said quietly through the service window. The pizza guys were already exchanging bets. The wager was always the same—whether or not Vinnie would finish out the evening once his date returned from the bathroom or if he would stand, make some excuse, and leave. Either way, every time his date went to the restroom, and for some reason they always did, Vinnie would begin having an entire conversation with himself. It was full of hand gestures and strange facial expressions and sounded like a critique of his date. Vinnie was entertaining to watch, although the first time it happened, one of the servers thought he was having some kind of seizure. It wasn't until she moved closer that she realized it was a highly animated conversation for one.

Tonight things were different because the redhead returned from the bathroom and they even had dessert.

"Vinnie may have found a keeper," Logan said as he placed two salads in the serving window.

They were all smiling, and money was exchanged among the pizza guys as Vinnie put on his date's coat, left his usual dollar-fifty, and waved good-bye.

Travis took Makenna's arm and walked her to the back kitchen. He pulled off his apron with the hand not holding her and threw it over the hook. When he saw Todd chopping carrots to whatever song was on his iPod, Travis let out a quick breath, pulled her into the dry storage, and closed the door. His eyes were wild with what looked like excitement as he paced in front of her.

"Would you like to go out? You know, like on a date?"

"Excuse me?"

"I'd like to take you on a date. Dinner, a movie. I know you said you're not exactly dating anymore, but I never got a chance to participate. I think I'd like to participate."

Kenna started to laugh and then realized he was serious.

"You're serious."

"Well, not if it's that funny." He turned to leave, but she took his arm.

"Travis, come on. We don't . . . we're not . . . you don't date women like me."

"Forget it." Travis pulled away easily and was at the door.

She knew once he walked out and that damn apron went on, he'd be back in front and she wouldn't get another word in for hours. Which was great. She should have let him go because he was talking crazy. They had nothing in common. Physically they appeared to work, sure, but Travis McNulty was complete freedom and motorcycle driving and she was all about responsibility and field trips. It was perfect that he was going back to work. She should do the same and all would be right with the world. That's what should have happened, but instead, she grabbed him again, spun him around, and pulled. Her body responded as it always did lately and promptly started to go up in flames, so she kissed him. This time, she was in charge. She was the one starting and finishing the conversation, and it was as if she were showing him that this, kissing, was all they were really good at. Her hands found their way into his hair, and when he pushed her up against the closed door, she could hear voices in the kitchen. He pressed his body into her and his hand traveled up the curve of her side. It was simple, innocent even in certain circles, but her entire body begged for more. *They were at work,* a stupid voice in the back of her head said. Anyone could come through that door at any minute, but she didn't care. She was kissing a beautiful man in a pantry. When was that ever going to happen again in her life?

Finally finished with him, she pulled back and pushed at his chest.

"Is that a yes?" Travis asked through barely open eyes and a smile so wicked she almost went back for more.

"This is crazy."

"Hey, that time was all you. Really fine skills there, by the way."

"I'm not your type. Dating isn't like making lunch or cookies even. Dating could lead to complications and, well, what if you don't even really like me?"

"Pretty sure I do." Travis looked down at the front of his pants, and Makenna blushed. She wondered if the blushing would ever stop.

"I'm not like this, Travis. I'm different."

"I know."

"Then let's just call that a kiss. We've had a couple of them, we've made some cookies, and now let's get back to our normal back-and-forth teasing. You have clearly lost your normal, so maybe you should call up someone, a model or someone who enjoys wearing heels, and walk away. Because I'll want a second date. And a phone call. I'm all about commitment. I have a daughter."

"Yes, you do, and she's incredible."

"I need someone who knows . . ."

"Knows what?"

"Someone who knows what I need, not just what my body wants."

"That's why we need a date. Just you and me, no lunches or work, just the two of us so we can figure this out. This isn't about getting in your pants, although whether you know it or not, you're sexy. Smart as hell too, which is a major bonus. I'd like to take you out."

"What has gotten into you? What about work and Logan?"

"I don't want to date Logan."

She smacked his shoulder. "You know what I mean."

"I've already talked to him. He knows I've got a thing."

"You've talked to him? You have a thing?"

"Makenna, relax. It's just dinner. Sunday, I'll pick you up around two?"

She felt herself slip further.

"In the afternoon? Two in the afternoon?"

"Yeah, unless you want me to stop by in the middle of the night." He wiggled his eyebrows.

Her face flushed again.

"I'll have to get a sitter for Paige."

"I'm sure Logan and Kara would love to have her for the day."

"Why are you taking me on a day date? What, do you have a real date that night?"

Travis laughed. "No. I want to spend time with you. Get started early."

"Holy hell, who are you?"

Travis smiled, kissed her gently, and walked out. "See you Sunday at two."

He closed the door behind her as if he knew she needed a minute. When had he started knowing her? Her heart was racing and she'd never been more confused in her life.

Chapter Nineteen

At first she thought she was looking up at a full moon, but Makenna looked closer and realized it wasn't quite full. It was the one right before full—when all the glow was there except a tiny sliver—and it lit up most of Makenna's small backyard as she stood on her patio with a cup of tea. Kara had given her a new citrus-mint green tea that she was actually starting to enjoy. Paige was thrilled and had begun spouting the benefits of green tea almost daily.

Makenna warmed at the thought of her daughter. She was up at the farm for night two of Gracie baby watch, and Kenna missed her. *She missed her noise,* she thought, taking another sip and a deep breath.

Looking up at the moon, as she often did at night, she felt small. It was strange how daily life could consume a person so much that even the little things seemed huge, like they were matters of life or death, when really they meant nothing. She'd learned what was huge and what wasn't when Adam died. The lesson had faded over time as doctor's appointments, clean toilets, and whether she was wearing the right shoes or should get one of those Louis Vuitton bags owned by all the mothers at St. Christopher's took on greater importance, but when she was quiet with herself, looking at the moon, she remembered.

Almost a full moon, she thought. Maybe that's what she was. It was possible a sliver would always be missing, left there by her mother or Adam or all the things she told herself. Maybe all that stuff combined kept her from being a full and glorious moon. Tears filled her eyes at the thought, but she swallowed them and held her hands to the warmth of her teacup.

A breeze rushed through the trees and she closed her eyes, listening to the tinkling duet between her wind chime and the one next door. She loved it here, loved her home. She and Paige lived in a section of Pasadena known as Bungalow Heaven. They'd moved into their little house a couple of years ago once Kenna figured out which school she wanted Paige to attend for kindergarten. Their home was just over 1,700 square feet and it was a Craftsman, as were all of the homes in the area. When they were looking, she had loved that about the neighborhood; the houses were all built the same way, but on the outside they were so varied. Some had porches; others were shingled. Some properties had big trees and others had small manicured shrubs. The neighborhood had it all and yet there was a thread of similar.

"Reminds me of a family," her father had said when she brought him to see the house. "Similar, but no two are the same." After his lovely metaphor, he proceeded to spout statistics about the crime rates and where the closest fire department and police stations were. He had come right out and said he was uncomfortable with a single woman and a little girl living alone. Kenna hadn't had the energy to be offended at the time, and now looking back, she only saw the love behind the comment. Makenna's mother had run off with "some rich asshole," as her brothers liked to say on the rare occasions their mother's absence came up in their adult lives. She was five when her mother left. With the exception of a pair of brown-and-cream colored heels with a tiny ankle strap and a silver ring with a bright blue stone her mother had worn on her middle finger, Makenna didn't remember her. Not what she looked like or smelled like. She had no memory of bedtime stories or bath time. Every now and then when she was growing up, she would try to reach back, but there was nothing there.

It had always seemed strange when people expressed sorrow for something she didn't even remember. As she grew older, she realized it was the void, the absence of a mother that struck so many as tragic. When she became a mother herself, she understood what she had been missing, and yet she didn't ever remember feeling unloved or neglected. If the emptiness had been filled by her father or her brothers or even Libby at the diner, why did it matter that one person decided not to show up for her? There were people who never showed up or those who did and made life worse than it would have been without them. Makenna knew it was human nature for people to sigh and put her in the poor abandoned girl category, but quite frankly, she never understood it. She was loved deeply by the people in her life and she had a beautiful, healthy little girl with a man she loved who had been taken away. If Kenna wanted to dwell on the unfair, she'd probably look to losing Adam before her no-show mother. That had been more tragic and had taken her longer to accept. Part of her knew she was changed when she lost Adam. She would always be missing a piece. It was all right; life wasn't fair and the moon, even missing its sliver, was still glorious.

As she walked back into the house, Makenna felt that calm again. Maybe after all this time, her life was slowing down, just a little.

Chapter Twenty

Travis picked Makenna up at two o'clock on that Sunday for their first official date. At least, it felt a whole hell of a lot official because he was there at her house and the nerves that hit his stomach when she opened the door reminded him that this part, the show-up-and-stick-around part, was not exactly his strength. *It's just a date, no big deal,* he heard from somewhere in the back of his head.

She surprised him by taking the helmet he offered and climbing on the back of his bike like a pro. No concerned looks or whining about helmet head; she simply slid her arms around him and gave over control. He wondered whether her mind was moving a mile a minute and she was keeping it to herself, but as they pulled into the parking garage, he felt like she was genuinely relaxed. They parked and Kenna looked confused. He was counting on that.

"Is this the library?"

Travis nodded.

"How? Why?" He saw it in her eyes the moment she realized it.

"When you guys were in on Friday, I asked Paige what one of your favorite places was, and she said—"

"The library." Makenna smiled as he helped her off the bike and took the helmet.

"Yup, but she said you guys went to the Pasadena library, so this is sort of like a date-level library."

She laughed and then pulled him into a kiss so hot he lost his breath.

"Who knew you library chicks could kiss like that?" He took her hand and they walked toward the huge main entrance.

"Do you have a library card?" she asked, looking over her shoulder at him.

"I do." Travis pulled out his wallet, flashed his card, and held the door open for her.

"You just got that, didn't you?"

"Yesterday."

She laughed and then fell silent at the sight of the lobby. Looking at him, mouth still open, she slowly turned in a full circle like she was on a field trip. Travis offered up his thanks to Paige because this was probably the best date idea ever. He took Makenna's hand and tried to remember some of the stuff on the walking tour brochure he'd looked up online.

"Okay, you are standing in one of the largest publicly funded libraries in the world."

Kenna raised her eyebrows, most likely at his mad tour guide skills, so he kept going.

"The interior is a big draw because of . . . well, look at it."

"Do you know what these murals represent?" She walked over to the colorful paintings.

"I do. They show the . . . history of California. The library opened in 1926 and there are tile mosaics on top of the building. One of them has a torch, which is supposed to mean the light of knowledge." Travis took in a big breath.

"Is that the tour?" She stopped and faced him.

"It is. I'm afraid it's a free tour, so it's . . . really short."

She went up on her toes and kissed him again, right there in the lobby.

"Okay, we'd better get started or things are going to get naughty in the library and I don't think she would approve." Travis glanced at the older woman in the black cardigan sitting amongst a stack of books and felt like he was in junior high again.

Kenna grinned, warm and teasing, and he really wanted to get in trouble.

"See, now stop doing that." He took her hand, but before they moved to the elevators, she looked at him. Her eyes were soft and no longer full of surprise. It was almost as if she was seeing him for the first time—or maybe for the first time, he was letting her.

They sat quietly among the stacks in four different reading areas of the library. When they got to each section, they found two seats together and each picked a book from the shelves at random and read. It wasn't planned; they just did it. It was silly and even though it was a library and they said nothing to one another for well over an hour, it was the very best date Makenna had ever been on. Ever. When they left, Travis used his new library card and checked out *The English Spy*.

"You will love it," she said as they walked to the parking garage.

"I'm sure I will. I already know most of it from listening to your excitement."

She bumped his shoulder and he handed her the helmet.

"Have you ever been on a bike before?"

"No." She fastened the strap under her chin.

"Huh." He swung his leg over and steadied the bike for her.

She wrapped her arms around his chest, which she had recently discovered was the best part of riding on a motorcycle. "Why did you ask if I'd ever been on a bike before?"

"No reason. People aren't normally so comfortable."

"You mean women."

"I didn't say that." He started the bike and they were pulling out into traffic before she had a chance to say another word.

She smiled and pressed her cheek against his back. Her hands traveled over his chest, and Makenna found herself lost in the curve of him, fascinated by the way their bodies fit together. When they turned into a restaurant called The Library Room, she wondered why she hadn't given a second thought about the bike before she climbed on. She was a mother; she probably should be cautious, but something told her there wasn't anything to worry about. She didn't feel in danger, not once, since he had picked her up at the house. That was strange, wasn't it? She usually felt out of place or, at least, nervous in new or unfamiliar situations, but everything about him felt safe. Something in the back of her mind told her she should pull back, take it slow, but by the time they parked the bike and he looked over his shoulder at her, her mind was still. He didn't move and just looked over his shoulder at her, one eyebrow raised.

"What?"

"You totally felt me up all the way here."

She shook her head and swung her leg off the bike. "I did not."

He followed and stood facing her. "You did, and I was completely at your mercy because I had to drive. I'm shocked, I mean there I was all vulnerable, innocently giving you a ride from the library and you just, well, you attacked me, that's what that was."

Kenna shoved the helmet at him, fluffed her ponytail, and walked away. She felt herself swing her hips and heard Travis laugh as he ran up behind her.

The Library Room was a cool little restaurant up the road. It was owned by another friend of Travis's from culinary school. They sat at a corner booth and ordered whatever the chef wanted to serve them, which proved a great idea because their waiter brought over a plate of meats and cheeses and poured them both some local beer.

"So, what's it like when you go to different restaurants?"

"It's nice. I enjoy eating other people's food. It's a constant learning experience. What's it like for you?"

"I never think anyone is as good as our place. I'm a little blinded when it comes to my brother and you." The beer warmed her cheeks and Makenna suddenly felt the nerves she avoided before.

This was too easy; they were too easy. "Nothing in life is easy," she heard her father's voice. *Shhh...*

Travis laughed. "Well, we do have a great place, one of the best, and I enjoy making food, but at the end of the day, it's food. With all of the cooking shows and celebrity chefs, it's become this weird drama. We've gone from knife-sharpening, farmers market-obsessed nerds to bleached blond rock stars. Which is great if you're trying to get laid, but in the cold light of morning, we're just making food. Just like my grandmother did. Hell, with all my experience, I still can replicate my grandfather's tri-tip, and he had a crappy little barbecue in the backyard and marinated it in a Ziploc bag. I guess what I'm saying is food is just food unless it's about something, about a connection."

"That could be a life analogy."

"I guess, sure."

"That's why you make Paige lunch?"

Warmth slid across Travis's face. "Absolutely. I know it sounds ridiculous, but making her lunch is really what it's all about for me—feeding someone's day and getting that little piece of construction paper."

"That doesn't sound ridiculous. It sounds..." Makenna looked down at her beer glass because there it was again, the fear. She knew Travis was fun, but the more she sat with him, the more things changed from fun to—"Real," she said out loud. "It sounds real."

"She has saved me. Making lunch for her has saved me a couple of times now."

Makenna laughed and then noticed the emotion that seemed lodged in his throat, so she stopped, reached across the table, and took his hand.

"Me too, in very different ways, but me too."

Travis grinned, and Kenna saw him shake away his feelings, the ones that were so right there on the surface, she could almost touch them.

"Anyway, my point is, it's not rocket science. We're not geniuses. People who cure disease, who can get a heart beating again, or even teachers, that's work. When it's all over for us, we are left with a dirty plate."

"Yeah, but you still get the piece of construction paper. That's what you're working for, isn't it? The reaction, the applause?"

"Oh sure. Hey, I'm a Leo. We love praise and I love the reaction, but I don't want it to confuse people or make things so convoluted that people can't relate. I want a genuine warm smile or that pursed lip thing people do when they taste. I love that. I never want to overshoot just to satisfy my own ego. It's sort of like books. Yeah, you know how you read certain books and at the last page, you're filled with the story and you sort of don't want to leave the characters?"

Kenna nodded because no one knew that feeling better than she did.

"And then there are other books that are a challenge. Maybe you needed to look up words or re-read sections until you got it. Those books are like an endurance test and they're great, but I want my food to be like the first book. A fresh, human story that leaves people with the memory of a fun journey. Simple and really so hard to do all at the same time. Anything else only serves me and an ego I've been running from my whole life. I grew up with all of that. You know when people say they don't want to turn into their parents? Yeah, that's why I eat other people's food most of the time."

"Well, I can see why you work well with Logan. You two see things pretty much the same way. Although he says you're the better chef."

Travis laughed. "He's full of crap. Your brother has passed me; he's no longer just a chef, he's a damn movement. I'm his lowly little helper slaving away in his organic, local kitchen."

Kenna shook her head. "I've tasted your food. He's right. You're creative. I like that."

"Thank you."

It was delivered straight, through sexy eyes, but that was her growing need for him. The sentiment was genuine. He was too.

"Damn, this is turning intense. My turn. Who's your favorite brother?"

Kenna laughed. "I don't really have favorites, and even if I did, there's no way I'm giving you that ammunition. They're two of my bestest people, as Paige likes to say, for different reasons, but the thing they have in common is they are both really solid men. Of course, I love both of their stupid faces, so I'm not exactly objective."

"I'm pretty sure you're right. Did Adam get along with them?"

Her face must have flinched, because Travis instantly looked like he'd stepped over some invisible line.

"Sorry, I don't know why I keep doing this. I guess it's just different. He's not like an ex-boyfriend or even an ex-husband. He's . . ."

"Dead," Makenna said softly.

Travis winced.

"It's okay, he is. My husband, Paige's dad, died. You don't need to tiptoe around it. It's there and if we are going to . . . be or, if we want to . . . damn it." Makenna huffed and averted her eyes.

He smiled. "If we are going to date?"

"Seems so strange, doesn't it?"

"Not really."

"Really? If we lined up all of the women you've dated, where exactly would I fit? I mean, if we are going to discuss our histories."

"Oh, hell no, we are not discussing my history. There's no point. You don't fit in there anyway."

"See? Why not? Because I'm some sort of departure for you? Like an experiment maybe."

"Excuse me?"

"That might have been a little harsh, but I'm still trying to get my head around this." She gestured between the two of them. "Us."

"So there is an 'us'? You want an 'us'?"

"Don't mess with me, okay? I'm already a basket case; I don't need to be danced around. You go first."

He leaned into her. "Gladly. This is the best date I've ever been on, ever. You are beautiful and funny and smart. You're nuts and bossy, but you're a great sister, an incredible mother, and you have a near perfect ass."

Kenna laughed.

"So yes, I want to date you. Be with you."

"Sleep with me?" Kenna almost put her hands to her mouth, she was so shocked at what came out, but then she wanted the answer so she went with it.

He almost choked. "One more time?"

"In addition to all the warm and fuzzy stuff, and the fact that I'm your favorite almost-six-year-old's mom, you'd like to take my clothes off and sleep with me?"

"Yes." If that smile was a precursor to sex with Travis, she probably wouldn't make it out alive.

"I would like to sleep with you. Well actually, not sleep . . . with you, because when we get there, once that's on the table, I'll probably need a whole weekend."

Makenna had been around men her entire life; she knew their ways, but this man was—*Did he say a whole weekend?*

"Okay, well, let's talk about something else," she said.

"Probably a good idea." Travis was simmering, or smoldering, or something because it felt like he was actually touching her with his eyes.

"Right. So I answered your brother question. That was the last one, right? Before you started to look at me like that."

"You brought it up. You said you wanted to have sex with me. I'm not sure how I'm supposed to finish up the evening with polite G-rated conversation now."

She laughed. "Let's get back to food then. One thing you can't imagine cooking without?"

"Garlic."

"Really? I thought you'd be a cool chef and say something like salt and pepper."

Travis laughed.

"Why garlic? It's so tricky."

"That's why. I can do so many things with it—tone it down, let it bite. You can warm people and piss them off with garlic. It's kind of like sex."

"You weren't kidding—you can't move on." She shook her head.

"I told you."

"So garlic, huh?"

Travis nodded as if he were slowly taking off her clothes. It had been forever since anyone had taken off her clothes or she'd even thought about it, but she was thinking about it now.

"Yeah, garlic, but you know, salt and pepper are good too." Travis got the check.

After ice cream at Churn, he dropped her off at her front door and kissed her silly. He had said it was not a good idea for him to come in. Paige was at the farm waiting for Gracie, but it still wasn't a good idea. Makenna wasn't going to throw herself at him, but as he pulled away, she couldn't remember ever wanting garlic more.

Chapter Twenty-One

Makenna had never been to Travis's house, but she couldn't sleep so she looked up his address in his employee file. As she pulled into the visitors' parking lot, she was on her third or fourth round of second thoughts. *Did women do this? Just show up at a man's house unannounced, especially a man like Travis?*

She sat in her car, engine running, and just knew Gracie was going to have her babies soon. Her dad had said by the end of the week for sure. When would be the next time she'd be alone, able to play single spontaneous woman? This was it: her moment to be free and get her man. Makenna laughed at the thought of her sex life being dependent on a goat giving birth. Seemed about right. Her man, what did that even mean? She was a mother, a sister, and a daughter, but being someone's woman, lover, was so forgotten that doubt stopped her cold.

No, she was doing this, she thought, turning off her Jeep. She clicked the lock and walked toward the elevators. She wanted him and it didn't need to be more than that. Want was enough for now, wasn't it?

By the time she got off on the ninth floor of the retro, hip apartment building, Makenna's heart was charging and she was questioning her choice of jeans. They were the tight ones, which were fine for a date, but she wasn't so sure about taking them off and she didn't want to be silly or mess up. Walking toward Travis's apartment, she had a scary clear picture of her jeans getting stuck mid-leg, causing her to do that penguin walk. Not sexy, and then she told herself to shut up. Not every detail could be planned out. Some things just needed to happen and maybe Travis would re-move her jeans with his—Oh, now that was a much nicer image. She felt the wild butterflies in her stomach.

At her knock, the dark wood door next to a concrete slab with 9-1-6 etched into it opened and Travis stood looking about as shocked as Makenna had ever seen him, and that included the time last week when Todd had managed to slice an entire flat of mushrooms without his headphones on.

"Hi," she said quickly before she lost her nerve.

"Hi." He smiled, which was a good sign.

She was suddenly feeling super in control, creator of her own destiny and all, until she looked down and noticed the top button of his jeans was undone and he was standing in his bare feet. They were nice feet, but nothing compared to that button and the other two barely holding his shirt closed.

Lordy, had buttons been this sexy the last time she wanted to get naked?

"Makenna."

"Right, sorry. I was distracted for a minute by your buttons."

Travis laughed.

"Aren't you going to invite me in?"

Travis stood back and pushed the door open for her to enter. She took a deep breath; her cheeks were burning, but she rolled back her shoulders and reminded herself that Gracie wouldn't be in labor forever. *Get your man, Kenna.*

"Everything okay?" Travis asked, running a hand over his face and leaning up against the wall of his entryway, clearly keeping his distance.

Oh, maybe this was a mistake. Maybe women don't do this, or I'm supposed to play hard to get, or—Stop!

"Yes, everything is fine. The thing is, Gracie, you know my dad's goat?"

Travis nodded.

"Good, right. Well, she's ready to have her babies and Paige is up at the farm, spending the night. Dad thinks the babies will arrive any day and I was just thinking before she delivered that it was time for me to put it on the table, you know?"

Travis tilted his head a bit as if he were trying to connect the dots and was getting lost somewhere along the way.

"I, okay, let me try to figure this one out. Paige told me about Gracie and that is . . . exciting. So, you drove down to tell me in person? I mean, I'm happy to see you again, it's been a couple of hours. The part that's really throwing me is the table. You want to put Gracie on the table?"

"No. I want to put 'it' on the table. You said on our date that once 'it' was on the table, you'd need a weekend. Remember?"

He nodded, smiling now.

"I don't have a weekend because of Gracie, but I'd like, I want it on the table."

His smile deepened, and Makenna just about melted as if he'd already touched her.

"Not like you to beat around the bush." He waggled his eyebrows. "What are you trying to say, Makenna?"

She let out a huff. "Of course you're not responding to my subtlety. I'm trying to be coy, cute even."

"As cute as you are right now, I'm not really into that. I much prefer knock-me-over-the-head Makenna. Out with it. Why are you here, and please don't mention the goat again." He pushed off the wall and moved closer to her.

"Sex. I'd like . . . I'm thinking that we should . . ." His hands slid around her waist and, no matter how blunt, she could only find three words. "I want you."

"Makenna," he said again. This time, his voice was a little smoky and a whole lot sexy.

He pushed her purse off her shoulder and it fell to the floor with a thud, followed quickly by her jacket. He didn't say anything and just looked at her.

"Are you . . . going to say anything?" He started kissing her neck.

"I'm pretty sure you've said enough for the both of us."

"But, do you . . ." Her heart was thundering in her chest and then her stupid mind kicked in. What was this? What were they doing? Did he have a condom? Oh no, why was that video she watched in high school playing through her head at a time like this? The one where the stern voice says, "When you have sex with a person, you are having sex with everyone he's ever slept with." She always thought that was a creepy way to put it, but now that he was kissing her—Oh sweet Lord—she couldn't shut off her mind. How many women had Travis slept with?

"Wait!" She shook herself free, and Travis closed his eyes and stepped back. "Shouldn't you say something? I said that I wanted to put it on the table, that I wanted you. Don't you think you should respond? Or not, right, maybe we just rip each other's clothes off and go at it."

Travis laughed.

"You're laughing." Kenna turned to pick up her purse, and Travis stopped her by holding her arm gently.

"I didn't mean to laugh. You're just so out of your element here and it's incredibly sexy."

"Oh, so you want me, too?"

He laughed again, pulled her into his warm body, buttons still in place, and kissed her in a way that told her Travis was definitely more of a show kind of guy.

"I do want you, but you need to think about this." He touched her face. It was simple, but her entire body hummed. How did he manage that? His fingers ran down her neck and her arm before he kissed her again. Slow and soft, like she was delicate. Makenna had never been called delicate. Even Adam had always told her she was solid and if there were ever a zombie apocalypse, he wanted her on his side. Delicate felt incredible, right next door to cherished, and when Travis moved down her neck, pulling her into his warm waiting body, she felt herself step closer to the edge. She was going to fall for him; it was simply a matter of time.

She'd planned on maybe meeting someone sensible, someone she could love in a fringe sort of way. Relationships could work on the fringe; they didn't all have to be dive in head first or cannonball leaps of faith. People fell in sensible, safe love all the time, but at the moment, Travis was kissing the sensible right out of her. Apparently, sensible wasn't in her cards.

She pulled back and looked into his dark brown eyes. They were almost black, but they turned down at the edges, making them warm and a little tender. Travis was tender. Another detail she'd missed.

"What if I don't want to think? What if I just want to feel and not worry or chart it out?"

"Then I'm probably your guy, but I'm not sure you can shut things off like that. Why don't you come in and we can sit, I'm watching—"

"No."

He looked confused.

"I'm here for sex." Makenna almost laughed at herself. "I mean, yeah . . ."

He laughed. "You're always coming up with the better ideas, aren't you?"

She took his hand, gently pushed him into the big red chair only a few steps away, and climbed into his lap facing him.

"Makenna."

"Yes," she said softly, unbuttoning his shirt.

"I—" He reached out, pulled her shirt over her head, and froze.

Kenna felt his body shift and looked down at herself.

"What?"

"I, I—"

"Jesus, Travis, what?"

"Where the hell does someone who wears muck boots and jeans ninety days out of a hundred get a bra like that?"

"Oh." She smiled and appeared to turn him on further by putting her hands to her breasts. "I like lacy."

"Apparently." He carefully touched the sheer, plum-colored bra. It was one of Kenna's favorites because it was basically see through, save the small swirls of darker lace that covered her nipples. No padding and soft silky straps. She loved lingerie because of the way it made her feel. Light. Not much in Kenna's life was light. Nice bras and panties were easy.

"Please tell me you're into matching," Travis said, kissing her shoulder.

"Oh, no. Sorry. Nothing but grandma panties down below. I'm a huge fan of cotton down there. Breathability and all." She stood up and started unzipping her jeans. "I really like flowers, or I have this great pair with butterflies. Let's see which ones I have on."

Travis laughed as she made a big show of wiggling out of her jeans. With her back to him, her jeans slid off with surprising ease, not like a penguin, to reveal the matching lace of the cheeky panties that covered just enough. Thongs made her ass look weird, but cheekies worked some amazing magic that made her butt look just a smidge smaller. On her extra pancake days, Kenna needed that smidge.

She turned to him and would forever remember the look on his face. Even if things didn't work out. Even if later on, she needed to pretend this night never happened so they could be civil for the sake of the restaurant or her ordered responsible life. Even if all of that came to pass and Travis wasn't the lunch-making, stick-around man and he really was the party guy in line at Lux she'd pegged him for; she would forever remember the look on his face. Travis McNulty, sexy as all hell, was enchanted, not cool or sarcastic. Sure, his eyes skimmed her scantily clad curves and he was clearly turned on, but Kenna imagined Travis had seen many women in their panties before. Probably women who had clocked plenty more hours at the gym. The look he gave her seemed to hold more. He hadn't expected this side of her, and surprising him turned out to be incredibly gratifying.

"You are so beautiful." That was all he said, and then he stood from the chair and swept her up in his arms. There he went again making her feel delicate. "I need to take these off in a bed—my bed."

He could see her go from playful and determined to uncertain the moment her hair fell across his pillow. *Holy shit, what am I doing?* He was out of his league, but she somehow felt so right that he couldn't shut it down. He found himself needing her, and not just her body. She was so real and funny. For the first time since he'd met Makenna Rye, she didn't seem unattainable. In fact, she was right there, half-naked on his bed and looking for him to simply show her a good time. So, why was he hesitating? He was all about a good time.

"Are you okay?" *Oh yeah, that's super sexy, Mr. Good Time.*

Kenna looked up at him, moonlight on her beautiful face and the curves of her body. "I . . . yes, I'm fine. Why?"

"Nothing." Travis unbuttoned his jeans.

There were no sexy oohs and ahhs; she just quietly watched him. He could tell she was thinking, running through things in her mind he couldn't even imagine. He didn't know if she'd been with any other men since her husband. He wanted to ask, find out what he was dealing with, but she reached for him and pulled him down on top of her. He rested his weight on his forearms.

Her lips went to his ear. "It has been a very long time. I'm on the pill, but we should still use a condom. Other than that, I'm fine. I want you and I'm trying to enjoy this. I'll sort the rest out later. Can that be enough?"

Travis wasn't sure he could breathe. It was one thing to deal with to-the-point Makenna at work, but he'd never felt this level of honesty in his bed. She needed and she came to him, wanted him. The thought of it filled him with the same question she'd had. Was it enough that she wanted him?

He could give her this, show her passion, have fun, and then they'd see what happened, right? He had no idea, but she was waiting for an answer, waiting for him, so he opened the drawer of his nightstand for protection. Her eyes followed him and a little of her playful sexy returned.

"That's more than enough, Makenna," was all he said. Then, despite wanting her to stupid distraction, Travis took his time. He savored every minute of her hands on his body, the warm tangle of them together and soft moan of her voice, because he'd lied. He'd been with his share of women, but this was — she was — something more than he could even define. He had no idea what he was doing, but there was no way this one night was ever going to be enough.

Chapter Twenty-Two

I t had been what felt like ages since Makenna had awakened in a bed other than her own. After the initial panic of wondering where she was and then where Paige was, she settled into the warm man nestled behind her. It was Monday morning, but still early, probably around five o'clock from the shade of darkness she could see through the window. Her father was dropping Paige off at school, but she quietly slid out of bed to call and say good morning. Grabbing the first piece of clothing she found on the floor, Kenna slipped it over her naked body, closed the bedroom door gently, and went into Travis's living room. She was in his T-shirt, she realized as she waited for Paige to answer the phone. Her mind began trying to sort out the two worlds, her responsibilities vs. the smell of him, the pull of her heart, but right as she started to feel dizzy, her daughter's voice came over the phone.

"Mama! Good morning, silly boots. Do you have your silly boots on yet?"

Kenna laughed and could tell her daughter was tired. "Not yet. How's Gracie?"

"She's so brave. We check on her all the time and Donk said we're close because she started panning last night."

"Panting," Kenna corrected and then felt emotion build in her chest first. Paige was so alive and interested; it was spilling through the phone.

"Right, she was pant—ing. And me and Donk were talking to her and giving her love. Donk is a good friend to Gracie."

"He really is." Kenna's eyes began to tear. "Did you get any sleep?"

"A little bit, but Donk said we are stopping at Libby's for breakfast so I can fuel up."

Kenna laughed and wiped her cheek. "Okay, make sure you get chocolate chips."

"I will. How's Popcorn? Did you feed him?"

She felt a tinge of guilt at her daughter's assumption that she was home, which was silly. She certainly wasn't going to share anything with a five-year-old.

"I did. He's still sleeping."

"Yeah, he likes to sleep in."

Kenna laughed again and turned to find Travis standing behind her, arms crossed over his bare chest and smiling.

"I know he does. Okay, Peach, I have to get ready for work. Have a super day at school and I'll see you at pickup."

"Okay, Mama. I have more pictures to show you. I love you."

"I love you too." Kenna heard the kissing sounds coming through the phone. She returned a few and touched the end button. She turned to Travis and should have felt awkward standing in his T-shirt, talking on the phone with her daughter, but didn't. "No babies yet."

"I heard." He moved toward her. "Are you still glad you put 'it' on the table last night?"

"Did you just use air quotes for what we ... what happened last night?"

Travis nodded and she stepped into him.

"Looks good on you," he said, touching her hair and pulling her in to close the last of the space between them.

"Oh, yeah? I'm still a little flushed and my lips are supremely well kissed, so even though I'm sure my hair is a mess, thank you. It feels good on me too."

He kissed her neck and she felt him smile. "I was talking about my T-shirt, but the rest looks good on you too."

Kenna blushed, which she honestly didn't think was possible after last night, but her mouth had done it again. He meant the T-shirt and she blabbered on, but before she could analyze too much, he kissed her. Her hands traveled up his warm back and even though she wanted to be casual, cool, her knees weakened. When he pulled back from the kiss, Kenna was sure all of her feelings were right there. She'd shown up last night in an attempt to be daring, to get her man, but as often happened with Travis, the tables were turned and he'd gotten her too.

Travis sat on the counter of his kitchen and watched her make him breakfast. She'd insisted, and if he wasn't halfway in love with her already, her scrambled eggs and diagonally cut toast with jam just about finished him off.

"I'm not sure a woman has ever cooked for me before."

"Your mom," Kenna said, biting into a triangle of toast as they sat across from each other at his small round dining room table.

He laughed. "Okay, yes, my mother has cooked for me, but I don't usually put her in the woman category."

"True."

He reached out, wiped some strawberry off the corner of her mouth, and licked his finger. Her eyes fell to his lips and lit with a passion he now recognized.

"I like your place." She crunched into her toast again. "It's very . . . uniform."

He laughed. "Nothing like your house?"

"No. There's not much uniform in my house right now because there are clothes all over my bedroom. I might have had a hard time figuring out what to wear yesterday. I was nervous and before I knew it, you were at my door looking your usual calm, cool self."

"You didn't seem nervous."

"Oh, trust me, I was. Still am, actually."

He took her hand. "You don't need to be." He wasn't sure why he said that because he was past nervous, but he supposed she didn't need to know that. It was their first morning together; she was sitting at his breakfast table in his T-shirt. As far as fantasies went, this one just about topped his previous Makenna farm girl fantasy, so he didn't want to spoil it.

"Don't I? This is all so strange, don't you think?"

"Not really. I think it's been brewing for a while," he said with a collected cool that surprised even him. "This was our next step, don't you think?"

"I guess it was, but we're sort of suspended here, you know, the rest of our worlds aren't at the table."

"You mean Paige isn't at the table."

She looked at him, her eyes uncertain, and then her shoulders rolled back as if she was preparing for something. "Yes, that's what I mean. She's my life and this feels strange. I mean it feels, it felt—"

Travis smiled and knew he wasn't helping her find her words, so he took her hands across the table. "Let's try this one step at a time. This is our first morning, I'd like another one sometime when it works for you, but again, Kenna, your world is still your world. I don't want to mess with that." He squeezed her hands and she was right, the whole thing was weird because his words sounded good, but he could see she wasn't buying it. Her order was being toppled, he was shifting her normal and as much as he didn't want to hurt her, the urge to love her was becoming too damn strong.

Chapter Twenty-Three

The next week flew by in a blur of last-minute catering details. As Kenna helped load the last of the prep work onto one of the trucks, she decided she would take the Depression glass and the punch bowl over in her car. In less than eight hours, Grady and Kate would be married, and Kenna was the one with butterflies.

She felt his now-familiar hand at her back and the warmth of Travis's body as he stopped behind her and spoke into her neck. "In case today's a complete disaster, I wanted to kiss you one last time as a successful and employed chef." His lips touched her skin, and Kenna laughed.

"Yeah? Well, today better not be even a little disaster. We've triple checked everything and I can't imagine anything—"

He pulled her over to the side of the truck and wrapped her in his arms. "It was a joke. A reason to touch you because it never seems to be enough."

He kissed her, and Makenna almost dropped her clipboard. One touch of his tongue and somehow all the details could wait, and when his hands slid into her hair, the whole damn wedding could wait. She knew all about needing more and was so grateful Gracie was now almost a week past her due date. Paige had insisted on going up each night after school and last night, according to her Donk, she fell asleep in the barn. Kenna missed her daughter being home at night, but what was supposed to be one night with Travis had turned into four, and Kenna still wasn't quite sure how she was going to introduce him into their life. It was good that Paige was still watching Gracie because it gave Kenna more time to try to sort things out.

The horn of one of the trucks sounded, and Travis pulled back from the kiss to touch her face, as he always did. It was kind of like he was checking to make sure she was real.

"All right. Showtime." He kissed her gently again. "I'll see you there."

She was pretty sure she actually sighed as her mind returned to the clipboard now dangling from her hand.

"Right, I'll be there in a couple of hours. I want to finish going over everything with Sage. Last time I checked, she was rolling her eyes at the fill-in bartender we got so she could do my job tonight."

"Yeah, even though we spent last week with Larry going over the menu, I'm pretty sure he's praying people only order pizza all day. At least Logan will be here through lunch." He smiled. "I'm sure they'll all be fine holding down the fort. It's one night. I've got Todd with me, so we know the place won't burn down."

"Right. I'm trying not to think about it. I can only focus on this wedding right now. How are you always so calm?"

"It's all an act, or it's that I woke up with you in my bed again this morning, so not much else matters."

She blushed. "Oh, really? Well, two hundred fifty guests aren't going to care about that." She laughed. "Get going."

Travis pulled away and turned to leave but turned back. "Hey, by the way, about those heels. Any chance you have multiple pairs of those, too?"

His eyebrows wiggled up and down. Kenna realized he was happy. Sure, Travis was always casual and relaxed, but this was different. He seemed almost youthful and happy. She was part of that, and the thought almost knocked her over.

He was still standing waiting for an answer, so she shook her head and looked around to make sure the entire staff hadn't just heard them. "You're impossible. I have one pair of heels, well, one pair of black heels."

Travis stood still, waiting.

"Fine, I have several pairs of heels. We'll do a shoe tour later, much later."

"Yeah, we will," Travis said with an enthusiasm that had her already feeling naked.

She hit his back with the clipboard. "Now go or it's Crocs and cotton unicorn underwear for you from now on."

He laughed, leaned in to steal one more kiss, and was gone.

Kenna stood watching all three trucks pull out of the parking lot on their way to the Wayfarers Chapel grounds. *Sexy, that's how he made her feel,* she thought, holding the clipboard to her chest as the truck disappeared into Saturday morning traffic. When she was younger, she was more insecure and not quite sure what to do with herself as a woman. But with Travis, she was almost flirty and that was fun, Kenna decided. Maybe she'd needed some fun for a while now. Smiling, still standing in the morning air, she brushed her hair off her face and turned to get back to work.

Travis was stupid happy. He should have known he would never stand a chance once he allowed himself to want her. She was more than he ever imagined, and he was certain she was going to bring him to his knees. But right now, he needed to focus.

He'd never seen anything quite like the Wayfarers Chapel or the two acres of incredible redwood forest he was now marveling at from under the tent of their temporary kitchen. So far, everything had gone smoothly: warmer drawers were working, hot things would be hot, and cold things would be cold. That was half the battle with cooking. Since the first moment he stepped into a kitchen in high school, Travis knew this was his thing, what he wanted to do for the rest of his life. Everything since that moment had been an adventure, an ever-changing set of challenges and milestones he wouldn't alter for anything in the world. Contrary to his family's ignorant beliefs, being a chef was never boring and rarely involved a hair net. He was about to serve a wedding in a huge white tent under the stars. Travis recorded the moment in his mind and then got to work.

Chapter Twenty-Four

Grady Malendar and Katherine Galloway were married just after sunset on Saturday evening at the Wayfarers Chapel on the edge of the California coast. Peter Everoad was Grady's best man, as Grady had been for him several months before when Peter had married Samantha Cathner at the Huntington Library. Kate's best friend Reagan, wearing a floral halter dress, was her maid of honor. The ceremony was by candlelight under the open-glass canopy of the chapel. Guests, only the one hundred that would fit in the small chapel, much to the chagrin of the senator and his wife, were tucked in among the grove of redwood trees. Kenna stood outside between the chapel and the huge billowing tent that had been set up for the reception to follow. The Wayfarers Chapel didn't normally have wedding receptions on their adjacent grounds, but ever since the media revealed that Grady was the head of the Roads Foundation, which had provided funding for some much-needed repairs at the chapel a few years ago, they made an exception. Kate and Grady were careful to leave the smallest footprint on the grounds.

Makenna watched as the happy couple kissed and were presented with thundering applause from their closest friends and family. That was her cue; they had exactly ten minutes, according to Sloan, before the guests would start filing into the tent and forty-five before the wedding party would make their entrance. Everything was timed, which appealed to Makenna's love of specifics, but the wedding was so whimsical, she found it difficult to turn away from the closest she'd ever come to a real-life fairy tale.

The warmth under the white sailcloth tent supported by wood beams stood in contrast to the chill of the night air. Rustic metal lamps hung throughout the hundreds of wooden seats padded with small cushions, casting a glow that Makenna had only ever seen in magazines. As she instructed their staff to begin lighting the table candles, she reviewed everything one last time before walking over to check on the two bartenders Sage had hired for the wedding. They weren't Sage, but seemed to know what they were doing.

Makenna clasped her hands together, filled with nerves and excitement as she looked toward the parking area, which was beginning to fill with car headlights as guests who were not able to fit into the chapel began arriving for the reception. Senator and Mrs. Malendar, along with Police Chief and Mrs. Flanagan, Kate's parents, had made their way to the end of a path that joined the parking area and the reception tent. Lit by tiny candles, from a distance, the path looked like hundreds of fireflies, flickering along a dark evening under a gorgeous full moon. Makenna couldn't help but think that Paige would have definitely loved this magical forest.

Kenna had never really been one of those women who swooned over weddings, but she loved this one. It seemed like more than a wedding. Maybe that was the couple getting married, their energy, or maybe it was the location, she wasn't sure, but she was aware that this was special.

Guests began arriving and leaving their coats with the two women working a makeshift coatroom that looked like a small cabin made of branches. The buzz of voices began to fill the tent and the band, a jazz quartet with a huge bass, started playing in the corner. Everything seemed to be going smoothly.

She looked over toward the catering tent just as their servers, dressed in linen slacks and vests, began filing out with trays. The Yard was certainly representing itself well so far and even though Logan rarely thought about advertising, Makenna recognized that they couldn't buy exposure like this.

As if her mind had conjured him up, Makenna glanced toward the entrance just as Logan and Kara made their way into the tent. Her brother wore dark slacks and a tweed blazer with a matching vest and an open collar; he looked so relaxed that it almost took her breath away. There was no question that the source of his smile, the one that emanated from him lately, was laughing and holding his arm. Kara Malendar's dark golden hair fell across her shoulders in loose natural curls, and she wore a rust-colored dress that looked like silk and matched one of the darker shades in Logan's jacket.

"Looking good, sis. I see we haven't burned the tent down yet, so that's a positive."

"So far, so good," Makenna said as she leaned in to kiss them both on the cheek. "You two look incredible."

"Thank you," Kara said. "It was a really wonderful wedding. I think it's the best I've ever been to. That may have something to do with the groom being my brother, but still." She smiled. "Did you notice they kissed throughout and held hands?" Kara sighed and Logan shook his head good-naturedly.

"What?"

"Nothing." He leaned in and kissed her.

"Well, you two enjoy. We've got this," she said in a way she hoped would allow her brother to continue enjoying himself even once his food began circulating.

He nodded then led Kara over to the bartender as the one with a shamrock tattoo on his wrist was twisting the top off of sparkling water for a glowingly pregnant Samantha Everoad. Makenna stepped outside and turned toward the catering tent. She could hear Travis's voice calling out directions as she approached. The table of appetizers was being cleared according to a text she received from one of the waitstaff. They were on schedule. She peeked in and even though she'd seen them swamped at the restaurant before, she had never seen so much food.

Huge platters of roasted ham, surrounded by colorful vegetables, beautiful fish, and lettuce were served on cream-colored serving dishes that were made for this kind of event. Travis was spooning dressing into a serving boat, his eyes intently scanning the plates of food as they were carried out. He looked so intense, almost serious, and Makenna caught a glimpse of the importance of his work. Since she'd known him, Travis was synonymous with casual, relaxed, fun, but the guy she saw in front of her was something else altogether. He had something to lose, something to prove, and Makenna discovered one more layer to love.

Peter Everoad gave a toast that made just about everyone cry, and then Kate's friend Reagan gave another toast that spoke to a side of Kate not many people knew. She was hilarious and clearly loved her dear friend. After Makenna helped one of the servers find more olive oil for the tables and relieved one of the bartenders for a much-needed bathroom break, she grabbed a glass of champagne and walked outside for a breather.

About an hour later, linens were wrinkled, ties were undone, and everyone was well fed. Travis took a deep breath of satisfaction. Other than Todd dropping an entire bowl of smashed potatoes on the grass, everything went off without a hitch. Kate and Grady cut their cake, and rather than feeding it to each other, they used the opportunity to serve each of their guests a piece. Travis thought that was a great touch and decided if he hadn't already liked Kate and Grady, their wedding would have convinced him.

The Yard staff had survived serving their first wedding, and almost everything would now be handed over to the cleanup crew. Once things were cleared, Travis would send out the coffee and set up the cereal bar, complete with just about every sugary cereal he'd ever heard of, a special request from Grady for his new wife.

Looking out over all of the people now dancing and celebrating, Travis was reminded again why he loved to cook. Food brought people together; it allowed them to connect and share around a table. Nothing, in his view of family and friendship, was more important. He wiped his hands and went to look for Makenna.

"Do you like weddings?" he asked, coming up behind her as she stood just outside the tent. He slid his arms around her waist and noticed her pulse quicken as he kissed her shoulder.

"I like this." Her voice was thick with emotion as they watched Kate and Grady dancing to a slow lilting song. "I haven't been to many weddings. I don't have one of my own to use as a reference, and I'm not sure if all weddings are like this, but whatever you want to call this, I love it."

"I'd rather have a tiny wedding and a happy marriage."

"Can't you have both?" She put her hands over his, and he noticed she was cold.

"I'm sure some people do, but I've been to my fair share of big flashy weddings and most of them are bullshit—for show. This is definitely not like most weddings. See the way he's looking at her? They could be in the middle of a grocery store and they'd probably still have that. This is not a normal wedding," he said, realizing he sounded jaded. Some things never really went away, did they?

"You're a real romantic, huh?" She looked over her shoulder at him.

"I can be, but the big show always seems like too much work. At least in my opinion."

"The big show?" She laughed. "And since when are you afraid of hard work?"

"I'm not afraid. Wow, how did we get on this again?"

"You asked me if I liked weddings. I said I liked this and you went all wedding Grinch right before my very eyes." She laughed and handed her empty champagne glass to one of the servers cleaning up in preparation for coffee and tea. Travis needed to get back to work, but she kissed him and he decided he had a few more minutes.

"I didn't mean to be a Grinch. I'm just not a fan of phony," he said, watching Grady dance with his mother.

"I can understand that, but there's also nothing wrong with working at something, making it special."

"I guess."

"You don't agree?"

"I like simple."

"Simple meaning minimum effort?"

"What are we talking about here?" *Shit!* Maybe it was time to go back to work.

"I'm just trying to understand."

Travis laughed. "Understand what? Life doesn't have to be complicated, Kenna."

"Really? I don't find anything about life to be simple."

"Why do I feel like I came over here to kiss you under the stars and you're feeling me out, and not in a good way?"

Makenna sighed and pulled him back in close to her. "I'm not meaning to. Maybe the champagne is bringing out my questions. I find myself wanting to understand a lot of things lately."

"Like?"

"Like . . . if I make things too complicated or if you don't make them complicated enough? I wonder why this thing between us seems so easy when there's no possible way it can be. I'm trying to figure out a whole slew of new feelings I haven't had in a while. Some of them I'm not sure I've ever felt. You appear to fit perfectly into my world right now, but things are rarely simple for long. It's been my experience that I always need to prepare for complicated."

"Okay. I think I can understand all of that, but let's not make ourselves crazy. How about you stand here looking beautiful and I get back to the tent so we can finish up this wedding?"

She smiled and kissed him, and Travis walked back to work as simple actually vanished right before his eyes.

Chapter Twenty-Five

The wedding had been a huge success, with write-ups in just about every major national newspaper. Kenna had been so busy making sure they didn't screw things up that she sort of forgot the celebrity of the couple they were celebrating. She'd hoped for word-of-mouth exposure and expected local media attention, but what followed the wedding far surpassed her expectations. Phones were ringing and her e-mail was packed with well wishes, requests for interviews from bridal magazines, and inquiries about future catering. The week had been a whirlwind, and the Rye family Wednesday meeting was consumed with celebration and Logan obsessing about keeping things small and limiting what they did so it would stay within their vision. They'd spent Thursday and Friday working out menu changes and finalizing the garden expansion.

By early Friday evening, Makenna was packed and ready to head to the farm to pick up Paige. Gracie finally had her babies, so they would probably be spending the weekend up there while Paige played big sister to Gracie's three new additions. It looked like they would be having Paige's birthday up there after all. Kenna threw her bag over her shoulder and left Paige's lunch box on the kitchen counter on purpose.

Looking up, she noticed Travis masked by a cloud of steam in his dance alongside Logan, clearly doing what he was meant to do. The feeling washed over her like one of those warm waterfalls on some exotic island. She had been in love before, but the first time it slammed into her so unexpectedly, she barely had time to catch her breath. And while this time was just as scary, it was different. She watched him laughing at Larry, who was telling some animated story to Logan, and knew she loved him. Maybe she'd always loved him on some level, but now it was front and center. Kenna let out a slow steady breath and while her mind had yet to figure out the details of a life with him, her heart seemed content in the knowledge.

She pushed through the doors and into the bar, surprised to see it now flooded with women in tiny dresses, tiaras, and boas.

"My God, what the man can do with his tongue." Barbie, actually Bride-to-Be Barbie as her sash read, was fanning herself with the hand not holding her drink. Kenna often wondered how Sage stayed sane; no wonder she did crosswords for fun.

"I know that tongue," another Barbie said, and they all laughed.

"Oh, oh, girls, show of hands, how many of us have had some piece of Travis's anatomy in us?"

Sage looked up from serving Barbie number six or number seven some stupid umbrella drink and met Kenna's gaze. She shook her head and rolled her eyes. Kenna took a seat partly because she couldn't look away from the gaggle of feathers currently making it almost an embarrassment to be a woman, but also because she was curious again. More than half the Barbies raised their hands. Kenna had to stop herself from leaning back and forth to count.

"You heading out?" Sage asked, finally making her way over.

Kenna stared at Bride-to-Be Barbie who was now using her hands to describe a certain part of Travis's anatomy.

"Kenna?"

"Oh, sorry. Yes, I'm heading to the farm. Who are they?"

"Bachelorette party. Pamela, the soon-to-be, and her merry band of drunk divas. They were already a few drinks into the party when they got here, lucky me. We should probably warn Travis before they call for him to come out and entertain them. I always thought it was only men objectifying women, but these lovelies are giving the Hooters crowd a run for their money."

"Yeah, is it true?"

"Is what true?"

"He was with her, the bride-to-be one? They dated?"

"I'm . . . pretty sure they were together for about a minute, but I wouldn't call it dating."

"And the rest of them, you think they're making it up?"

"Probably not." Sage started to laugh but stopped when Makenna didn't seem amused.

"Hey, it's not a big deal. We all have a past, right?"

"Right. Yeah, sure. I need to get going, so be safe and try to have a good night."

"You too. Are you all right?"

"I am. Oh, I almost forgot, could you bring ice and soda for Paige's birthday on Sunday?"

"You got it."

Makenna went back through the kitchen to avoid hearing the end of what Travis did to Barbie number four on the hood of her car one night. Yikes, the guy was a legend. *What does that make me? Another customer at the drive-thru?* Makenna's head was spinning with questions, most urgently—*What the hell am I doing? I have no business with a man like Travis, and how on God's earth is he ever going to fit into my very real world?* She looked back toward the kitchen one more time and saw Travis talking with two older ladies who were clearly smitten. Mr. Smooth, she thought, just as he looked up and then appeared to be excusing himself to walk toward the back kitchen. Makenna grabbed Paige's lunch box and left out the back door.

By the time Travis made it to the back kitchen, she was gone. She'd seen him, but even from that distance, there'd been something in her eyes. He wasn't sure it had anything to do with him, but she hadn't said good-bye. He pushed through the back door and found Kenna just as she was putting her seatbelt on and starting her Jeep.

"Hey, no good-bye?" He kept it casual and leaned in to kiss her. The minute his lips touched hers, he knew something was wrong. He searched her eyes and found nothing. She stared blankly, as if right through him. *Shit!*

"You okay?" He touched her arm and could have sworn she wanted to pull away.

"What do you mean? I'm just in a hurry because I've got to drive all the way to the farm tonight."

Yeah, something was wrong. Kenna never cared about driving, especially to the farm, and never when it concerned her daughter.

"One of the night shift dishwashers called in sick and Carl is back there up to his elbows in suds. I'm fine, just busy."

"Uh huh." He leaned over and noticed Paige's lunch box on the passenger seat.

"Are you forgetting to forget Paige's lunch box on purpose?"

She met his eyes quickly and put her hand on her daughter's lunch box. Travis felt a chill, almost like a protective back-up-asshole chill, but that couldn't be, right?

"Oh, well, I thought with the weekend and since we'll be at the farm that I'd—Oh damn, why can't I be good at bullshit. I need some space. There. I need to think about things and I need a little space, so I took her lunch box. I'll make her lunch for Monday." She was look-ing at the steering wheel, and Travis felt a pain in his chest.

"Okay, space . . . why? Did something happen?"

"No, I'm just busy, I need a break and"—she whipped her head up and met his eyes—"and, I think we need to think about this, us."

She might as well have slapped him, because he liked to think he was pretty perceptive and he didn't see this coming. It had been only a few hours ago that they were wrapped in each other's arms. She had woken him up in the middle of the night to show him how the moon lit up her backyard, and he'd made love to her right there on her back patio. And now she wanted space?

"Makenna, what's going on?"

"Nothing. Well, not nothing. We're just different. Don't you have to get back in the kitchen?"

Travis looked toward the restaurant; he did need to get back. It was pretty slow, but Todd should never be left alone for too long.

"Did something happen?"

"No. It's nothing out of the ordinary really, I . . . maybe I forgot who you were."

"Who *I* was?"

"Nothing, it means nothing. No judgments, okay? But I need to get going. Paige is waiting for me. Can we talk about this later? I'll see you Sunday for Paige's birthday."

He didn't know what to say. He couldn't even fight with her because he had no idea what the hell was going on. He let her go and went back to work.

After having to make and remake two salads because he couldn't think straight, Travis left Todd with two pizzas to finish up while he went to find Sage.

"What's going on?" he asked a few minutes later while Sage was shaking a drink.

"Oh no! Why do you always come to me when things hit the fan?"

"Because you always have the intel. Let's not waste time. What things and which fan? Kenna took Paige's lunch box with her when she left, and something's wrong."

"Oh, now see, that was plain mean. I sort of thought she was pissy."

"What did I do? Spill it."

"Hang on." Sage flipped up a martini glass, poured the bearded guy on the other side of the bar his drink, and returned to her register with his credit card.

"You didn't do anything. Well, you did do something, quite a few somethings actually."

"Sage."

"Right, sorry. So Kenna was getting ready to leave. She came in-to the bar to ask me to bring ice and soda and overheard these

dipshits at a bachelorette party. The bride-to-be was Pamela. Remember her from when we first opened?"

"Brunette with the beauty mark?"

"Yup, good memory, Romeo. That's the one." Sage turned and
left a leather folder with a pen next to the bearded guy, who was
now glued to the football game over the bar. "Anyway, Kenna was
almost gone when the dipshits, there were like twelve of them, all
started talking about you."

"Me?"

"Yeah, Pamela was drunk and babbling on about how you were
the best . . . well, 'fuck,' her words, certainly not mine, she'd ever
had."

Under normal circumstances, he would have laughed at one of
Sage's bar stories, but not this one. He peeked back in the kitchen
to check on Todd, who appeared to be working.

"So there was that, which was bad enough, but then a few other
dipshits chimed in that they too had 'had' you." She used the
quotes as if he needed them.

Travis took a deep breath. It wasn't deep enough because he
felt his chest squeeze. "Okay, so that was it? Kenna knows I've
slept with some women."

"Some? Romeo, this was like half the bridal party, and they were
rowdy. Giving details and talking about how you were their favorite drive-thru."

"Excuse me?"

"Yeah, that you would never be the sit-down-and-commit type,
but you were fun for a few drive-thrus."

"Holy hell, why do I feel dirty and not in a good way?"

Sage laughed but then grew serious. "Kenna didn't say anything,
but she seemed a little weird. I think she's all over the place and
she's clearly fallen for you. Maybe hearing all this messed with
her."

"She has fallen for me and I've fallen for her. We're together.
I'm not getting why these ladies, and I use that term loosely, would
rattle her."

"She has Paige."

His eyes met Sage's and he saw exactly what she meant. He didn't just feel dirty and used; apparently he was.

"I'm well aware she has Paige."

"I think she wants to make sure that a man in their life is worthy of . . . I mean . . . that's not what I meant to say."

"Sure you did, someone who's good enough to be in Paige's life. I'm fine behind the scenes, making lunch or while Paige is waiting for Gracie, but not quite good enough to play in the big game."

"That's not what I said."

"You didn't have to."

Travis returned to what he knew, his work.

By the time they closed around 10:30, he'd calmed down. He tried to imagine what it would be like if he'd sat down at a bar and heard men talking about how great Kenna had been in their beds. The simple thought of it pissed him off, so he tried really hard to keep that in mind. Just because it seemed more acceptable for women to joke about men, it didn't make it any easier to listen to. Sage apologized again before she left, but the truth was she hadn't said anything Travis didn't already know. Makenna and Paige were special, and they deserved a good guy. Although his father's critical voice seemed ever present in his mind, he knew he was a good guy. But, that didn't mean Kenna needed to hear the sordid details of his life before her.

He needed to talk to her. There was no way this was waiting until Sunday, and so instead of heading home, he turned his bike onto the freeway and drove north on the I-10.

Chapter Twenty-Six

*M*akenna started awake to find Travis standing in the entrance of the bedroom she grew up in. He was leaning against the now-closed door. He must have been watching her sleep because he didn't say a word.

"Travis."

"I didn't mean to scare you. We need to talk."

She looked at the clock on the nightstand, and her blurry eyes registered that it was one-something in the morning.

"Is everything okay?" She sat up.

"No, I don't think it is." He sat next to her on the bed, and Makenna clicked on the light.

"I didn't have sex until my junior year in high school," Travis started without warning. "My girlfriend, the same one I'd had since my freshman year, and yes the woman who is now my brother's wife, wasn't ready. I cared about her, so I waited until she was ready. She was a cheerleader and I was on the football team. It all sounds a little sickening now, but that was my life. We finished high school and we both got into UCLA. I was even a damn honor student. Squeaky clean, all-American."

She could see him building up, the tension seeping into his

face, and she instantly felt bad that he felt the need to explain. He stood up from the bed, but she stayed where she was. Everything about his body language said he needed room.

"You don't need to do this."

"No, I think I do. By the time we graduated, I thought I loved her. Her parents loved my parents and we were the perfect couple, destined for a big wedding and a house in the same suburban neighborhood. It's hard for me to remember who I was back then, but when I want to kick my old self in the face for being so stupid, I try to remember it's all I knew. I was raised to be that. My point in telling you all this is that I used to be a one-and-done guy. I wasn't always, well, what you heard at the bar tonight."

"I understand."

"No, you really don't, because here's where it gets good. Everything fell apart when I hurt my knee. I know it sounds stupid, but that was all it took for the whole damn house of fake to come tumbling down. One knee. Up until her boyfriend blew his knee out, not much had happened to Avery. Her life was pretty... shopping-at-the-mall fantastic."

When his voice shifted to his version of dipshit, Kenna held back a laugh.

"Anyway, this is getting boring fast, so I'll give you the condensed finale. After our freshman year in college, Avery dumped me. I wasn't going to be a college athlete, let alone a professional one, and that's what she wanted. She didn't want me, she wanted the same thing my dad wanted: a winner. She found one in my brother John, who was a senior by that time. As with all great romances, they'd been screwing each other behind my back for... about six months before she broke it off."

Makenna tried to keep him from continuing, but he held up his hand. It almost seemed like he needed to finish, like telling her all of this was some sort of cathartic flush.

"Fast-forward to less than a year later. John proposed to her the week after he graduated. They were married the following April. I was in the wedding, brother of the groom, best man."

Kenna put her hand to her mouth. She'd always been acutely aware of her own pain. She'd lost her husband and her mother had left her when she was five. Her pain had been on display, but this, the private pain of someone she loved, was worse. It was almost unbearable.

Travis felt the same sting of stupid every time he reflected on his past. His story was taking longer than he'd planned, but he suddenly wanted to answer her questions, needed her to know.

"I think I've only ever told this whole sad tale to your brother, and I'm pretty sure we were drunk when I let it slip. Anyway, I know it sounds pathetic, but I'd never been with anyone else. I was twenty-one years old. My body was broken, an obvious disappointment to all the people I thought were important in my life. When my brother married my ex-girlfriend, he slid into my place. Without a word from anyone, I was done."

"Travis, please stop. You don't need to say any more."

"No, I want you to know everything. You need to understand."

"I understand, please." Makenna wiped a tear from her eye.

"Things get better, I promise." He sat next to her on the bed. "Please don't cry. I quit school, traveled some, learned to cook, and figured out what I wanted. I also put women where I needed them to be—I'm sure that's what a shrink would say. I didn't need them and even though I swear I've always been honest about who and what I was, I guess it's fair to say I've used my share of women."

Makenna said nothing.

"So, that brings us to a few years ago when I met a woman and her little girl. I enjoyed the mom's ass from afar and started making the little girl's lunch. Things started shifting around for me and then when I kissed you, nothing else mattered anymore. There were women and then there was just you. I'm not perfect, Kenna. I do have a past, and I can't help it if you run into it from time to time. But you need to understand how I got where I am today. We all have history. I'm thirty-two years old. I'm no longer ashamed of who I am, and if I had to go through some stuff to get to you and Paige, then I'm good."

"I'm sorry."

"You don't need to be sorry. You have a lot to protect. I was pissed, maybe a little embarrassed at first. I get why you ran off, but I'm not some sleazy manwhore. I guess I played that part for a while because it was easier than being dumped, or being some broken loser."

"Please, stop."

Travis took her in his arms. "I love you. I'll work my ass off to deserve you, but I won't live my life ashamed."

"I don't want you to be ashamed." She touched his face, leaning in to gently kiss his lips. "I was being stupid and now that you are here, I couldn't care less how many women you've slept with. I think it fed my own insecurities: you know, the tiny dresses and the experience. I just—"

"Took your lunch box and went home?"

She shook her head. "I shouldn't have done that. I just got all turned around. This is new for me too . . . Hey, before I kiss you, could you say that last part again?"

"The lunch box?"

Kenna shook her head.

"The part about how great Paige is?"

She smiled and shook her head again.

"Oh, you must be talking about the part where I said . . . when I said that I love you."

Her lips did that quiver thing, but before her tears fell, she took his face and kissed him. Soft and healing, as if by touching him she could fix him. He sure as hell hoped it was that easy.

"I love you too," she said, still holding his face, and he could have sworn she slid right down into his soul. Turned out when Makenna Rye said she loved someone, she meant it.

He went to kiss her again, but she held her finger to his lips and said, "And just for the record, I loved you before you told me about stupid Avery and your dumb brother with the bad we're-no-longer-in-college-asshole haircut."

Travis laughed and then kissed her. "Wow, that was good. He really does have a bad haircut. Maybe you can mention that to him the next time you see him, you know, just like that with the asshole part in there too."

"Oh, that would be my pleasure. You know how things just flow right out of my mouth."

"I do know that about you," he said, laying her back on the bed and caging her between his arms. "Blunt, I think that's what we call it. I really do love you when you're to the point."

"Really?" she said as she pulled his shirt over his head and threw it on the floor.

"Absolutely."

"Good, because here I go again. Take off the rest of those clothes and get in here because under this robe . . ." She playfully pulled the silk off one shoulder.

Travis reached out to touch her. "I'm all ears."

"Serious unicorns await you if you get naked and hit that light."

Travis leaned up off the bed, dropped his jeans, and clicked the lamp off in record time. When he slid under the covers and pulled her on top of him, moonlight filled the room, as if it'd been put there just so he could keep looking at her.

He pushed the hair off her face as she straddled him and let her robe fall open.

"I love you," she said, nothing short of stunning in all her open abandon. She lifted and slowly they filled each other with warmth that had nothing to do with their pasts. They were connected in a now that no longer confused him. He had no idea if he could be the "right" man for her world, but he knew he was in love with her and would be for the rest of his life. As the moonlight spilled over them, with each pull and every glide, she seemed to fall farther and he followed.

Chapter Twenty-Seven

Makenna opened her eyes, somehow knowing exactly where she was, and then pulled up the duvet she was nestled in to check for clothing. Panties and camisole in place, her next thoughts were filled with wondering if Paige was awake, what time it was, and then . . . Travis.

He had been there last night, right? The whole thing felt like a dream, not *the* dream, but an entirely different dream. He loved her, she knew that already, but he'd said it and so had she, and they'd spent some time showing each other just how much.

Before she'd fallen asleep in Travis's arms last night, she'd gotten up and put her clothes back on. She remembered now. Even though she'd been exhausted, some things were automatic for Kenna. There was no way she would allow herself to sleep naked in her family home or with her daughter two doors down. Sure, she made love to a gorgeous man until almost sunrise, but there were still rules. She sat up and realized it was nine o'clock. This was clearly some version of a dream because there was no way she was at Ryeland Farms and allowed to sleep past five o'clock. She hadn't even heard the roosters. Makenna wondered if Travis had left as she tightened her robe and made her way downstairs. Before she even entered the kitchen, Paige plowed right into her.

"Mama!" she yelped, dancing around in her sweatpants, cowgirl boots, and a Dodger's T-shirt that was about four sizes too big. "Guess who came to visit us and to see Gracie's new babies?" She pulled Makenna into the kitchen, and with a big sweeping gesture of her little arm, said, "Tada! Mmmmy Travis!"

And there he stood, looking like he'd just arrived and scooping Paige up with one arm when she charged at him. Travis was holding a coffee cup in the other hand and, from what Kenna could hear as she went to the fridge, discussing gumbo with her father. She made herself a cup of tea and kissed her father on the cheek.

"Morning. Is it the end of the world? You let me sleep in."

Her father grinned and picked his hat up off the table. "You had a fill-in." He gestured to Travis, who met Kenna's eyes and gave her that rich melting smile he'd perfected.

"Really? You let a city boy play 4-H?"

Her dad nodded and took Paige from Travis, throwing her over his shoulder as she squealed. "He did a pretty good job too. I think I've got him convinced he needs to sell that bike and get himself a proper truck."

Makenna laughed and took a sip of tea. "Is that so?"

"I'm thinking about it," he said, drinking coffee and looking right at home in their kitchen, in her life.

"That's a shame. I love that bike."

Travis looked at her father, who promptly dropped his head and laughed as he filled one Thermos with coffee and the other with hot chocolate.

Kenna watched her dad and knew he was taking Paige on the tractor. Coffee and cocoa always meant a tractor ride was in the works. The first memory she had after her mother left was coffee and cocoa. She'd been crying in her room when her father came in, big cowboy hat firmly in place, and told her to get dressed. She'd looked up at him, wiped her eyes, and when she hesitated, he said, "We've got a Thermos of coffee for me and one with cocoa for you. Let's not dillydally or it'll get cold. We don't have time for crying; there's work to be done."

She'd gotten dressed quickly and when she ran down the stairs, her father held out her coat and pulled up her hood. She remembered swallowing back her remaining tears and taking her father's hand. She'd ridden with a big wool blanket across her lap as her father delivered mail and equipment to some of the houses the farm hands lived in on the property. Standing in the kitchen, a grown woman now, she could still feel the scratch of the blanket and the fuel smell of the tractor. After their deliveries, her father had parked them under one of the pecan trees and poured coffee and cocoa into the green metal cups of each Thermos.

"It's good to get out and get some air in your lungs."

Kenna, who was just about six, nodded up at her father.

"Who's going to sit next to me at the table now?" she'd asked.

Her father must have hesitated and at least allowed a moment for his own emotions, but as a little girl, she hadn't noticed.

"Well, there are five chairs, but one of them is loose."

"The one Garrett sits in?"

"Yeah, that one. It's wobbly, so let's break that one up and make it firewood. That'll leave four chairs, just enough." Her father took a gulp of coffee. "In fact, since we're changing it up, let's not have set seats anymore. Instead, let's just grab whatever seat we want."

"What if Garrett or Logan push and I don't get a seat?"

"Well, we know there will always be four seats, so it might be a little crazy, but eventually everyone will find a seat. It'll be like an adventure every morning."

Kenna remembered nodding and could still feel the warmth of the cocoa as it hit her little stomach. "Sure, I like adventure."

"Me too." He'd kissed her on the forehead, and that was the last time Kenna cried about her mother. After that day, her father kept her busy and life with her brothers and her father became an adventure.

"Well, the almost birthday girl and I have a tractor ride waiting for us, so we'll leave you two now."

Before he could grab Paige under his arm, Kenna put her arms around her father, kissed him on the cheek, and held on.

"Thank you," she whispered in his ear.

"What for?" he whispered back.

"For taking me on the tractor."

Her father pulled back and looked at her through weathered green eyes that had seen more than their share of heartache. She didn't need to explain it; he knew what the tractor meant, and again, he took off his hat and kissed her on the forehead. He turned to Paige and Travis, who were locked in an intense thumb war, scooped her up under his arm, and was gone.

Kenna watched them go down the path, her daughter giggling and squirming, and for what felt like the thousandth time in her life, she was so grateful.

Travis checked the door then leaned in and kissed her.

"You did chores for me?" she asked, returning to her present.

"I did. I was a very good boy." He backed Kenna up toward the counter, but before she had a chance to be playful and tell Travis what a good boy he had been, Garrett walked into the kitchen with dirty hands extended.

"Aw shit, it's clearly mating season for all the animals." He turned on the sink and lathered his hands.

Makenna huffed, sure her face was flushed. "What are you talking about? Travis just got here. He came to see Gracie's babies."

Garrett nodded and dried his hands. He stared down at her, not moving, eyes giving nothing away.

"He let me in last night," Travis leaned into her and whispered.

Makenna closed her eyes. "Right, sure. Well, good morning, my least favorite and always rude brother."

Travis said nothing. It was probably best because Garrett seemed poised and ready to use anything that came out of his mouth for his next smart-ass assault.

"Least favorite? Yeah, I don't think so."

Kenna nodded her head like a child and drank her tea.

"Well, that's a shame, because your least favorite brother just got done installing the new top you ordered for your Jeep. Maybe next time you should ask your favorite brother—that is, if he's not too busy melting butter with this guy." Garrett gestured with his thumb to Travis.

Makenna all but jumped into her brother's arms and planted a big kiss right on his mouth. Garrett set her down, rolled his eyes, and Travis laughed.

"Did you really put on the new top?"

"Dirt on my hands proves it."

"Thank you, my favoritest brother," Makenna said, using a Paige word and wide eyes.

Garrett shook his head and flicked her hair. "Not quite as cute when you say it. What are you two doing, other than feeling each other up?"

"Travis did chores for me this morning," Makenna said playfully. Raising Paige had restored a youthfulness she never really felt growing up, but playful without chasing her daughter around their home was something new. Kenna felt giddy, silly, and crazy in love.

"I noticed. A sure sign of a whipped man." Garrett laughed, patted Travis on the back, and left out the front porch.

Travis didn't normally lean toward comparisons, but there was no denying the contrast between the Ryes and the McNultys. It was obvious to him just working with Logan, but the contrast was even greater in their personal lives. Always plenty of teasing and pushing around, but it was tempered with what Travis could only describe as fun, joy maybe. The teasing was the fun and he'd seen it get pretty intense, especially between Logan and Garrett, but Makenna was right—it wasn't hurtful. Watching the Rye family, Travis started realizing his family members were bullies, as she'd said. He remembered reading some self-help book a long time ago that said, "You can't choose your family," and hanging right in the McNulty family kitchen were the colorfully stitched needlepoint words, *Family is Family*.

Travis knew what he had been born into, the inevitable pull of his blood, but for the first time in his life, he was beginning to envision his own family, people of his choosing who loved him. Love. He loved her and her daughter . . . and wanted them in his life. Even if he wasn't yet sure what that meant or if he was even up for it, the need was there. He tried to push it back and steady his heart. One more cup of coffee and a few more stolen moments with Makenna, and Travis needed to get a move on if he was going to make it to The Yard in time to meet Logan and start prep for lunch. Paige grabbed him on his way to his bike and pulled him back into the barn for one more look.

"The one in the back is shy. I named her Kitten," Paige whispered.

"Kitten is a clever name for a goat."

Paige nodded. "I know, it's not somefing you expect, but she's soft like a kitten, so Donk said it was perfect."

"That it is. Okay, I've gotta get going, but I'll be back tomorrow for the big day."

Paige pulled him down, kissed him on the cheek, and whispered that they were having her favorite cake.

"What kind?" Travis asked.

"It's a surprise."

He nodded. "Right, of course."

Paige held out her hand, and Travis took it as they walked out of the barn. He left her with Kenna and started his bike. The woman he was in love with and her daughter stood waving as he drove away.

Waking up with a woman, doing chores, talking with Paige, and then heading off to work. Could his family, his version, be different, or did it all eventually melt into the fake Folgers commercial that his parents tried to portray? He'd had a great time and would look forward to seeing Kenna and Paige again the next day, but when he opened up his bike on the empty country road, he had to admit freedom felt nothing like family, and that felt good too.

Chapter Twenty-Eight

Garrett and Logan carried Paige on their shoulders like a minia-
ture Cleopatra. They made their way out to the grassy patch
under the largest of the pecan trees they had on the farm. After a rousing, male-dominated version of "Happy Birthday,"
Makenna's sweet baby girl blew out the six birthday candles atop
her hummingbird cake. As their friends and family clapped, Kenna
kissed Paige and realized her daughter was kneeling at the same
picnic table she had sat at when she turned six years old. Her life
had been different than her daughter's at that age, and Kenna found
herself with a mixture of pride and sadness for them both. Her
mother had abandoned Makenna shortly before her sixth birthday,
and Paige had spent most of her life without a father.

Makenna handed out pieces of cake and amid the laughter and
celebration, she understood that joy and love came from so many
places and often went hand in hand with pain.

"Oh my goodness!" Paige exclaimed as she tore open one of her
presents. "Thank you, My Travis!"

Travis leaned in for a high-five and a kiss on the cheek.

"What is it?" Makenna asked, stepping closer.

"I get to grow butterflies. It's a kit." Paige held up the box.

"Wow, so fun." Kenna looked at Travis.

There was no doubt he understood Paige, got her quirkiness, and encouraged it. Kenna somehow loved him more for that. She'd only been in love with one other man and that was Adam, whose memory was always fresh on important days like these, and yet today there was somehow enough room to love Travis too. She wasn't quite ready to unravel all of these new feelings because buried way in the bottom of it all, she found herself thinking about her own childhood, her own mother. Kenna didn't want to go there, didn't want to have to look back. Instead, she accepted the love surrounding her daughter and went inside to grab a trash bag for the quickly mounting wrapping paper.

"Need any help?" Travis asked, walking in behind her.

"No, I think we are good."

By the time Kenna grabbed two black trash bags and closed the pantry door, she was wrapped in his arms.

"Very cool gift," she said, gently kissing him.

"Thanks. I think it takes like ten weeks for those things to grow, so that should hold her busy mind for a while. Great party by the way. Did you see that chair your dad made?"

"I did. He knows more about Marrakech now than I ever thought possible."

They both laughed and Travis played with the hair around her neck. "So, how are you?"

She laughed because he almost looked uncomfortable, which of course was ridiculous because this was Travis. Granted, it was in love Travis, but the man still had moves Kenna had just started to understand. "I'm good, I'm great. Paige is happy and it's gorgeous out today. Things are good. Aren't they?"

"Yeah, they are."

They stood watching the party through the screen door.

"Why is this so . . ."

"Awkward, first date, meeting-the-parents weird?" He looked at her.

Kenna laughed again. The man could make her laugh. Without fail, no matter the situation, he always managed to get right in there. Part of her, the part that thought of Travis in her future, in their future, knew his humor was a good thing.

"I have no idea. Maybe it's the birthday party. Our first . . . family function as . . . "

"A couple?"

"Is that what we are?" Kenna turned to him.

"I . . . well yeah, I mean I love . . . Damn, why can't I get this out in the daylight?" He held her arms and studied her as if he were looking for some secret that would help his heart. "Makenna, yes, we are a couple. I love you and your daughter and we are not just having hot, holy hell, sex. I love you." He let out a breath. "There."

She smiled, and they both turned and stood side-by-side watching the party. Kenna reached around and put her hand on his very lovely ass. She had no idea what had gotten into her, but if he was going to play the adult, the responsible one, she wanted to be the fun one. "I'm glad we cleared that up, babe." She squeezed and then gave him a kiss that left him gaping as she walked through the screen door.

"Babe, did you just call me babe?"

Kenna nodded, and then it was his turn to whip her around for a kiss. The wind blew and at her daughter's squeal, Kenna turned to see Paige blowing bubbles. *See*, she told herself, *you can have both, this works.*

"I've just agreed to help out with Paige's field day next week. Is that okay?" Travis asked after things had been cleaned up and Paige was playing Twister with the men of the Rye family. That was a treat Travis wouldn't soon let them live down. He thought of taking pictures but really wanted to keep his ass whooping restricted to the gym.

"Really?" Kenna almost tripped over Garrett's dog, Jack, who was lying on his back taking in the sun.

"Huh, is it that bad?" he asked, steadying her arm.

Makenna grinned, as if she knew something he didn't. "You volunteered for field day at St. Christopher's Private School?"

"Well, hell, it sounds ominous when you say it like that. It's a field day."

Makenna raised her eyebrows, clearly deciding to play with him.

"She's in kindergarten, how bad could it be?"

"You're going to pull up on your bike, in the parking lot?"

"I . . . was. I'm sure there are other guys there with—"

Makenna shook her head.

"Okay, so there aren't other guys with bikes. I do well with up-tight crowds." He laughed. "Paige said it's in the morning, so I figure I'll pitch in for a couple of hours before we open. Come on, you're making me nervous." He helped her bring in the last of the glasses.

Makenna set the napkins down on the counter and faced him.

"Don't be nervous. I'll be there to protect you when all the mommies try to tear your shirt off with their teeth."

"What?"

"Oh, you're clearly just an innocent when it comes to the car-pool crowd. These are the women buying *Fifty Shades*, my friend. You'll look like a walking, talking fantasy." She put her hand on his shoulder and winked at him. Travis laughed so hard he almost cried.

"Where do you come up with this stuff? Maybe we could have a late breakfast after, or we could do that you ripping my shirt off with your teeth thing too. That sounds interesting."

She blushed and just like that, he turned the game around on her. Smiling up at him with the wind and the setting sun playing with her hair, he wanted her more than he'd ever thought it was possible to want another person. She was perfect in every detail. She made him laugh because she was able to laugh at herself. She was sexy and blushing at the same time. She was Paige's mom and no doubt the love of his life all rolled into one woman. Travis leaned back on the counter and held her around her waist as they watched Paige easily defeat three grown men groaning on the floor in a pile of twisted limbs.

He kissed her neck, and the awkward from earlier fell off them. Time, it just took time, that's what he told himself.

Chapter Twenty-Nine

*T*ravis knew exactly how many times Avery Price, now Avery Price McNulty, had called him in the past ten years because that number was exactly zero. The last time he'd spoken to his ex was a few days before she married his older brother. She'd called him drunk after her bachelorette party. Sort of like Pamela, who'd made an ass out of herself in front of Makenna, but in a much more pro-football wife classy way. She'd called to tell him how sorry she was for the way things had "played out," and she hoped he'd forgive her and they could one day be friends. She went on for what seemed like hours with her purely self-serving attempt to clear her conscience before marrying the man of her dreams. Travis had done what he'd always done since sinking to the position of family loser—he took one for the team. He'd told her it was fine and that he understood. After he hung up, he'd gone home with the sexy woman sitting across from him at the bar.

That was the last time Avery had called him, so it took his brain time to click on when her name appeared on his phone after he got out of the shower Thursday morning.

"Avery?" he answered, drying his hair with a towel.

"Oh, great, I'm glad I caught you. Do you have a minute?"

"Yeah, I'm on my way out, but sure. Is something wrong?"

"No, why?"

"I just . . . well, you don't normally call me, so—"

"Right." She laughed. "I know this is probably awkward for you."

"Not really."

"Okay, well, that's good. I mean, we are family and we should—"

"Avery, what's this about?" There was no way in hell he was going to be late for Paige's field day so he could listen to his ex go on about what a big happy family they all were.

"Sorry. Well, I have happy news and I just wanted to kind of share it with you, you know, before the whole family was together."

"Why?"

She let out the breath she seemed to be holding, and then the real Avery came out to play. "Trav, please don't make this more difficult for me. I'm trying to be nice and extend a courtesy."

He laughed. "I certainly wouldn't want to make things difficult for you. What's the good news? I need to get going."

"Your brother, well, John and I are pregnant."

Travis never understood that stupid phrase. "We are pregnant." What the hell did that mean? Sure, two people were having a baby, but the woman was pregnant. He wanted to yell that back into the phone, but he'd always thought if he started yelling at Avery, he might never stop.

"Huh, well, congratulations."

"Thank you. We've been trying for a really long time, and you know after the first miscarriage—"

"Avery."

"Yes?"

"Why the hell would you—You know what, forget it. I need to go. Thanks for calling and sharing your news. I'm sure the whole family is thrilled."

"They are and—"

He hung up before one more word slithered through his phone, wondering if he had the most screwed-up family in the world because it sure as hell felt like it at the moment. He threw the phone on his bed, as if that might help distance him from what just happened, and got dressed. After tying his tennis shoes, Travis put the phone in his pocket and grabbed his keys. He needed to leave if he was going to make it to Paige's school by eight.

He tried to shut down his mind and let go of the anger bubbling inside of him, but by the time he reached his bike, it was in full force. He knew it was sick, but on some level he used to think that John and Avery's inability to get pregnant was some twisted version of karma. Apparently not. It seemed everything was golden for the golden couple.

As he turned into traffic, what pissed Travis off the most had nothing to do with his actual family. The anger came from the way they affected him, that they could still get under his skin and pick at wounds he was trying to ignore for the sake of keeping the peace. Why couldn't they just leave him the hell alone?

Travis barely noticed he'd pulled into St. Christopher's Private School, which spoke to his current state because when he looked toward the school, it was intimidating as hell. The damn thing looked like a mini Stanford. He sat on his bike, helmet hiding his face, while he tried to put everything and everyone back in their spots. He was consumed with memories and disgust that in all these years, with everything they'd said and done, he'd never really said a word. He'd just gone along, smiling, because he didn't want to be any more of a disappointment than he already was.

Travis reached the field on his way to the front office to check in as Paige had instructed. Some of the events must have already been underway because he could hear parents cheering—or was that shouting? Christ, was there a difference? He looked over the fence and saw four men huddled with a group of kids, older than Paige, with flags hanging from their waists.

"Okay, so that was weak. Let's get out there and show them what Mrs. Bank's class is all about," one of the men shouted, and the kids cheered.

Travis stopped. It was an innocent game of flag football, but his eyes scanned the field. He couldn't find Makenna or Paige and he suddenly started to sweat as a memory, his past, began strangling him.

It was the day of John's wedding. Travis had been in the bathroom throwing up when his father knocked on the door of the stall.

"Just a minute."

"Trav, are you in there? What the hell's going on? We're about to start."

Travis was standing in the parking lot of St. Christopher's Private School a grown man, his brother had been married over ten years, and yet there he was in a full-color version of that day. He struggled to get his shit together, could still hear the parents and kids cheering in the present, but the memory moved forward. Travis leaned up against the cool stone of the building as if he could somehow brace himself.

He'd come out of the stall a few minutes later and splashed water on his face. Wrestling with the cinch of his tuxedo necktie, his father took him by the shoulders.

"Were you throwing up in there?"

Travis had nodded. Jesus, he'd only been twenty-two years old and still broken and in a knee brace.

"Okay, I want you to listen to me. Your brother deserves this day. This isn't about you, got it? We're a team and when one of us is winning, we're all winning."

He'd blinked at his father, smelling the beer on his breath, and given up that day. There had been times before their little bathroom chat that Travis had been defiant, "spirited," as his mother used to say with her PTA smile. But that day, minutes before his brother was about to marry his ex-girlfriend, was the day his father finally cashed in all those years of football practice and "go team" bullshit. That day he'd been strangled, and not just by his tux. It was the day he caved, gave up, and started taking it for the team.

Travis squeezed his eyes closed, trying to drown out the sounds and kill the memory, but when he opened them, he suddenly remembered why he'd run from all of this bullshit. His life would never be about this—dads living through their sons, cheering crowds, and happy team picture bullshit—ever again. It didn't matter what school or which field, he wouldn't spend one more minute on anyone's team.

He pushed off the building, looked for Kenna and Paige one more time, and then turned to leave. He knew with every fiber of his being that what he was doing was wrong, that he needed to get a grip and get in there for Paige, but he didn't, couldn't.

As his bike roared away from the school, his mind began to clear. He wasn't sure what the hell happened back there, but something was very wrong. His freshman year in college, he'd gone to see a counselor to help get over his injury. He remembered her saying that once a problem started to adversely affect your life, your present life, it was time to deal with it. He pulled into the parking garage of his apartment, and he had a feeling he'd arrived at that point.

The idea of a field day for kindergartners sounded absurd to Makenna until she walked to the back field of the school and saw her daughter dressed in a black-and-white T-shirt that said Conroy across the back. She was standing with her class and when she turned around to wave, she had a little black line under each eye like Tom Brady, but cuter and with pigtails. That sight alone was worth signing up to volunteer and standing by the long jump to watch tiny legs do the impossible.

She was manning her station with Kim, Brianna's mom. Makenna noticed when Paige started school that all of the women introduced themselves with their name quickly followed by their child or children's names. Makenna had gone from simply, "Hi, I'm Makenna," to "Hi, I'm Makenna, but you probably know me as Paige's mom."

Being a parent was interesting, Kenna thought. The caring, mothering part had come naturally to her, even organically, but the public persona of a "mommy" was proving a little trickier. She'd never thought of Paige as an extension of herself. When she was born, it was as though she was this magical person who, by some fate, Kenna was allowed to borrow for a while. There wasn't anything wrong with being connected to her daughter—it was just change. Her baby was now becoming a tiny person in her own right, which filled Kenna with pride, but also put her in uncharted waters, with no one to share it with. She noticed the "single" part of single mom a little more these days, especially in the larger context of school. Kenna knew she sounded weird, which was why she normally kept to herself and simply smiled. She would probably never know if other women felt the same because for as long as she could remember, she was younger than most of them and always on the fringe. She wasn't willing to risk looking like the crazy widowed farm girl. Dear God, it would be so nice if her mind would take a break every once in a while.

Paige ran over and grabbed her arm.

"Hey, you look great. I'm at the long jump, so I'll get to watch you in a little while."

"Okay. Is My Travis here yet, because Coach Sweaters needs him for the relay."

Kenna looked toward the entrance to the field and then to the parking lot.

"I don't see him yet. Maybe he was caught up at the restaurant."

Paige looked around with a mix of frenzy and excitement as two of her friends joined her.

"Mama, this is Kiley and Amanda, they're my friends."

Kenna shook hands, and then one of the teachers called the girls over to their starting point. It looked like Paige would begin with the beanbag toss.

Kenna glanced at the parking lot again and then took out her phone. No messages.

"Did you want to work the measuring tape or the clipboard?" Kim, Brianna's mom, asked.

"Oh, I'm sorry. I'll take the clipboard." Makenna tried to smile and slipped her phone back into the pocket of her shorts.

234

Thirty minutes later, they were on their second batch of high jumpers and Kenna took one more glance toward the entrance to the field. She knew he wasn't coming and even though there could be a completely understandable reason, she also knew there wasn't.

He wasn't coming because he didn't want to be there. It seemed things had finally gotten too complicated for Travis McNulty. It was one thing to make lunches, sneak sex here and there, show up at a birthday party, or even go out on a handful of great dates, but field day represented the R word. Responsibility was the unsexy part of life. It was often bigger than what could fit on the back of a motorcycle.

Kenna shouldn't have been surprised, but when one of the gym teachers came over to ask her if "Paige's friend" would be there for any of the relay station shifts, something hit her square in the center of her chest. Pain, anger, probably a mixture of the two. She apologized, said something had come up at the restaurant, that Travis wouldn't be able to make it. Then she pulled her baseball cap down and did what she'd done her whole life—she moved on.

After two more hours of "working the clipboard" as Kim had put it, Makenna had only seen her daughter for about five minutes. Wasn't seeing your child the only reason parents volunteered for this stuff anyway? She took a sip of the water bottle someone had given her and sent her father a picture. She looked for Paige at the other stations and realized that St. Christopher's field day was huge. There were activities on three different fields and the basketball courts. She scanned the crowd for their name on the back of a T-shirt or for Paige's pigtails. They'd tied green ribbon in them that morning, but as she looked around, it seemed other parents chose green too.

Kenna recorded another little boy's three-foot long jump, which was pretty impressive because he was barely over that height himself, and finally found Paige. She was at the relay station and her pigtails were flying as she approached another girl and handed her the stick. Kenna leaned forward to get a better look because it seemed like her line was winning. She turned back to her station. Even though her heart was threatening to do a long jump of its own, she wrote down the last little girl's distance. Kim said she was "going to run and use the little girl's room."

Happy for the break, she stood there wondering why it had become so important for Travis to be at St. Christopher's field day. What did it say about her parenting skills, her survival skills for that matter, for her to have let love creep in and disrupt her world? She sat down at one of the picnic tables. She would have put her head between her legs the way they illustrated in the emergency landing instructions, but she didn't want to scare the children.

A guy who had introduced himself earlier as the gym teacher blew a whistle and then instructed everyone through a megaphone that field day was now over. He thanked the parents and guardians for all of their help and then told the kids to return to their homeroom teachers. Paige ran over and gave Kenna a hug.

"Did My Travis call?"

"He did," she lied, not even flinching because there was no way she was telling her little girl that she'd been left, ignored. "There was an emergency at the restaurant and he had to stay there. He was so sorry he missed it, but he said to bring your lunch box by and he'd make something special for lunch."

Paige looked concerned at first. "Is he okay? He's not hurt?"

Not yet, Makenna thought. "No, he's fine."

"Okay, good. It's not a biggie; we have a field day every year, so maybe he can come next year. Or, you know what he could do? The carnival. That would be fun," Paige said and kneeled to tie the laces of the new purple tennis shoes they'd bought for field day. It was good Makenna had a minute, because she was stunned by her daughter's recovery time. Paige was such an incredible energy, a light in her life, that sometimes Makenna wondered who was raising who.

"Did you see me run? My new shoes were lightning bugs!"

"I did. I think you won some of those prizes."

Paige nodded and took her hand. "Thanks for coming, Mama."

She brushed off the front of her shorts. "I have to go back to my classroom now."

Makenna bent down and kissed her daughter. She held her in a hug until Paige squirmed; then she watched her run back to class. After making her way through the front office and apologizing again for Travis not showing up and leaving them short on volunteers, Makenna climbed into her Jeep. She sat for a moment and put her hands to her face. She was pissed at him, angry that he hadn't even bothered to call, but it all felt like so much more than simple anger. She was filled with a need to "circle the wagons," as her father would say, and there was this weird sense of protectiveness. The only problem was Makenna wasn't sure which child she was protecting.

Chapter Thirty

*M*akenna could feel him circling the next morning. He'd called her last night, a few times, but she and Paige had made spaghetti and watched *Monsters, Inc.* She'd ignored his calls. After tucking Paige in, complete with burrito extra cheese, Makenna had moved the couch to the other wall in their living room. It looked good and made the whole room new. She proceeded to do every bit of laundry in the house, including the dish towels and bath mats. After hosing off the patio, she crawled into bed and tried to read. Her house was clean; her daughter was asleep and tucked into her magic forest room. She set her book aside, clicked off the light on her nightstand, and stared up at the ceiling. This was her life, she told herself, her perfectly restored world, and everything was in order. She cried herself to sleep, woke up early, and made breakfast. At The Yard, she silently ran through the back kitchen as Paige picked up her lunch from Travis. He was standing there, Paige's lunch box dangling from his finger as if nothing had happened. He and Paige talked while Makenna grabbed invoices off Logan's desk, and then they were back in the car on their way to school. Makenna had not said a word to him; she wasn't sure where to start. It wasn't until two hours before opening when Travis finally took a seat across from her at the corner bar table.

"I'm sorry." He tried to take her hand across the table. She didn't pull back but didn't move at all. "I'd just finished dealing with Avery and when I got to the school—this is going to sound so strange—I couldn't go in."

"Wait, you were there? Why were you dealing with Avery?" Kenna could have kicked herself. She had decided to say nothing, to not give him the satisfaction of a conversation, but some part of her, probably her heart, hoped he had an explanation.

"Yeah, long story short, Avery and John are having a baby and she wanted to deliver the news personally because that's totally healthy, right?"

She didn't laugh. She could barely look at him. *Was I supposed to laugh, really?*

"So, I was kind of reeling from that conversation and then I had this weird flashback memory thing. I just left, and I'm sorry."

Makenna finally looked up from her laptop, her face now burning.

Travis ran his hand over his clearly sleep-deprived face and continued. "I'm not sure what happened to me, but being at the school and hearing those parents, those fathers cheering, I lost it. I know I sound like a complete idiot, but I couldn't go in. How'd it go? Paige said she got two ribbons."

She couldn't form words. Was he thinking that was it? He was sorry and they'd just resume talking about their day? It was entirely possible that what they were discussing was a guy with some daddy issues who took a pass on a kindergarten field day. Somewhere in her mind, that scenario played, but in the forefront of her mind, spilling out of her thundering heart, was something completely different. She was sitting across from a guy who was so wrapped up in his own mess that he left her daughter waiting. Without a second thought, a text, or a phone call, he bailed. Makenna was left having to explain why he hadn't bothered to show up. She'd lied to her daughter for him. Lied. Travis continued to ramble on as if nothing was wrong, like it was some blip. If she had to listen to one more word, she was going to lose her mind.

She looked at him, unable to find any kind of expression, closed her laptop, and stood to leave.

"Where are you going?"

"I think I'll work from home today."

"What?"

"Yeah, it's probably best that I'm not here today because I'm about to lose my shit all over you and that . . . well, we open for lunch in about two hours. Crazy pissed-off woman is never good for business."

Travis took her arm. "Makenna, I'm sorry. I know it was the worst not to show up, but I'm trying to explain."

Kenna looked at his grip and then back to his eyes. He let go of her arm. *Smart man.*

"I honestly didn't expect my reaction. I've obviously got some stuff to deal with, and I will. Paige mentioned a carnival coming up and I'll be there, I promise."

She turned on him so fast he had to step back.

"Here's the thing." She stepped toward him and looked right up into his eyes. "You're not going to her carnival as some make-up day. That's not how this is going to work. You told Paige you would be at her field day, and then you didn't show."

"And I talked to her this morning. I came in early, made her lunch, and apologized."

"You didn't show and you didn't call."

"I thought you'd be busy working field day and I was in a really bad mood, so I just let it go."

"Right. Fine."

"I get that you're pissed and I'm sure I would be too, but I'm not sure what you want me to do."

"I want you to stick with what you do best—making lunches." She saw the pain hit him, which was exactly what she wanted. Something was fueling her, years of something, and it felt like nothing was going stop the anger. "That's what I want. I told you at the beginning of this that we were different, that I was different."

"I know, but what—"

She held up her hand. "I have responsibilities, someone counting on me, and I will not . . . will not allow anyone to screw that up. Do you understand me?"

"Kenna, it was one field day. I'll make it up to her."

"Oh wow, do you hear yourself? Here's the thing, Travis. It doesn't matter what kind of morning you were having or what was going on in your very adult world. She was waiting for you. You promised, so short of a story that has you lying in the street bleeding, I'm not interested." As soon as the words flew out of her mouth, she had visions of Adam in the hospital after he'd died. Why would she say something like that? She was out of control and angry at things that seemed far deeper than "one field day," as Travis had put it. She'd started out a pissed-off mom, but somehow some of her own pain had seeped in. Maybe part of her was sticking up for the little girl her mother had left. Images of her childhood, Adam, and the feeling of waiting for him. God, she was so tired of waiting.

Travis ran his hand over his face again and shook his head. "Again, I'm not sure what you want me to do here, Kenna."

She went from angry to numb in a matter of minutes. *She should have left her life alone,* she thought, as tears welled up. In that moment, Kenna would have given anything to go back to simply bantering with Travis. She wanted to go back to being Ken, before the stupid notion that she needed to date anyone. What the hell had she been thinking? She wanted to curl up on the couch with her daughter and read or watch another movie. They were fine, and she didn't need any of this.

Travis was trying to hold on, to fix this, but she was slipping through his fingers. Her eyes were wild and he was afraid to move because she was so angry one minute and he would have sworn he saw fear flash across her face the next. He said nothing and searched her eyes for some clue that would explain why it felt like the woman he loved beyond reason looked like she was saying good-bye.

"Stop looking at me. I can't breathe," she said, breaking the weighted silence between them.

He moved toward her, and Makenna held up her hands in what looked like a gesture of survival.

"No, please stay where you are."

"I know I screwed up. It won't happen again, but we'll get past this." He let out a slow breath and scrambled for calm.

Travis knew her, knew the curves and turns of her body and, he thought, her mind, but this was new; this was pain she had yet to share. It felt like more than one field day, and he didn't know how to help.

"I'm not minimizing." He kept trying. "I know Paige was waiting for me, counting on me to be there, and I discussed it with her and apologized. That's the best I can do, and now I just have to move on and be there for her carnival, right?"

"She's a child," came out in a whisper.

"I know. Why does this feel like more than a field day? If you're pissed about other things, let's get them out. Tell me what you want, how we get over this."

"We don't, we don't get over this. What we do is figure out how to move on and get back to the way things were before . . . before—"

"Before you fell in love with me? Before you knocked me to the ground and I fell in love with you and your daughter?"

And there it was. He saw the first tear hit Makenna's cheek and even though he was pissed and confused, all he wanted to do was hold her.

"Yes, before that. Before I started needing you. Before you promised and didn't show."

"Kenna."

She shook her head. "Maybe you're right. Maybe this is deeper, but whatever it is, I can't do this. There's a reason I've been alone since Adam died."

"Please."

"No! I'm tired of being left behind and so damn tired of waiting," she blurted out in a voice somewhere between a yell and a cry that he barely recognized.

At the sound, Sage appeared in the bar, wide-eyed. She'd clearly been chosen to check on them by the rest of the staff. They were all probably huddled in the back kitchen because it was entirely too quiet. Sage went quickly back through the door again without a word.

"I should go."

"I think we need to figure this out."

"There's nothing to figure out, Travis. You're you with your family issues or stuff with your dad. That's what kept you from field day, from us. You're all about easy and simple, remember? That's not who I am. I'll always plan the details. I'll always be complicated. I don't want the pain of waiting around anymore. The need, wanting someone to pick me up from school or come home or show up at a damn field day. I don't want it. I want my old life back. I was happy there." Makenna wiped her tears away. He sat down and she let out a slow exhale.

"Please, come here." He'd honestly never felt more helpless in his life. She seemed hell-bent on running, and he had no idea how to make her stay.

"No. I can't make it go away. I can't love you because, as it turns out, we're both broken."

He stood and managed to close the space and wrap her in his arms. She allowed the hug and rested her face against his chest.

"It's okay." God, he loved her.

She said nothing and he knew despite his words, what was coursing through her was anything but okay. She was going to break his heart. He braced himself and waited for the blow.

"I need to leave."

He didn't let go, so she eased out of his arms.

"Thank you, I'm fine, we'll be fine. Really, this is all for the best."

"Best for who?" he asked.

"Both of us."

"Not really, seeing how my life without you and Paige is going to work."

"We *are* in your life, we'll always be here."

"I'm not giving up, Kenna. This isn't over."

"I'm sorry. Things will get back to normal. It'll just take time."

Travis shook his head.

Makenna nodded and moved toward the door. He put his arm up on the wall next to her, boxing her in.

"Please, let me go."

"We're just going through a mess right now. This is what it's all about, right? Figuring each other out. We're doing the work."

Makenna swallowed and shook her head.

"Don't do this. I'll bust my ass. You're right—it's complicated, but I want you anyway."

Nothing was working; he could see it in her face.

Makenna put her hand on the front door.

"Have a good night, Ken." Travis turned before he could fall to his knees and walked back to the kitchen. He paused at the door while what seemed like everyone who worked there, including Logan, busied themselves as if it were any other day. When he heard the front door open and close, Travis grabbed his apron and went to work.

And just like that, she got her wish. She was back to being Ken. She walked out into the warm sunshine and by the time she reached the Jeep, her tears were dry. Makenna rolled her shoulders back, started her car, and got on with it. She had payroll to do, Paige to pick up that afternoon, and details to tend to. Her heart would find its way back to where it belonged. It always did.

Chapter Thirty-One

The next two weeks were business as usual, and Travis was slowly losing his mind. Makenna was civil. He even saw Paige a couple of times, but she hadn't forgotten the lunch box for fifteen days straight. He would never be able to explain it to someone, but not making Paige's lunch was almost as painful as not being able to touch her mother's face. Logan hadn't said much, and Travis imagined the whole thing was awkward for him too. If he knew his friend, he was letting it play out and hoping, in the end, he still had a friend and his sister in one piece.

Kenna seemed perfectly fine, on time, focused on her job. He had no idea how she did it, how she shut it all down, and he would admit seeing her buzzing around hurt. He didn't want her to be miserable, but he was now boxing every morning, which meant he was dog tired because it was honestly the only way he could fall asleep at night without seeing her, wanting her, wishing he could somehow undo what he'd done. So it might help if she, at least, looked a little sad, but she didn't.

"Do you know where Kenna is?" Logan asked as he directed a guy with a goatee, wearing a yellow sweatshirt, to put the boxes on his dolly in front of the office.

Travis shook his head and looked back down at his red peppers.

"She's in the bathroom," Sage said. "Yeah, is my salt in there?"

Yellow sweatshirt looked at his list and nodded.

"Great."

"Is she using the bathroom?"

"No, cleaning it. She went in there with a toothbrush, something about the grout."

"Jesus, she's moved on to cleaning the grout now?"

"You"—Logan looked at Travis—"could you please fix this because I'd really like to have my sister back, not to mention my restaurant manager."

Travis wrinkled his brow. "What are you talking about? She's cleaning. Isn't that a good thing?"

Logan shook his head and signed for the delivery.

"See that? Did you see me signing that? I've got chicken legs braising and I had to stop to sign for supplies. Not my job, but because you fucked up, my manager has locked herself in the damn bathroom. Fix this, God damn it!" Logan pushed through the kitchen doors.

Travis dried his hands and went to the bathrooms. The men's door was locked. He put his hand on the door as if he could somehow reach her.

"Kenna?"

"Busy."

"There was a guy here with a delivery."

"Just sign for it." She sounded out of breath.

Travis leaned up against the locked door and then slid down the wall until he was sitting, his boots resting at the base of the opposite wall. He could hear her scrubbing, the water sloshing.

"Kenna?"

"What?" she yelled, and he heard something fall to the tile.

"What are you doing in there?"

She let out a sigh he could hear through the door. "I'm cleaning."

"The bathroom is pretty clean already."

"Yeah, well, that shows what you know. This grout is dirty. Just leave me alone."

He said nothing, just sat there wanting to be near her.

She wasn't scrubbing.

"Should we talk about anything?" he said quietly, somehow knowing she was on the other side listening.

"No." Her voice was soft and close. She was sitting directly on the other side; he could feel her.

"Okay, well, since you've moved on and are clearly fine . . . you're cleaning, so you're obviously fine, I'd like to get a few things out."

She was right there; he could hear her breathing.

"I miss you." Three words and his eyes were already threatening to tear up. "And even though it's not going to work and you're doing fine, I want you to know that I'm still not giving up. I'm still loving you. Can you feel that, Kenna?"

Nothing.

"Maybe we both have things to learn. You know, we're different, but that doesn't mean this won't work. Paige showed me this video once. It was an owl that was friends with a cat. I guess it was on some farm, she didn't tell me, but it was pretty cute. There was a picture of this black cat with his paw around like a barn owl, I think. Weird, right?"

Nothing.

"I remember because I told Paige if those two could get along, maybe she could be friends with Sierra." He laughed and wiped the tear from his face. "She scrunched up her face, you know how she does, and said that was different because Sierra was a predator." He continued laughing and then he heard her through the door. At first, it sounded like she was breathing heavily again, back to cleaning, but Travis realized she was crying. He thunked the back of his head against the door. "Christ, Kenna, please talk to me."

He heard a sniffle and then the scrub brush. Travis ran a hand over his face, stood, and went back to work.

Makenna couldn't breathe. She heard him walk away, and now her sobs were coming in gulps of air as she continued scrubbing. She missed him, wanted him, but she wanted her sanity, her order even more. That's what it had come down to for her over the last couple of weeks. Every time she looked at her phone or walked past him, she vowed to maintain her normal. She needed it for her daughter and for her own heart. It served neither of them if she was some mushy basket case, but her heart hurt every time she saw him and it wasn't getting any better. She kept trying to move forward. It had worked before, but he was still there, still loving her, as he said. *This will pass*, she told herself. All she needed to do was to continue being complicated and he would eventually move on too.

Makenna sat Paige down that night and talked about the lunches and her Travis. She explained that he was part of her life, but maybe not as big a part as she was making him. She tried to direct her six-year-old back to Logan, Garrett, and her Donk. Of course, she didn't say it, but she wanted Paige to know that these were the men in her life; they had always been there and would continue to be there even if things became complicated. She also wanted her to understand that while her Travis made great lunches, so did her Mama. Paige said she understood. Kenna knew it was as much as a six-year-old could understand, but things seemed to be under control. Kenna started putting carrots and little cups of buttermilk dressing in her lunch, and apparently Sierra asked her where she got the little cups. Major points!

Chapter Thirty-Two

Sage was already sitting on the yellow couch when Makenna arrived at Lux on Sunday morning.

"Where's Paige?"

"Gracie and the babies. She never wants to leave the farm now." Makenna took out her phone and showed Sage more pictures.

Sage took the phone and thumbed through the pictures, oohing and ahhing. "Can you blame her? I wouldn't want to leave the farm either." Sage held up the phone, and the screen was filled with a shot of Paige sitting on Garrett's lap.

"Oh dear Lord." Kenna snatched her phone back and threw it in her purse.

Sage laughed, and Makenna got in line for her tea. She was still trying to like the damn tea.

"So, how are things?" Sage asked tentatively and sipped her latte as Makenna sat down.

"Things are good."

Sage tried to catch her eye, but Kenna was certain if she looked at her friend, she'd start to cry.

"That's not incredibly convincing."

"Well, it is what it is. We're fine." Makenna broke open her cranberry muffin and took a bite. "It'll get better. I just need more time."

"You know, you've been my friend for a long time and I love that you call me out on my bullshit, so I'm going to return the favor. You love that man. Did he screw up? Absolutely, and you should be enjoying watching his ass grovel, but what you're doing has nothing to do with him. You're blaming him for every letdown in your life, and that doesn't seem fair."

"Aren't you supposed to be my friend?"

Sage laughed. "I am being your friend. You're not going to be able to just clean him out of your life. He's deep inside you, honey, and I think you have to face that, don't you? Maybe you need my therapist. Do you want to talk?"

"No. I just want to go back."

"Yeah, well, you can't. What's done is done. You love him, he loves you, and now the work begins. You're all about work, so get in there. You've already had one great guy. I'm not sure you're going to get another one if you two can't figure this out."

"I'm fine on my own. Paige and I are actually better than ever."

"Again, babe, bullshit. You're a sulky, distracted mess, and last week you hit the bathroom tile with a toothbrush. If that's not a cry for help, I'm not sure what is."

Makenna laughed. "I was just trying out this stuff I bought from an infomercial. I hate the grout in that bathroom."

"Find a way to forgive him."

Makenna started to cry and Sage pulled her into her arms.

"Fix this, honey, because I love you so much. Sure, you'll survive without him, but it'll break my heart to watch it, and after all, it's all about my heart."

Makenna laughed and wiped her tears on Sage's orange sweater. "Have you always been this smart?"

"I really have."

They both laughed.

"That, or I just read too many of those 'be your best self' books." Sage finished her coffee and got up for another.

Makenna finished her muffin and split the side of bacon Sage returned with. They played a couple of rounds of their "What's his story?" game, and Makenna cried again when Sage asked her to describe Travis if he walked in. He was no longer the hungover bachelor; his details were so vivid and she missed him.

"Did you really close your profile?" Makenna changed the subject.

"Yup, I'm officially off the market. I never liked shopping anyway."

They both laughed.

"Besides, my cocktail contest is coming up. Can you believe it's already October?"

"No. Any ideas yet on what you're going to make?"

"I'm thinking of making something with rye."

Makenna looked at her and Sage put on her very best confused face, but she wasn't buying it.

"Maybe you should just tell him, you know?"

"Tell who?"

"Cut it out. Just be honest with him and say, 'Garrett, even though you smell like a cross between dirt and sweat most of the time and even though I will never get you in a suit unless it's for a funeral or a wedding and even though you have never shown one moment of interest in giving a woman what she needs or wants, I'm desperately in love with you and would like to have your children.'"

"Yeah?"

"I think you should go for it."

"Oh, shut up." Sage ate the last piece of bacon.

Travis spent Sunday letting Brick kick his ass again. He'd scheduled an extra session because he needed something to do, something to get his mind off of how the hell one field day had blown everything up. He still wasn't sure how to deal with his completely jacked up panic attack or his family. He needed help, so after he crawled out of the gym shower, he called the one person he knew would have some ideas.

He watched Logan walk past the front window of Libby's and then take a seat across from him.

They both ordered coffee, and suddenly Travis didn't know where to start.

"You look like shit."

"Thanks."

"So, how are things?" Travis winced at the stupidity of his question, but it was all he had.

"Huh, well, things are great with me, but you've been in a pretty big shitstorm lately. I'm hoping that's what we're here to talk about; why I left my warm fiancée alone in our bed on my one day off. Please tell me you have something more than stupid chitchat."

"I don't know how to get her back. It's like there's all this space between us and she won't let me in."

"Right, well, you left her."

"What? Oh man, are you going to bring up the damn field day?"

"No. Maybe. It's not the field day, but I'm guessing it's how she's processing it. Maybe I should back up. I'm not sure what you know and what you don't know. You know the story of our mom. She left and blah, blah."

Travis nodded.

"You might not know Makenna's side, though."

"Her side?"

"Yeah, she was a little younger than Paige. She was in kindergarten and our mom picked her up at half day. She was always late, so that was Kenna's norm, but on the day she left, she never showed at the school."

"Shit." Travis ran a hand over his face.

"Kenna sat in the school office for four hours until someone told me and Garrett and we went to pick her up."

Logan told the story pretty matter-of-factly, but Travis could still sense the pain—Logan's and Makenna's—and then it hit him.

"School. She was left waiting at school."

"Bingo." Logan took a bite of his toast. "I think that's what this is all about, and if I know Kenna, it's pretty deep in there, so she's already buttoned herself back up."

"What does that mean?"

"The week after our mother left, remember she was only five, Kenna cleaned her room from top to bottom. Lined up all her animals, folded all of her clothes, like she was getting ready for something."

Travis said nothing and pushed away his breakfast. There was no way he could eat anything.

"She's been that way since. When she's bruised or hurt, it's like she absorbs it, cleans up, and moves on. That's the mode she's in now with you. I'm pretty sure she knows it makes no sense that she shut you out for missing a field day, but I'm not sure she knows how to be any other way."

Travis ran his hand over his face. His eyes burned. "Then what am I supposed to do?"

Logan sat back in the booth and crossed his arms over his chest. "Not sure. She's not talking to any of us. Dad tried, but she insists she's fine. My best advice is to use what you have."

Travis leaned in, hoping his friend had something.

"You're always around her—you guys work together. Just keep showing up. Keep being there, you know, sort of 'up her ass' as Kenna would say. It's like when we make a reduction and it gets too thick: we just keep adding liquid until it smooths out. Try that with Kenna. Dilute one field day with a whole lot of showing up."

Travis sat there staring at his friend.

"Food? You're giving me food?"

"Hey man, you were the one who told me food was sexy, remember? It's just an analogy. Try showing up, being there for her, and maybe she'll work through her crap and trust you."

It wasn't a bad idea, Travis thought. It was the only idea he had, so it had to work.

Logan took the check, threw some money on the tray, and stood to put his coat on.

"You're leaving? That's it? Show up is all you've got?"

"Yeah, that's it. Oh, and while you're waiting for her to figure things out, you might want to deal with your own family. Having a nervous breakdown over a field day can't be good. I'm guessing you'll have a few more field days in your future, so you'll want to figure that out."

Travis laughed and stood. "You think this will work?"

"It has to, man. She's your strawberries, right?"

Travis felt his heart jump, and there was no way he was losing it while his friend was so damn right. He hugged him quickly and they walked out of Libby's. Travis might not have been able to choose his family, but he was damn good at picking his friends. He drove home and did a few loads of laundry. He could get ready too. For the first time since Kenna broke things off, he was feeling optimistic; at least he had something to do. Operation Show Up was about to commence.

Chapter Thirty-Three

*M*akenna started her Monday morning by helping to hand out school newspapers as parents dropped their children off in the roundabout. St. Christopher's asked that parents give at least forty volunteer hours a semester. Kenna signed up to help the paper, so she was now smiling and handing copies of *The Thunderbolt* to parents she'd only ever noticed before as passing cars. It was interesting to see inside people's cars, the intimacy of their morning commute. Kenna noticed McDonald's wrappers in backseats, and it occurred to her that maybe she wasn't that different from the Jaguars or the BMWs after all. With only passing glimpses into her fellow school parents' cars, she felt like maybe they were all doing the best they could. As she drove to work, it finally hit her how important showing up was to her. Dirty car or messy hair, showing up was most important and it was a common ground, a respect she found in just a couple of volunteer hours. *Life was so strange*, she thought, as she parked her Jeep and walked into the back kitchen.

"Good morning!" Travis said in a voice that was so peppy, she jumped.

"Damn! You scared me. Good morning." She glanced at him

quickly and made her way to Logan's office to get the three boxes of stove knobs their vendor was picking up this morning. They were the wrong size, and she wanted to put them on the bar for the guy when he arrived. She looked in the office, and they weren't on the chair where she'd left them before the weekend.

"Did Grant already pick up those returns?"

"No, I put them out on the bar since he's coming in this morning to exchange them." Travis kept chopping.

"Okay. Thank you."

"No problem. I showed up early, so I thought I'd help out." Still chopping, no eye contact.

Kenna went to the bar, poured herself some tea, and got to work.

For the next two weeks, Travis seemed to be everywhere. Before she knew she needed anything, he was right there to help. He'd started making Paige's lunch again, even without the lunch box, and handing it to her in a paper bag as she left for the afternoon. He kept saying some version of "just showing up." It was maximum effort and while Kenna tried to tell him a few times to stop or wanted to be annoyed, she wasn't. She loved him and with each passing day, she found herself putting in the work too. Sage had her reading a book about loss and Kenna had started a journal that seemed stupid at first, but she now found herself pouring her feelings into it every morning.

Whatever she and Travis had fallen into lately, they were getting back to friendly, funny even. They were healing, and Kenna was starting to feel that no matter what happened, they would be in each other's lives and they'd be fine.

Chapter Thirty-Four

Operation Show Up was a huge success, but they were slammed during week three and by the time Travis caught his breath, it was Saturday and they were heading into a second wave of dinner. Todd had called in sick, so they were shorthanded, but Makenna brought Paige by so she could show him her first school pictures. Just as he helped Paige off the counter and watched them leave out the back door, Sage came up to the serving window.

"Your brother is in my bar."

"What? I need that pizza for fifteen now." He held out his hand. Larry gave him a ten-inch mushroom, and Travis called for a runner.

"You heard me. It's the younger one, and he asked me to get you. I wanted to tell him I'm not a messenger, but the bar is busy and I didn't want to cause a scene."

"Tell him I'll be there when I can."

Sage nodded and walked back to the bar. They were an hour away from closing by the time his hands were free.

"Hey, I didn't know you were coming up," Travis said, taking off his apron and walking into the bar.

"Last-minute thing. I met with some people today, well, Dad and I met with them, and it looks like that restaurant is a go."

"Really?" Travis was gearing up for another round of acceptance when he remembered the feeling of his chest tightening when he walked up to Paige's school. He remembered that his whole world hit a tailspin after that day.

"Yeah, weird right? My brother's a cook and I end up opening a restaurant."

"Bar."

"What?"

"It's a bar."

"Sports bar slash restaurant, that's what the investors are calling it."

"Right, well, I'm guessing since you're a football player that there's a stronger emphasis on the bar part. Oh, and for the hundredth fucking time, I'm a chef. Trained actually. I'm not a cook." Somewhere in his mind, Travis actually heard a cheering crowd. He smiled at the look of complete shock on Drew's face.

"Hell, what crawled up your ass?"

"You know, lots of things have crawled up my ass over the years. Where's the rest of the crew?"

"They're back at the hotel. There was a game this afternoon, so we all—"

"Came down like a team?" Oh, this felt good. Travis was almost drunk with freedom.

Drew looked a little scared. "Yeah, we go home tomorrow morning. I wanted to talk to you before we left, but since you're being a dick, maybe I'll just go."

"You show up here, without any notice, during the dinner rush, and you want me to drop everything to congratulate you on putting your name on yet another strip mall sports bar?"

"I guess that means you don't want to be one of my cooks or chefs or whatever you called it?"

"What?"

"They told me I could have a say in hiring, and I thought you might want to work for a family place."

"What is wrong with you?" Travis felt like a whole new man, like he was finally hearing things. "I have a better idea. Why don't you call Mom and Dad and get the rest of the team down here. Are John and Avery with you?"

Drew nodded.

"Great! Get them all down here. I'll head back to my kitchen and work on my cooking thing and once they're all here, tell Sage. We'll all have a little powwow in the private dining area."

Drew, who was an incredible athlete but not too bright, looked downright confused as he pulled out his phone. "Okay . . . I think they've already eaten."

"Oh, that's fine. I have no intention of feeding them. Just tell them to get their asses down here." Travis grabbed his apron and allowed years of angst to surge from his chest. He welcomed it and returned to his kitchen.

Less than an hour later, Travis rounded the wall into the private dining room Makenna loved. He felt her everywhere, remembered the first time he kissed her, and knew this family meeting was all part of getting her back.

"Okay, so I want to start by telling you all that I love you."

"Sport, what's this all about?" Travis's father said as he stood in front of them.

"Dad, I might as well start with you. This won't take long. First of all, stop calling me Sport. Sports really didn't work out for me, so that name no longer applies, unless you count boxing, which I'm sure you don't, so just cut it out."

"Hey, wait a minute."

"No." Travis held up his hand. "I'm done waiting. Sit down." To his surprise, his father took a seat next to his mother, who looked like she was about to pass out. "Okay, so thanks for coming down. Recently I've had some issues that have messed with my life, messed with the woman I love and her little girl who I'm crazy about, so it's time for me to clear the air. I need to find my A game, and for that to happen, this needs to be said."

Not a word, not one movement from his entire family. Travis couldn't help but smile.

"So, in a nutshell, it was completely screwed that you dumped me, Avery, and then married my brother. Weird, like Jerry Springer kind of crap."

Drew started to laugh, and John looked down at the table.

"I'm over it though. I think you two are a perfect couple, and I'm looking forward to being an uncle, but Avery, please stop looking so damn guilty. No one cares anymore. Be happy, okay?"

Avery nodded.

"And John, you could call me once in a while. You're a dick and we have next to nothing in common anymore, but I'm willing to overlook that if it means we can have some kind of normal conversation."

"I . . . sure. I'll call."

"Great, so I guess that's it. Oh, wait, Drew. Quit being such a cocky asshole. I would work as a line cook at Denny's before I would ever work for you. Got it?"

Drew laughed again. "Got it. This is fun. Do I get to go next?"

"No," they all said in unison.

"All right, so one last thing. I'm a chef, a damn good one, and if any of you decide to open your eyes, I'd love to have you come in for dinner."

Travis slapped the table and turned to leave because his heart was racing and he couldn't get a full breath.

"Hold on just a damn minute," his father said, standing and walking up to him.

Right when Travis thought he might have a heart attack, his father put his arm around him.

"Good talk, son. I'm glad you got some stuff off your chest. Maybe we'll swing by for dinner next week."

"Absolutely!" His mother stood up and hugged him. "You're not on drugs, are you?"

Travis laughed, hugged his mother back, and walked the whole screwed-up lot of them to the front door. There was no question most of what he said went in one ear and out the other. They'd still call him a cook and treat him like the bastard child, but it no longer mattered because he was different. Doing without was no longer an option for him, and that felt incredible.

Travis needed to do something with all his newfound energy. It was time to chop, every chef's go-to stress reliever, and then he remembered seeing Paige go into Logan's office. Hope sprung in his chest as he flicked the lights on and there, sitting in the center of the desk, was Travis's salvation. The one thing he'd been missing for weeks—Paige's lunch box.

He felt the smile crawl across his face as he bent and grabbed the light blue woven and plastic handle of the Daniel Tiger box. He actually looked over his shoulder because he was being ridiculous. Seriously, how sad had his life become that what a newly minted six-year-old ate was up there on his priority list. He realized he didn't care. After weeks of showing up, things were good. Travis walked back into the kitchen, pulled the zipper, and when he saw the folded piece of construction paper, he unfolded it. This time, it was yellow. There was a big smiley face made into a sun. Around it were flowers with big eyelashes and green grass. Across the top in blue crayon, it said—*MAMA SAID I COULD. MAYBE YOU SHOULD MAKE HER LUNCH TOO. I LOVE YOU.* The words were surrounded by the usual hearts and smiling sun, but at the bottom, there were three stick figures holding a bunny in front of a house.

His eyes filled and Travis cried. He quickly wiped the tears with his sleeve. Something about a little girl's genuine expression, her happiness, bulldozed right over him. She was so incredible and there was no question he loved her, always would. He loved her mother too, to desperation if he was honest with himself. He looked at the drawing again and thought maybe he would make it to holding that bunny, that picture, someday. Paige's drawings had taught him so many things. Love was simple. Holding hands, resting a head on a shoulder, flowers, and a smiling sun. He'd never known such love, even as a child, but he knew it now, and now was what mattered.

Lasagna, he thought. Yes, that would be Monday's lunch. Take that, Sierra!

The last hour was blissfully slow, so Travis decided to make the lasagna before he left so it could sit all day Sunday. Pasta was always better after a little sitting. He started chopping for his sauce. He could use the sauce left over from dinner, but he was going to use beef instead of their usual pork sausage to cut down on the richness. Travis put down his knife, wiped his hands, and walked out front to grab some basil from the garden near the entrance to the restaurant. He waved goodnight to Mr. and Mrs. Ferguson, regulars, and clipped his basil and a sprig of oregano. When he entered the back kitchen, Logan was grabbing something out of the pantry.

"Hey, I was looking for you. What'd your brother want?"

"Nothing."

"Are you okay?"

Travis nodded, said nothing, laid out the basil, and tried to focus.

"What are you making?" Logan asked.

"Lasagna."

His friend glanced at the big kitchen clock, and then his face became puzzled. Travis grabbed several cloves of garlic and went to the walk-in for Parmesan and some of the mozzarella they had pulled right before lunch. They did their own mozzarella for all their pizzas and a couple of the featured salads. Travis and Logan both agreed it was what set them apart. Often, mozzarella was either too loose or like an eraser. They'd perfected it when they worked for Benji in Seattle. Logan was still standing in the kitchen, confused, and then he looked over and must have seen the lunch box because he grinned.

"You going with our sauce or ground beef?"

"Ground beef, cutting a quarter of the garlic, and adding a bit more sugar." Travis was back to chopping. The rhythm—his friend understood the rhythm and Travis never appreciated him more than in that moment. No lecture or psych analysis, just rhythm.

"Fresh tomatoes instead of canned, especially with that extra sugar?"

Travis nodded.

"Yeah, she'll love that."

Travis felt a sting in his eyes again and shifted to cutting onions just in case he started losing his shit again. Logan walked out the door connecting the back kitchen to the bar and a few minutes later, he returned with two frosted glasses of beer. Travis didn't even have to look twice; he knew it was Knucklehead Red from Beachwood Brewing. They'd starting carrying it a week into opening and it was their favorite. It had turned into their go-to beer. Logan passed a glass across the chopping block and then raised his glass. They clinked and drank. Travis went back to chopping and Logan left again. The next time he returned, he was wearing an apron and AC/DC was now spilling through the speakers. "Thunderstruck" started building, and Logan grabbed a knife and began chopping right next to him without saying a word. Travis was again grateful he was chopping onions.

They worked through most of the *Back in Black* album and by the time "Shook Me All Night Long" came on, they were layering their creation for the oven. Sage brought in two more beers for them and one for herself.

"We're all closed up out there. You boys need anything?"

"No, I think we're good." Logan closed the oven door and leaned against the counter next to Travis. They all three clinked and sipped their beer.

"So, you finally told your family where to go. Well done. I almost jumped over the bar when I heard your asshat brother's offer."

"Do you have super hearing?"

"Hello, I'm a bartender. We can hear a pin drop out there in the jungle. Anyway, you two look like you're having fun, but I wanted to say if you ever want me to poison Drew, just say the word."

Travis laughed. "You know he's a superstar in the football world, right?"

"Eh, who cares? He's obnoxious. Night, guys." Sage waved and the kitchen doors swung closed.

Travis and Logan sipped, still leaning on the counter. They had about an hour to kill and Travis knew it was coming.

"His offer?"

Never fails. Thanks, Sage.

Travis took another sip and once again affirmed that he loved a good beer. "Drew stopped by to tell me he was opening a restaurant and asked if I wanted to work for him."

Logan almost wasted perfectly great beer, but he managed to swallow. "What the hell does that mean?"

"Some investors are backing a sports bar. They'll put it near the USC campus and call it Drew's or McNulty's and make a small fortune."

"Yeah, I got that part. I'm a little fuzzy on where the hell he thinks you fit into all of that. Does Bozo not know that you were the single reason Benji got his second star?"

Travis laughed. "Lo, are you thinking Drew knows what Michelin stars are? I'm sure he would recognize the Michelin man, but that's about where it ends."

"Well, he should fucking know. His brother's a chef."

"Yeah, well, I agree, so I called the whole fam down and we had a talk."

Logan's eyes went wide. "Seriously?"

Travis nodded.

"That had to feel good."

"It did. Cards?" Travis took out a deck of cards from under the counter.

"We've still got forty-five minutes, so sure."

After a few hands of Hearts, the lasagna was cooled, covered, and placed into the walk-in until Sunday night. They both shut off the lights and grabbed their stuff.

"Hey, why don't you come up to the farm tonight?"

"Are you feeling sorry for me?"

"No."

"Is your sister up there tonight?"

Logan nodded.

"You think she'll have a problem with me showing up again?"

"Probably."

Travis laughed. "Can I borrow a T-shirt?"

"Yeah." Logan clicked open his truck.

"Okay, I'll see you up there." Travis put his helmet on, swung his leg, and started his bike.

Chapter Thirty-Five

*W*hen the rooster let out its strangled cry the next morning, Travis rolled over and pulled the covers over his head. They'd gotten to the farm a little after one and he had crawled into one of the guest bedrooms. He grabbed his phone off the nightstand and even though every part of his body wanted to stay in bed, he had spent enough time with Logan to know that there was no point trying to sleep past five. He pulled on his jeans and already smelled the bacon as he headed downstairs.

Makenna shuffled into the kitchen without looking up. She was in pajama bottoms and wrapped in the same sweater Travis recognized from cookie morning, as he'd come to call it. He wondered if that white tank top was under there again. She walked straight for the refrigerator and held her hand up to her brother Garrett, instantly silencing him, which was hard to do. Logan was at the stove and once she'd cracked open her can of Coke and taken her first drag, she said, "Gentlemen," to which her brothers replied in concert, "Lady," and raised their coffee cups. She was back on the Coke again; he wondered if that meant she was just as miserable without him.

Makenna stood next to her brother and still hadn't noticed Travis sitting at the table. He was looking forward to her surprise.

She accepted a bite of the potatoes Logan was making and nodded her approval.

"Where's your better half?" Garrett leaned his chair back onto two legs.

"She's immune to the damn—" Kenna looked up, and Travis got the look he was hoping for. It was surprise, but not exactly a bad thing. Her eyes softened in what he thought might even be humor. "Rooster, Paige is immune to the rooster. She's still sleeping." Makenna finished answering her brother, but her eyes remained on Travis. "You. What's with you and kitchens?"

Travis laughed and felt incredible relief. She was coming back to him. He could see it on her face.

"Morning, Makenna."

"Morning, Travis. Are you still working your 'showing up' plan?"

He nodded and took another sip of his coffee.

"Sage told me you had a busy night last night."

"I did. I'm shooting for great these days."

She smiled, and Travis felt like his chest was opening up right there on the kitchen table. She was so beautiful. He'd missed her, and all he wanted was to pull her into his lap.

"I thought that was too much work. The leap and all, remember?"

"I do, but I'm all about leaping these days."

She grabbed a piece of bacon and sat at the far end of the table, next to Garrett, who had his face in the paper.

"Are you helping us harvest the apples today?" She took another gulp of Coke.

Logan turned from the stove, emptied his skillet of potatoes into a white oval dish, and tried not to look guilty.

"I don't remember you mentioning apples last night."

"Didn't I?" Logan set the dish on the table.

Travis laughed. "I don't mind helping."

"Your girlfriend will be there," Kenna added.

He knew she was talking about Paige, but his girlfriend was already here, he thought. She was only a few feet away from him; he could reach out and pull her into his lap with little effort. She was wearing sweatpants and big red socks. Her hair was a mess and she was still drinking soft drinks first thing in the morning. She made him crazy, and she was the great love of his life: his person, or his penguin as Paige had once said. She'd given him strength to ask for more, demand more. Now he just needed to keep showing up and wait for her to let him back in.

"Iguanas grow back a new tail every time they lose theirs, did you know that?" Paige asked about an hour later when Makenna went to wake her up and found her reading in bed.

She patted a spot next to her on the big yellow bed that had been in the Rye family for generations.

"Well, good morning to you too." Makenna lay down next to her daughter.

"It's true, I read it last night. Iguanas have these big long fat tails. Look." Paige flipped through the pages of her book and pointed to a picture of a big lizard with an even bigger tail.

"Huh, look at that. Very interesting. The tail falls off?"

"Yup," she said, sitting up and closing her book. "Sometimes it gets stuck like under a rock or a meanie pulls it and the iguana gets away by breaking its tail." Paige's eyes were saucers as she explained her latest discovery. She jumped down off the bed and went to the dresser across the room. Since Gracie's baby countdown and Paige's general interest in spending time on the farm, they'd started leaving clothes in both places. She opened the middle drawer and pulled out a pair of jeans. Makenna watched her daughter dress herself and once again was amazed by how big she was getting.

"You know what I think is so cool?" she asked, pulling a blue turtleneck over her head, her hair dancing with static.

"Huh?"

"That they keep letting it grow back. If it's just going to fall off or get pulled off again, why do they let it grow back? They should pro-lly just leave it off, right?" She hopped back up on the bed with her socks and boots.

Makenna took her little feet into her lap and pulled on the striped knee socks. "Well, I'm not sure about that. I don't think the iguana has a choice, Peach. Its body needs to regrow the tail or it would be incomplete. I'm sure there's something in there about evolution or survival, right?"

Paige was listening intently as she pulled on her boots and hopped off the bed. She ran into the bathroom, stepped up onto the stool, and brushed her teeth.

"I think you're right, Mama."

"You do?"

"Yup, when something falls off, we can't be scared. We have to be like the iguanas and just grow it back."

Makenna sat on the edge of the bed, watching her daughter tuck her shirt in, and wondered if they were just talking about lizards.

"I'm going to put breakfast in my tummy. We need to keep growing, Mama."

With that, her daughter was gone, on her way to the kitchen where Kenna was sure her Uncle Rogan had set aside a plate for her. She picked up the clothes on the floor, threw them in the hamper, and went to get dressed.

Makenna pulled on her jeans, her muckers, and a big cable-knit sweater. She washed her face and pulled her hair back into a pony-tail. Looking at herself in the mirror, she knew two things—it was one of her favorite days, the start of the apple harvest, and she was finished trying to fall out of love with Travis. Maybe it was because she was home, on the farm, and he was here. Maybe she was tired of waiting for that other shoe to drop or living in her past, or maybe it was as simple as Paige telling her they needed to be iguanas.

Kenna wasn't sure. All she knew as she ran down the steps and out into the morning air was that she loved him, needed him more now than she ever had. That would have to wait for the moment, though, because as her father liked to say, "There's work to be done."

She fell in step silently behind Travis and Logan as they led a small group toward the orchard.

"Ever pick apples, Travis?" her brother asked.

"I remember you talking about this a couple of years ago, but no, I've never picked an apple. Are there things I need to know?"

"Well, there's some history and a few odd little rituals that you might want to know about. Our family has farmed this land for, God don't let my dad hear my uncertainty, but I think it's five generations?"

"Wow."

"Yeah, we've really expanded in the last two generations, but there's a picture of a few great grandfathers ago with an apple on his head. I want to say eighteen-something? When was the camera invented?"

Makenna held in a laugh listening to the two of them. Sometimes, when they were together, she actually forgot they were grown men.

"Um, eighteen hundreds, late-eighteen hundreds, I think." Travis kicked a rock.

"So, way back then. I'm sure if my dad corners you today you'll get all the details."

"Okay, let's back up. Apple on his head?"

"Yeah, every season, one Rye family member goes into the orchard alone and picks the first apple. It has to be an apple from a tree, not one that has fallen. Then he, or she in recent years, stands at the entrance to the orchard with the apple on his or her head. You still with me?"

Travis nodded.

"Once the person, the opener as we like to call him or her, is in place, the rest of the harvest crew enters. One at a time, the apple is removed, polished with one quick wipe, placed back on the opener's head, and then the person entering gives the opener a kiss on their right cheek."

Makenna smiled because she truly loved the ritual.

"Aren't there dozens of people and workers that come to help harvest?" Travis asked as they arrived at the wood posts that marked the entrance.

"Yes," Logan said as they both noticed Makenna behind them.

"Each one kisses the opener? Some of those guys don't seem like they kiss all that much," Travis said, looking back at the approaching group.

Logan and Makenna laughed.

"For some of them, it's probably their only kiss, but I'm telling you it's ritual, maybe even a little superstitious. Every single man, woman, and child polished the apple and kissed Garrett on his right cheek last season," Logan said.

"Garrett? As in your brother Garrett?"

"The very one," Makenna answered.

"Wow. That's pretty cool."

"Oh, and I almost forgot—the opener then has to eat the apple," Logan added.

"Huh, that's great. When do the festivities start?"

As if on cue, Garrett walked up with Paige on his shoulders. She was still carrying a piece of toast and she'd put on her red puffy jacket. Her long blonde pigtails were braided.

"Your hair looks beautiful," Makenna said, touching Paige's braid. "I know your uncle didn't do that hair, did you get Kara to help?"

"He did! While I was putting breakfast in my belly, Uncle braided. He's super fast."

"You braided her hair?" Kenna looked at Garrett.

He wrinkled his brow. "Uh, yeah, that surprises you? I braided yours a time or two when we were growing up. Logan always gets the credit, but I did my share of braiding and feminine product purchasing."

They all laughed.

Paige reached for him, and after a warning glare Travis was sure he deserved, Garrett set Paige down next to him. She pulled her uncle down and kissed his cheek and then took Travis's hand. Her little hand nestled into his, and suddenly he went from existing to living again, just like that.

"Hey, I saw some flowers over by the barn. Maybe we should put some flowers in your braids."

Paige beamed up at him. "I love flowers."

"Most girls do."

"Yeah, what else do you know about girls, My Travis?"

He laughed, and Paige swung their clasped hands back and forth. She was looking up at him, waiting for an answer. "Oh, you want me to answer that. Okay, well, I know that girls like animals."

Paige nodded. "Not all girls like them. Some girls think they smell, but those girls are stupid." She quickly put her hand over her mouth.

"Is stupid not allowed?"

Paige shook her head. "Mama and I have a list now of words that are not allowed. She says it's because I'm getting bigger and sassier. I need to keep eyes on my mouth, that's what she says."

"Yeah, me too." Travis looked toward the barn and found the wildflower patch he remembered passing.

"So, what else do girls like?"

"They . . . like stories and pancakes. They like cookies."

Paige nodded enthusiastically.

"They like mac and cheese. They like drawing pictures. Oh, and all girls like to talk."

"Yes, we do. Mama talks a lot, sometimes to herself. And I've even heard her say a few words on the list."

Travis laughed, crouched down, and picked a few yellow and white flowers.

"Okay, harvest princess, hold still."

Travis put a few flowers down her braids and then tucked some in the elastics at the end. Paige stood stock-still, looking up at the birds and the wind blowing through the trees above them.

"I think that will do it. You look beautiful."

She swished her braids and smiled at him. The sun touched her tiny face, and Travis knew he would always want her in his life. If he had to conjure up some scenario without Kenna, he would deal with that, but he'd never met a little girl like Paige and he was pretty sure his heart would stop if he ever had to let her go.

"Can you lift me up so I can see?" she asked, walking in her little cowboy boots toward a truck parked next to the barn.

"Sure."

He lifted her and this time, when she smiled, Travis noticed her front tooth had grown all the way in. Another milestone he was there to witness.

"They look very pretty. Thank you, My Travis." She kissed him on the cheek.

He set her down, and she took his hand again as they walked back to join the group.

"I noticed your tooth is all the way in now."

"Yup." She nodded. "You know what else girls like?"

"What?"

"Boys."

He laughed.

"Is that so?"

She nodded. "I mean, not all boys because some are . . . not smart," Paige said, clearly trying to avoid another word on the list. "But nice boys, smart boys who cook for us and make us lunch — me and Mama, we like those kinds of boys."

Travis grinned and squeezed her little hand. Right before they reached the group, he leaned down and kissed her on the cheek. "I like you and your mama too, Paige."

Her cheeks pinked, and she swished her braids one more time and ran back to Kenna. Just like that, Travis knew two kinds of love.

"Impressive work, man," Garrett said after Paige showed him her flowers.

"Hey, thanks." Travis fell in step next to Kenna as they approached what looked like the entrance to the orchard.

"You ready to head in? You always take so damn long," Garrett said, handing Makenna a canvas bag with a leather strap.

She fastened the strap around her neck, letting the bag hang in front of her.

"Do I get one of those?" Travis asked.

Garrett handed him the other one he was holding. "You think you can keep up, city boy?"

Travis laughed, and Kenna walked toward the orchard as Paige cried out, "We're starting. We're starting."

"Hey, where are you going?" he asked, barely realizing he'd touched her arm.

"I'm the opener."

When she turned and walked into the orchard she'd been visiting since she was a little girl, younger than her daughter, Makenna looked up and felt whole. Her face flushed and her stomach was jumpy.

As she walked among the apple trees, she touched the trunks and listened to the crunching and the early morning birds overhead. The air was moist and chilled. She felt alive and grounded in the land that helped make her. When she was nine rows back, she turned right and counted six trees in this time. That would be her tree this year. The last time she'd been opener, her life had been a day-to-day struggle to stay sane. She remembered walking the same nine rows back, touching each tree and barely being able to continue. Nine had been Adam's lucky number, so much so that they were married on September 9th. He'd been crazy superstitious; Kenna smiled at the memory now. After she'd gotten to nine, she'd turned right and counted one tree for each year of Paige's life. He'd been gone almost three years back then and she was still drowning in grief. It may have been a morning much like this one, but she had not noticed. She'd stood in the middle of the orchard, listening to her trees and crying for what she had lost and the changes she wasn't sure she could handle.

This time, she counted six trees to the right, lifted her face to the sun that was now just starting to peek through the leaves, and sent a kiss up to him, her first love, the father of her sweet baby girl. He was always with her: sometimes it was an ache, but lately she'd found him more in a gust of ocean air or in the ice cream-covered smile of their daughter. Paralyzing sadness had turned to ache, and Kenna had learned a long time ago that ache was simply part of life. Good and bad, yin and yang. She reached up, picked her apple, and walked back toward her good.

Travis waited until last. He patiently watched what was really the coolest thing he'd seen in a long time. At least three dozen people performed the ritual and kissed a now beaming and laughing Makenna Rye. Paige was already running in and out of the trees with a smaller bag around her neck. Garrett, Logan, and Kara were chasing her. Her giggle echoed through the morning air. Travis stepped forward after a short man in a plaid shirt kissed Makenna and joined the others.

Their eyes met.

"Do you know what you're doing?" she asked quietly.

Travis stepped close to her, placed his cheek next to her cold cheek, and almost collapsed. It had been a month—four weeks since he'd touched her, and his body coursed with everything it had been missing.

"I know exactly what I'm doing now," he whispered in her ear and reached up to take the apple off her head. Makenna was silent as he polished it. He was the last one, so he handed it to her, allowing his hands to touch hers. He faced her and with his other hand, he gently pulled her closer. "Would it be all right if I broke with tradition just this once?"

Makenna shook her head. "I'm not sure that's such a good idea. We've been doing this for years, and you know any change could be bad luck."

"It's just a small one," he said as his eyes fell to her lips.

"Well, I guess, if it's small."

He could feel her heart pounding as if it had missed him too.

Kenna turned her cheek to him, just like she had done with everyone else, and he grinned. Right to the very end, she was going to make him work for it. Maximum effort. He gently took her face and turned her to face him.

"What are you doing?"

Her eyes told him she knew exactly what he was doing right before they fluttered closed and he kissed her. Travis, aware of the eyes peeking out of the orchard, only took a taste even though he was starving. He allowed his tongue to dip into her mouth and then when her lips curved, he pulled back.

Makenna let out a sigh. "You're getting really good at this showing up thing," she said and took a bite of her apple. The orchard erupted in applause and whistles. Travis grabbed her around the waist and kissed her again, right there in front of her family and people he didn't even know. He didn't care. Her cool lips tasted of sweet apples, and he was so happy to have her back in his arms that nothing else mattered. He'd shown up; Logan had been right. Travis looked back toward the trees and saw his friend smiling and shaking his head.

"About damn time," he shouted.

Travis laughed and hoped Logan knew how grateful he was for their friendship. Garrett moved next to his brother. "Well, hell, looks like she was checking him out after all." Both men laughed, and Makenna shrugged as if she'd been teased most of her life.

"I love you." He took her back in his arms.

"I love you too." This time, Kenna kissed him like she meant it, and Travis suddenly remembered something his father used to tell them during football practice. "Lock it down," he used to say. As Travis got older, he learned that was just a dude way of saying, "Hold on." Lock it down was exactly what he intended to do, for the rest of his life, if she'd have him.

Kenna fell asleep on the drive back to her house. They'd picked apples all day and Travis had offered to drive her and Paige home. Garrett would bring her car around in the morning before they needed to leave for school, so they all drove home in the warm bed of his truck. When they arrived, Paige invited Travis in and introduced him to her tuck-in ritual, and Kenna even let him take over as guest burrito maker. Everywhere she looked, he fit, and that no longer scared her. All she felt when she looked at him was warmth and love, a comfort she wasn't sure she'd ever feel again.

They closed the door as Paige was drifting off and even though Kenna invited him to stay, Travis said he had something to take care of. She kissed him and didn't even bother trying to read. She fell asleep as soon as her face hit the pillow.

Chapter Thirty-Six

Makenna woke up in her pajama bottoms and a tank top the next morning. She pulled on the fuzzy pair of socks next to her bed, brushed her teeth, and when she heard the low rumble of his laughter and the blissful giggle of her daughter, she tensed. But when she walked out of the bathroom, there was no cat and the walls were blue, so she walked out to the kitchen.

She turned into the kitchen just like the dream, but no one was there. Travis and Paige were in the living room, side by side on the couch. Still in her pj's, Paige sat, legs crisscrossed with Fritters in the space between them. They were both bowled over laughing and pointing at the television.

"Ewww," Paige exclaimed.

"Whoa, that one's worse." Travis winced and looked away. He caught her watching them and grinned.

"Hey, good morning."

Paige hopped up and ran to Kenna's side, taking her hand and pulling her toward the couch.

"What are you two watching?"

"Grossest bugs. It's awesome—come sit. Here, I'll move Fritters." Paige climbed back up on the couch and patted the piece of couch between the two of them.

Makenna sat as some black beetle-looking thing was biting the head off of some smaller green stick-looking thing.

"Oh!" Paige and Travis both bellowed again as if they were watching some sporting event. Makenna sat there, sandwiched between the two of them, feeling their warmth and laughter. She wasn't sure it got any better than this.

Travis leaned over, still watching the bug massacre, and kissed her on her shoulder. He was in sweatpants, not pajama bottoms, and unfortunately, his beautiful chest was covered by a faded-to-almost-invisible T-shirt. He cleared his throat and looked at Paige, who was enthralled with watching worms. It looked like they were possibly swarming an ant hill; Kenna wasn't sure, but she looked away.

"Why are we watching this so early in the morning?"

"Because it's awesome," Paige said, and then looked at Travis when he waved his hand in front of her face. "Oh, right. Okay, are we ready?" Paige stood up and put on her monster slippers.

Travis shook his head, laughing.

"Ready for what? It's Sunday, and I hope you two don't have big plans because I am not moving from this couch today." She propped her feet up on the coffee table to emphasize her commitment to lazy.

Travis looked at Paige, who promptly started to giggle.

"What are you two up to?"

"Oh nothing," she said, walking toward the kitchen. "My Travis bought us new lunch boxes."

"He did?" Kenna glanced over, and Travis was smiling and nodding as if he knew what was coming next. "What was wrong with Daniel?"

Paige squished her face. "Well, he was getting a little shiny."

"Shabby," Travis and Kenna both corrected, which should have felt weird, but it didn't.

"Wait, did you say 'us'? He bought 'us' new lunch boxes?"

"I did. Yes." Paige was now speaking slowly like she was explaining something complicated. Her eyes moved back to Travis. "Now?" she asked him.

Travis nodded and was again laughing. She couldn't blame him because whatever Paige was up to was pretty damn cute. She ran into the kitchen and returned holding two lunch boxes. One looked like a newer version of Daniel Tiger. Maybe it had a different picture? Kenna couldn't remember. Paige handed her one of those modern-looking lunch boxes that seemed like it was made out of wetsuit material. It was black with tiny white polka dots. Kenna looked at Travis, who smiled.

"This one's for you, Mama, for your lunch."

Kenna slowly took the lunch box and set it on her lap. Travis picked up the remote and silenced the television.

"Is this a hint that I should take my lunch?" Makenna said, running her hand along the side of the material and looking to Travis for more information. "It's a fantastic lunch box."

"I know. I picked it out," Paige said, standing close and bouncing around like she had to pee.

Travis was abnormally quiet, but she could almost see the waves of energy flowing off of him. She set the lunch box on the table. "Are you all right?"

He took her hand and when their eyes met, his were soft and melty, almost as if he'd just finished watching a sad movie.

Paige huffed, picked up the lunch box, and set it back in Makenna's lap. "You have to open it. This only works if you open the box, Mama."

Travis laughed again but still said nothing. Makenna furrowed her brow, still confused, and slowly unzipped the lunch box. Inside was a piece of folded construction paper. She unfolded it and the letter was written in crayon, but not in Paige's handwriting. It was Travis's writing. She read the letter.

Makenna—

Please let me make your lunch too. I promise to always show up and I'll take suggestions.

I love you,

Travis

P.S. Open the box.

Surrounding the letter were flowers and hearts Kenna recognized as Paige's artwork. There were two stick figures kissing in the bottom corner and a smaller stick figure holding their hands. Kenna's first tear hit the orange construction paper.

"She's crying," Paige said, walking over to Travis. "Oh no, this is bad, right?" She crawled into his lap.

Travis kissed her cheek and whispered, "Let's give it one more minute."

Makenna reached into the lunch box and pulled out a ring box. She looked at Travis, eyes still melty, and then at Paige, whose hands were clenched and eyes were saucers. She let out a slow breath, wiped the tear off her cheek, and opened the box. The hand not holding the box went to her mouth. It was a square-cut diamond, set on a narrow band and framed in what looked like platinum. The ring sparkled even in the muted light of morning.

Travis stood, still holding Paige, and then deposited her on the couch. "This is my part. Be right back."

Paige nodded and clapped while Travis dropped to his knee next to Kenna at the other end of the couch. Her heart was pounding and as hard as she tried, she couldn't order her mind. Travis took her hand and the box.

"Makenna Rye Conroy, I love you. I know you and Paige have a great life, built on a really great dream." He cleared his throat and held her hand a little tighter because his was shaking. "That should never go away, but maybe there's room for another dream: our dream. You two are the very best things that have ever happened to me, my A-plus by a mile, and I promise to love you both and put in the work every day."

Makenna was now crying again, but she smiled over at Paige, who promptly flashed Travis the thumbs-up and ran to his side.

"It's working," Paige whispered at his ear. "Put the pretty ring on her now."

Travis took the ring out of the box. "Makenna, please marry me. Let me make you both lunch."

Makenna nodded her head because she couldn't speak, and

Travis slid the ring on her finger. She stood and he stood with her. She wiped her face and then held his between her two shaking hands. "Yes, yes to everything." She kissed him, and Paige danced around the two of them. Travis swooped her up with one arm and she gave him a high-five.

"Good job, My Travis. I was scared when she started to cry, but you did it."

"I did. We did it. The lunch box was a great idea."

Paige nodded and kissed Makenna on the cheek. "See, now I don't have to sneak My Travis. He'll just be here, living with us. Cookies all the time. Sierra better watch out."

They all laughed. Makenna met Travis's eyes and everything fell into place. It was different, but so right. She supposed it was just like her father had told her on the tractor that day. Things might get a little crazy, but it would be an adventure and eventually everyone would find a seat.

Acknowledgements

I would like to thank:

Katie McCoach, my editor, for keeping me sane. Relatively speaking.

The cities of Los Angeles and Pasadena for providing endless corners of discovery.

My family for putting up with my closed door, imaginary friends, and often absent mind.

My mom, and all moms who make time to play burrito, even when they are tired or doing it all on their own.

Tracy Ewens shares a beautiful piece of the desert with her husband and three children in New River, Arizona. She is a recovered theatre major that blogs from the laundry room.

Reserved is her fifth novel, and the fourth in her *A Love Story* series.

Tracy is a horrible cook, wishes she could speak Italian, and bakes a mean Snickerdoodle.

CPSIA information can be obtained at www.ICGtesting.com
Printed in the USA
LVOW11s2004200516

489247LV00006BA/617/P